Skin on Skin

Skin on Skin

Jami Alden
Valerie Martinez
Sunny

APHRODISIA
KENSINGTON BOOKS
http://www.kensingtonbooks.com

APHRODISIA BOOKS are published by

Kensington Publishing Corp.
850 Third Avenue
New York, NY 10022

All Kensington Titles, Imprints, and Distributed Lines are available at special quantity discounts for bulk purchases for sales promotions, premiums, fund-raising, and educational or institutional use.

Special book excerpts or customized printings can also be created to fit specific needs. For details, write or phone the office of the Kensington special sales manager: Kensington Publishing Corp., 850 Third Avenue, New York, NY, 10022, attn: Special Sales Department, Phone: 1-800-221-2647.

Aphrodisia and the A logo U.S. Pat & TM Off.

ISBN-13: 978-0-7582-1590-1
ISBN-10: 0-7582-1590-8

First Kensington Trade Paperback Printing: July 2007

10 9 8 7 6 5 4 3 2 1

Printed in the United States of America

Tempted

JAMI ALDEN

CONTENTS

Tempted   1
Jami Alden

Hot Wired   107
Valerie Martinez

China Doll   197
Sunny

1

"*My darling, I want to touch you everywhere,*" *Lars whispered.*

Miranda shivered as his long, elegant fingers slid down the flat plane of her belly, his skin so dark against her own pale flesh. His hardness stirred against her bare leg and she gasped. Soon he would drive that thick column of flesh inside her. Could she possibly bear it?

A soft mewl escaped her lips as his hand drifted to the delta of springy curls between her thighs. She squirmed in embarrassment as his fingers tickled the entrance of her body, finding her shamefully wet, aching for his touch.

"Oh, Miranda," Lars sighed, groaning in approval as he felt her wet welcome. "Have you any idea how long I've wanted to touch you like this, how I've ached to slide inside the sweet petals of your womanhood . . ."

Lauren put the book facedown on her bedside table and closed her eyes. Her hand slid down to the waistband of her pajama bottoms and inside her cotton bikini panties. In her mind, Miranda's silvery blond hair became a mass of cinnamon curls, and her petite, delicate figure became Lauren's own strong, curvy form. Lars morphed too, his burnished gold hair turning thick and black, his burning blue eyes melting into deep, dark chocolate.

She bit back a cry as her fingers found her slick, hot center, circling her clit, teasing herself so this wouldn't all be over in less than a minute. Her hand became his—huge, strong and callused from work, rubbing, circling her clit, sliding inside her just enough to tantalize. Just enough to make her ache to feel the hot, huge length of his cock driving deep inside her.

A muffled cry squeezed past her lips as she came, arching off the bed, pressing her hand firmly between her thighs to draw out her climax as long as possible.

Before the last tremors of her orgasm had subsided, she flipped over onto her side, hugging a huge down pillow against her stomach. Wishing with everything she had that it was him instead of a pillow.

These ridiculous fantasies about Tony Donovan had to stop, or she was going to put her head through a brick wall.

Never mind that Lauren had been telling herself the exact same thing for seven months now, ever since she'd met him. And, she scolded herself silently, her steady habit of romance novels wasn't helping matters. Could she help it if, no matter how the author described him, every damned hero ended up looking like Tony? She closed her eyes and allowed herself one more glorious vision. Six foot three, a body that should be on the cover of *Men's Fitness* magazine. Thick, dark hair with just the tiniest hint of curl and an adorable cowlick waving off his forehead. And his eyes, big, dark, and liquid. Eyes that made a woman think about drowning herself in chocolate so he could lick her clean.

Cursing, she reached for the remote control and flicked on Sportscenter. Maybe that would distract her.

Tony. Her best friend. Her coworker. But not her lover. Never that.

She listened with half an ear as the host made his predictions about tomorrow's Oakland Raiders game. But most of her brain was still occupied by Tony. Wondering where he was, what he was doing. Who he was doing it with.

She should go back to masturbating. At least those images of Tony didn't twist her guts until she thought she might throw up.

Stupid jealousy. So unproductive, especially given how he felt her. She cringed, remembering his invitation to join him and his brother Mike earlier tonight.

"We're going over to Pete's in Tahoe City later on," he'd said over wings and beers at Sullivan's pub. "Want to go?"

Lauren cast a glance at Mike's wife, Karen. "Are you going?"

"No," the other woman said. "I've been on my feet all day and I'm beat."

Mike rubbed her shoulders affectionately. "Maybe you wouldn't be so tired if you wore better shoes." He'd looked pointedly at Karen's stiletto-heeled boots.

"You love my shoes and you know it," Karen had replied and pulled Mike's face down for a kiss that made the room temperature rise at least ten degrees.

"Ugh, you guys are gross," Tony said, sounding like a twelve-year-old afraid of cooties. "So, Lauren," he'd said. "You want to go?"

Go shoot the shit with Mike while she watched Tony roll up on some hot young thing? No thanks. She'd done plenty of that since she started working with the brothers at their building and renovation company seven months ago. But all she'd said was, "Nah, sounds like you should have it be a guys' night."

"Aw, Mac," he'd said with a grin and a squeeze of her shoulder. "You're practically one of the guys."

She knew Tony loved to say things like that just to get a rise out of her, but that comment had stung. Even more than his usual jokes about her masculine profession as a carpenter and her customary workman's attire.

Lauren thumbed the volume up on her remote, trying to drown out the evil voices in her head. *Why are you surprised? You know exactly how he sees you.* Just one of the guys. An athletic, tomboy of a girl who's great to hang out and drink beer with, but not a girl he'd ever feel *that* way about.

She sighed and flipped over to *Saturday Night Live.* Hugh Jackman was hosting, and he was almost enough to keep thoughts of Tony Donovan at bay.

She'd see him soon enough, her friend, her buddy, her pal.

His friendship meant the world to her, so she would continue as she had, concealing any inkling of interest and enjoy the time she did spend with him. From the moment she met him, she'd wanted to be his lover, but knew it would never happen. So she'd settled for friendship. Like she always did.

Tony settled next to Lauren on the couch and stretched his arm along the back of the cushion behind her. He snuck a quick, jealous glance at his brother Mike and his wife, Karen, snuggled together on the short end of the sectional. Karen didn't even bother to pretend to pay attention to the game, but rested with her head in Mike's lap as she read a paperback. Mike settled into the corner of the couch, absently playing with his wife's hair.

It still surprised him every time he saw them together. Mike, the least physically affectionate person in the family, couldn't keep his hands off his wife. As though he needed to have constant contact to make sure she was still here. Although, Tony supposed, considering their rocky path to love, he supposed he couldn't blame them.

His lips pursed into a frown. This was *his* couch, *his* house.

If anyone should be snuggling down in front of the game it should be him.

But no, he had to content himself with sitting next to Lauren. Almost, but not close enough for his thigh to press against hers. His hand dangled off the back of the couch. Almost, but not quite touching the thick reddish-brown curls that hung down past her shoulders.

"Yes!" Lauren and Mike shot off the couch simultaneously, arms up in wide vees. "GO GO GO," Lauren shouted, and Tony finally focused on his 42-inch-wide TV screen.

"Did you see that pass?" Lauren looked down at him, amber eyes sparkling with excitement.

He'd missed the entire play. "Yeah, it was nice."

"Nice? It was a thing of beauty." She and Mike settled back on their respective ends of the couches, and Tony was hard-pressed not to pull her flush against him. An urge that became even harder to resist when Lauren stripped off her fleece pullover. The mountain weather had turned chilly in the past week, but Tony's house was plenty warm, just the way he liked it.

"It's a sauna in here, Ton," she said, fanning herself a little before she sat back against the overstuffed cushions.

"I like it hot," he replied, and took a long pull at his beer. He tried not to think about how good she smelled, soft and fresh. And she always smelled good, even after a hot day under the sun doing manual labor. The clean scent emanated from her pores until he wanted to bury his head between her breasts and soak her up.

Oh, bad idea, thinking about her breasts. He shifted and tugged at the leg of his jeans. He nonchalantly rested his foot on the coffee table and bent his knee to shield the rapidly grow-ing bulge in his fly.

But really, she did have a fantastic rack, showcased very nicely today in a T-shirt that read "JUICY." She had a fantastic everything, as far as he was concerned. He shot up off the couch to get another beer, hoping the alcohol would do its part to put his dick to sleep.

He didn't have much hope it would work, but it gave him an excuse to retreat to the kitchen and get a handle on himself. He remembered the first day he'd met Lauren. Mike had hired her after their youngest brother, Nick, moved to Palo Alto to live with his fiancée. Tony had been skeptical about hiring a woman, but she came with great recommendations and proved that first day to be a highly skilled, motivated worker.

Of course he'd been attracted to her, with her comic strip heroine's body, all juicy curves and nicely defined muscles. And that hair. A riot of reddish brown corkscrew curls tumbling around her shoulders. With hair like that, you just knew she'd be a fuckin' wildcat in the sack. Topped off with her wide smile and whiskey-brown eyes full of warmth, and she was almost irresistible. But unlike most women he came across, she showed absolutely no awareness of him as a man. Besides, they worked together, and Tony didn't sleep with women he was likely to run into on a regular basis.

And the real clincher had come later that week. They were finishing up on a remodel job out in the Lakeview Estates. Mike was pushing them to complete the job so they could have the rare privilege of telling a client they'd actually finished *ahead* of schedule. But at about six-thirty Lauren had started looking at her watch. And by seven she'd mustered up the courage to ask her new boss when he thought they might finish.

Mike's brow had furrowed and he'd shot Lauren that intimidating look Tony knew he practiced in the mirror. Tony knew because he'd once caught Mike at it. "Do you have somewhere you need to be?"

But Lauren hadn't flinched. She'd just smiled that wide,

laughing smile and said, "Not really. But the Sharks are playing and—"

"Ah, a woman after my own heart," Tony had said, looping his arm over her shoulders. "C'mon Mike. If we finish up tomorrow we'll still be two days ahead of schedule. You can come over and watch it on my plasma-screen."

Lauren's mouth had gone slightly slack and her gaze blurred. It was a look he'd only ever seen on a woman's face when he was buried deep inside her. "A plasma-screen?" she'd murmured lustfully. "You have a plasma-screen?"

At that moment Tony had a startling revelation. He'd finally met a woman he liked too much to fuck.

For the past seven months he'd shoved any and all sexual thoughts aside and settled into a comfy friendship. They did almost everything together, from work, to working out, to watching sports on the plasma-screen she so openly coveted.

Unfortunately the lust he felt every time he saw her was becoming exceedingly difficult to resist.

First he had to work with her through the hot summer, her long muscular legs showcased in cargo shorts while her D-cups strained against a tank top. The image was still vivid in his mind, of firmly muscled arms tan and glistening with sweat, khaki shorts hugging the firm curve of her ass. He'd spent the entire summer resisting the urge to yank down her shorts and bury his mouth in the moist, gingery curls of her pussy.

He grabbed another Dos Equis and held the nearly empty bag of chips in front of his crotch for good measure. He settled back on the couch, nearly groaning when she reached into the bag of chips he still held on his lap. Her hand brushed repeatedly against his cock as she rooted around for more than crumbs, and he wondered how the hell she could be so fucking sexy in a T-shirt and jeans hiding those world-class legs. And she had no fucking clue, he thought angrily, as her gaze remained guilelessly fixed on the game.

Karen and Mike were nuzzling and whispering on the other end of the couch and Tony bit back a demand for them to get a room. It was a good thing they were here. God knew what stupid moves he'd pull if he was alone with Lauren.

Moves, he grumbled silently, that had worked without failure in the past. But for whatever reason, Lauren was completely unaware of him sexually.

Which was a good thing, he reminded himself, because if she showed the slightest bit of interest, offered the tiniest bit of encouragement, he knew he wouldn't be able to hold himself back. He had no faith in his self-restraint. And then he'd be down one very good friend, which in his experience was much harder to come by than lovers.

He was startled from his musings by a shrill, electronic version of the William Tell overture. Lauren squirmed to get her phone out her pocket and he savored the sensation of her firmly curved hip rubbing against his thigh. Would have been nice if she'd been a few more inches to the left, but he had to take what he could get.

Lauren frowned at the caller ID display and flipped open the phone. "Hi Mom . . . yeah. Yeah. Of course I'm coming. No, I haven't asked for the time off, yet." She smiled tightly at Mike. "No, Mike's really great, I'm sure he'll let me," she grinned and winked at Mike, who grinned back and mouthed, "No way."

"I don't think so, Mom. I know, I know, I just . . ." Her gaze met Tony's for a half second before flicking away, hidden by a sweep of dark amber lashes. She went silent and cinnamon-colored brows knit furiously over her small, straight nose. "Motherrrrr!" She sounded like an exasperated adolescent. "I know there's nothing wrong with that! Jesus, Mom, give me a break!" She rolled her eyes at whatever her mother was saying. "Well, don't. It's fine. Fantastic, in fact. Yeah, I'll see you in a week."

She flicked the phone closed and let out an exasperated sigh and flopped back against the sofa cushions. "I don't believe it!"

All three stared at her expectantly.

"My mother thinks I'm a lesbian."

Mike and Karen laughed, but Tony just raised his eyebrows.

Lauren brandished her phone threateningly. "If you say anything, I'll pound you."

Typical Tony—he couldn't resist the opportunity to needle her. "I don't know where she'd get that idea. You're so girly and feminine in your denim and flannel." He choked on a laugh as Lauren launched herself on top of him and tried to pin him to the couch. She shrieked as he rolled over and knocked her to the floor.

She made a pretty good show of trying to get away while her struggles afforded her the perfect opportunity to rub against Tony like a cat in heat. She even got a full-second ass grab in there under the guise of trying to roll him over.

Sad, yes, but a girl had to get her thrills where she could find them.

And despite her masculine profession and affinity for flannel, she was emphatically heterosexual. She pushed Tony off her and climbed back onto the couch. Not that she could blame her mother for her suspicions. Her mother—well she had her own ideas about sexuality, namely, that if you were young and healthy you should be doing it as often as possible. Carly MacLean couldn't imagine a world in which a willing woman wasn't getting laid, and often. So if there wasn't a man in her youngest child's life, there must be a woman.

"I could give you a mullet and complete the image, if you want." Karen, a hairdresser, giggled and ducked when Lauren pegged her with a pretzel twist.

"Shut up, it's not funny," Lauren said, laughing. "You don't understand. My mom is obsessed with my sex life, or lack thereof," she said with a roll of her eyes. "And now she's telling everyone I'm a lesbian."

"Why do you care, anyway?" Mike asked around a mouthful of pretzels, "It's not like the gossip will reach here."

Lauren sighed. "My parents are having a thirtieth wedding anniversary in two weeks, with a big reception, renewal of vows, the whole thing. My mom keeps pestering me to bring a date, and now that she's got this idea in her head, no doubt she'll invite some prospects." She sat back and covered her face with her hands. "She even asked me if I go for the more butch or the more lipstick types."

"Oh, lipstick, definitely. And I want to watch," Tony said.

Lauren was about to punch him again, but something in his eyes stopped her. A heated glint lurked behind his amusement. Even teasing her, Tony oozed sexual heat. It was in the tone of his voice, the deep richness of his eyes, the way he moved with lazy athletic grace.

She couldn't believe it. The perfect solution sat next to her on the couch. "Tony, I need you to do me a huge favor. Be my boyfriend."

Tony inhaled a tortilla chip and started hacking.

Not so sexy now, she thought. "Not for real, dummy. Just come to my parent's party with me and pretend. You're perfect."

"Perfect, how?" Tony wheezed as Mike thumped him on the back.

She scrambled to find the right words. She couldn't exactly tell him that he was sex personified. His ego really didn't need any more stroking. "Ummm, you just have that look," she said evasively.

"What look?" He looked at Mike and Karen for help.

Karen rolled her eyes. "The look of a guy who's fucked half the women in California and left them all smiling, despite the fact that you never call them again." she said and promptly went back to her book.

"Yeah, that look," Lauren said.

"Huh." Tony's expression said he wondered if maybe he'd been insulted.

"Look," Lauren said reassuringly, "You know how you are. You're a player—a successful one, and it shows. You're not the kind of guy to be in a sexless relationship with a woman—"

"I'm in a sexless relationship with you," Tony broke in.

Lauren rolled her eyes. She wouldn't even dignify that with a response, seeing no reason to remind him that he didn't exactly see her as a woman. "If you show up with me, my mom will forget her concerns about whether or not I'm getting laid. And I won't have to spend the weekend politely turning down offers from other women." She pulled the best pleading puppy-dog face she could muster and opened her eyes wide. "Please, Tony. Pretend you're attracted to me for just one weekend?"

2

Pretend to be attracted to her. Lauren's request rang through Tony's head two weeks later as he threw a sport coat and slacks into his garment bag.

This was going to be torture. A weekend spent playing Lauren MacLean's oh-so-attentive boyfriend. He would have to touch her, kiss her, all in the name of convincing her family that they were enjoying hot and sweaty headboard-pounding sex.

He just had to make it through the weekend without letting it happen for real.

His blood hummed with anticipation as he pulled up in front of Lauren's house. They'd decided his suburban would be much more comfortable than her Jeep for the eight-hour plus drive to Newport Beach. He wondered what Lauren's parents would be like. He'd always got the impression that she was fairly close to them, but she'd never talked about them in detail.

In any case, he found it a little weird for a mother to be so concerned about her daughter's sex life, especially since, in his experience, from the time he hit fifteen, most mothers had been trying to keep their daughters away from him.

Lauren flung open the door before he could knock, and stood there looking hotter than Tony had ever dreamed. She wore a bright green V-neck blouse that emphasized her smooth, toned shoulders and deep cleavage. Her jeans were low-slung and tight, lovingly cupping her ass in a way that made him want to lean down and take a healthy bite.

"What?" she said sharply.

Tony tore his eyes from the visual feast of tits and ass and focused on her face. Damn, she actually had on makeup! He thought she'd worn lipstick to his brother Nick's wedding, but it was so close to her natural lip shade that she might as well not have bothered. But today she had on just the right amount to emphasize the strong bones of her cheekbones and jaw and make her eyes seem huge. He knew he was staring, but he couldn't seem to stop. "You look . . . different."

Her brows knit over the bridge of her nose and she crossed her arms tightly over her chest.

Smooth, Donovan. At least she wouldn't think he was trying to talk her pants off.

"I look stupid, don't I?" she snapped.

"No, honestly you look amazing."

"Really?" She wanted to believe him, he could tell.

"Yeah. Trust me, you clean up really well."

Lauren turned and walked back into the house. "Karen picked everything out for me. She said I couldn't pull this off if I showed up dressed like a lumberjack."

As she reached for her suitcase he took the opportunity to study her. "I'd say Karen did a good job. Did she do your hair?" Her usual ringlets had been tamed into thick curls that bounced softly around her shoulder blades.

"Yeah," she said, eyes lighting up as she stood and turned toward him. "She gave me this great stuff to put in so it doesn't frizz out. And it doesn't make it sticky, just really soft. Here, feel." She leaned her head closer.

He reached out and combed his fingers through the silky strands. As he did, the fresh citrusy fragrance wafted around him, sending a jolt of lust straight to his crotch. She licked her lips nervously and he wanted to nibble on the plump, glossy curves.

"Isn't it soft?" she asked nervously.

"Yeah, soft," he repeated, though he felt anything but.

She cleared her throat and stepped out of reach. "We better get going, long drive and all that."

He picked up her wheelie back and she tried to grab it from him. "I can carry it."

"I know you can, but if I'm supposed to be your boyfriend, you have to let me do stuff like carry your suitcase for you."

Lauren chuckled. "Ooh, chivalry. Be careful or I might start making you carry my toolbox."

"Oh, I'm carrying a tool for you, baby," he said with an exaggerated leer.

"I don't have my needle-nose pliers on me," she laughed. She locked up and walked out to his car while he tried not to stare at her ass. Damn, he just knew that image was going to taunt him for the next eight hours on the road.

Lauren sang along softly to the Foo Fighters playing on Tony's state-of-the-art sound system. That was something she loved about being with Tony—the fact that they could sit around in comfortable silence and just hang. She studied him from under her lashes, admiring the way the muscles of his forearms shifted and tensed as he drove. He steered with one hand hooked over the wheel, his other arm resting between them on the bench seat.

He reached out and patted her knee. "How are you doing over there? Need to stop for anything?"

She resisted the urge to push his hand higher up her thigh. When she'd first met Tony, his constant touching had made her uncomfortable. She wasn't particularly physically demonstrative, and it took a while to get used to Tony's habitual invasion of her personal space. But she'd realized quickly that he meant nothing by it, that he was just a warm, touchy-feely person.

Pretty soon she came to enjoy how he would sling an arm around her shoulders or give her an encouraging squeeze after a hard day. It wasn't his fault that his friendly touches had her hormones screaming for more.

"No, I'm fine," she smiled.

"So tell me about your family. You don't talk about them much."

"I told you, my dad's a director for television, and my brother does the same thing in New York."

"What about your mom? You've never talked about her before, so I thought she might be out of the picture."

She clenched her jaw and wove her fingers nervously. "My mom used to be an actress, before my brother and I were born."

"Really? Was she famous at all?"

She sighed. The moment of truth had come. She hoped Tony wouldn't get all weird and freaked out like every other guy. "*You* might know who she is."

Tony glanced at her curiously.

"Did you ever see that movie *The Rose Chamber?*"

Tony's brow furrowed. "Isn't that a p—"

"Adult film, yes," Lauren said. "My mother is Carlotta Banks. Or, Carly MacLean, as she's known now."

Tony's gorgeous brown eyes almost popped out of his head. "Your mother is—"

"A porn legend. She and my father met when he directed one of her films. Nowadays he does commercials and Lifetime movies of the week, but that's how he got his start."

Tony shook his head, stunned. "That movie was a classic. Right up there with *Behind the Green Door,* and *Deep Throat.*" His eyebrows raised and he got a wild look in his eyes. "And your mom—" he broke off, frowned. "That was *your* mom? That was your *mom!*"

Damn. He was going to get weird on her, just like every other guy she ever brought home. Oh well, at least this thing wasn't for real. She hoped Tony could still power through it. "Yeah, I know, I look nothing like her, I act nothing like her, and I am anything but a firecracker in the sack."

Tony's eyes left the road momentarily to study her. "I don't remember what her face looks like, but I think you might have her rack."

Shocked laughter erupted from her throat. Only Tony could say that to her without getting his ass kicked.

"And as far as the other . . ." his voice got deep and rich, the one that made her think of chocolate-dipped body parts. "I bet if a guy knew what he was doing, you'd show him a damn good time."

She barely had time to absorb that remark when he said, his tone more serious, "That must have been a heavy load of baggage growing up."

For all that he loved to needle people, Tony knew when it was time to stop teasing, and he often surprised her with his sensitivity. The same insight he used to mercilessly bust her chops allowed him to see what no other man in her experience had. "Yeah, being the daughter of a porn queen can leave you pretty confused about the whole sex thing."

Tony snorted at her understatement. "How old were you when you found out?"

"Thirteen. One of the kids at school found a tape in his parent's room and couldn't wait to tell the rest of the class that Mrs. MacLean was in a 'naked movie' and doing all sorts of crazy stuff. I told my mom, expecting her to deny it, but she got this look on her face and I knew it was true."

"How did she explain it?"

"Back when she was working, in the seventies, she considered what she and Dad were doing art. They were helping to free American culture from our puritanical hang-ups about sex." She sighed and looked out the window as they flew past the farms of the central valley. "Unfortunately, the kids in my school didn't really see the artistic value." No, instead they expected her to be the same. So she'd started wearing baggy clothes and acting tough enough that boys finally forgot she was a girl. Even when she'd gone to college and no one knew who her mother was, she'd continued to downplay her femininity. "I hope this doesn't freak you out too much," she said finally.

Tony smiled, his eyes so dark and warm she almost leaned over to rest her head in his lap. "Don't worry about it."

Relief coursed through her. "Thank God. I figured if anyone could handle this situation, it would be you."

"What's that supposed to mean?"

"Just that you have a casual attitude about sex, and don't seem to have any issues changing partners like you change your underwear," she stammered, surprised at his defensive tone. Had she inadvertently offended him?

"You know, I'm not the male slut you seem to think I am," he said hotly.

"I didn't mean to imply that you were." She was silent a minute, smarting at his unnecessarily sharp tone. "But you're not exactly known for being discriminating."

"At least I don't spend Saturday night curled up with a romance novel and my vibrator."

Five hours later, Lauren still hadn't said a word to him other than replying when he asked for directions. By the time they turned onto her parent's street the tension had evolved into a living force inside the car.

Tony rolled his eyes. He knew the vibrator crack had been an obnoxious thing to say, but it pissed him off that she saw him as some kind of major player. Damned if he knew why. Why should he care what she thought about his bedroom habits?

Besides, it wasn't even true, not recently, anyway. He'd slowed way down since all of his brothers had gotten married and engaged. Not only had he lost his wing man when Mike married Karen; he seemed to have lost his taste for casual encounters. Instead, for the past three months his healthier than average libido had been keenly focused on the woman seated to his right. Too bad his brain had been equally focused on resisting temptation, unwilling to let his dick fuck up a surprisingly deep friendship.

Lauren curled up against the passenger door, squeezing herself as far away from him as possible. Shit. If they were to have a snowball's chance in hell of succeeding in the weekend's charade, he needed to offer up a convincing apology.

"I'm sorry for what I said earlier," he said quietly. "I know it was a dick thing to say, but it bothers me that you think of me as some kind of slut."

She didn't unfold her arms, but she at least looked at him when she replied. "Tony, I don't give a crap how many people you sleep with, and I don't see why my opinion would matter, anyway."

Because maybe that's keeping you from wanting to sleep with me, he thought. To her, he said, "Yeah, well your opinion does matter. And on the off chance that you do care, I haven't been with anyone since Nick's bachelor party."

Her eyes widened in shock. "You? Go three months without sex? I don't believe it."

He shrugged. "Believe whatever you want, but it's the truth."

"What about last Saturday? I thought going 'out' was like your code phrase for getting a piece of ass."

"Mike and I met a couple friends at Pete's and listened to the band. I was home by midnight, *alone.*"

The corners of her mouth just barely pushed up. She was

pleased, for all that she tried to look like she didn't give a shit who he slept with.

Something suspiciously similar to joy burst in his chest at the thought that she cared, and Tony did his best to stifle it.

"That *was* a jerky thing to say," she said. "Unlike you, I don't exactly have members of the opposite sex breaking down my door—"

"Only because you don't want them to—"

"And for the record," she continued, "I don't use a vibrator. Turn here," she said, indicating a driveway to the right.

"Well, let me know if you ever need a hand," he cracked, then sucked in a breath as they pulled into the large circular drive of a beachfront mansion. Even in the dark, there was no mistaking it. Lauren's parents were *loaded!*

The cobblestone drive sported a fountain in the center, complete with a bronze statue of a cherub pissing. To the right was what looked like at least a four-car garage. Several more cars lined the drive, and in the glow of the outdoor lights, Tony counted two Ferraris, a Rolls, and a Humvee.

"You never told me your parents were rich," he accused.

Lauren's expression was sheepish. "I told you he worked in television."

Tony shook his head. "Why do you live in that shitty little apartment and drive that hunk of junk?"

Lauren shrugged. "I let them pay for college and they bought me my first really good tool set. But for the most part, I like knowing that I can make it on my own."

He couldn't help but admire her. He'd met a lot of trust-fund babes who came up to ski at the resorts near Donner Lake. Most wouldn't consider lifting a finger for a wage, much less choose a career of manual labor. "Damn, there's at least a million dollars worth of automotive gear in the driveway alone," he said on a low whistle.

She sighed heavily. "Unfortunately, they don't all belong to my folks. Looks like they're having another one of their gatherings." Lauren smoothed her hair and tried to brush the rumples from her blouse caused by eight straight hours in the car. "My mom will use any excuse to have a party."

At that moment, the front door was flung open and Lauren braced herself as an energetic bundle flew down the front steps and threw herself into Lauren's arms.

Tony had an impression of wild black curls and a lush body hovering just on the edge of plumpness, all packaged in a bright purple sundress. As she stood back, holding Lauren by the shoulders, he knew this had to be Lauren's mother. Though Lauren towered over her mother and had reddish hair instead of blue black, Tony could tell Lauren had inherited her wide, full smile, sculpted bone structure, and big eyes from Carlotta Banks.

Not to mention the spectacular cleavage, but Tony was trying to ignore that. Former porn star or not, Carlotta was, after all, Lauren's mother.

"Sweetie, you look absolutely gorgeous," Carlotta gushed, holding Lauren's hands out to her sides.

Tony stifled a laugh as Lauren begrudgingly turned in a circle so her mother could appreciate the full effect of her outfit.

Big dark eyes lit on Tony's face and Carlotta's grin grew even wider, if that was possible. "Oooh, you must be Tony," she said and caught him in a fierce, quick hug. She stood back and cast a sidelong glance at Lauren. "I can see why you'd want to pretty yourself up for this one. He's absolutely gorgeous," she cooed. Tony stood gamely as Carlotta ran her hands from his shoulders to his forearms. "And so delightfully *big*."

Lauren's expression dared him to make a lewd remark. "Thanks, Mrs. MacLean," was all he said.

"Oh, you must call me Carly," she said as she looped an arm through each of their elbows and tugged them into the house. The clacking of her heels echoed off the marble floors and Tony was so dumbstruck by the sheer display of wealth he almost didn't catch what Carly said next.

"I was so excited when Lauren said she was bringing you, Tony. And I can't tell you how nice it is to see her dating someone size-appropriate."

"Mom," Lauren said warningly.

"Honestly, Tony, the last guy she brought home was so spindly, you just know she would have broken his hips if she got on top."

"*Motherrrr!*"

Tony couldn't contain his laughter this time. Lauren's face got even redder when he said, "Nothing to worry about there, Carly. I'm built very . . . solidly." He followed this with a heated glance at Lauren.

She rolled her eyes.

Tony stopped and gently disengaged his arm from Carly's and grabbed Lauren around the waist. Knowing that Carly watched his every move with great interest, he said, "Come on, honey, don't be embarrassed," he said, and leaned in close to whisper, "Better start the show."

Before she could react, he caught her firm chin in his fingers and tilted her mouth up to his. He tasted her gasp of surprise, felt her shock as his lips moved over hers. Teasingly, he flicked his tongue against the soft curves, almost groaning when she suddenly remembered her role and obligingly parted her lips. Her hands slid up to wrap around his neck, and finally she kissed him back like the lover she pretended to be.

The hot slide of her tongue against his sent a bolt of heat straight to his groin. He'd imagined kissing her, touching her, for months, and the reality was better than anything he'd ever imagined. She tasted sweet and salty, and the tentative flicks of her tongue made him want to yank down his jeans and bury his cock in her right there in her mother's foyer.

His hand settled in the firm curve of her waist and slid it

slowly up her rib cage. His fingers tingled as they anticipated the soft heavy weight of her breast against them.

But Lauren frantically grabbed his wrist, stopping his progress north. Tearing her mouth from his, she leaned in as though to kiss his neck and breathed, "I think she's convinced we like each other."

Heat flooded his face as he reminded himself sternly that this was all supposed to be an act. "Right," he said and looked up to see Carly watching them with unabashed glee. He raked a shaky hand through his hair, very much afraid that by the time the weekend was over, he was going to have a record-setting case of blue balls.

"I'll get you two drinks and you can go say hello to your father. He's out by the pool with everyone else," she said, gesturing toward the back of the house. "Then you can go be alone," she winked.

Lauren clutched at Tony's hand for balance as they continued through the living room and down the hall to the pool deck. The combination of her flimsy kitten-heeled slides and Tony's unbelievable kiss were enough to throw her completely off-kilter. God, if that was the way he kissed when he was pretending, how would it feel if he meant it?

Not that it would ever happen, but she was pretty sure that if Tony ever turned the full force of his lust on her, she would spontaneously combust. Even now it was hard to keep her focus, and all he did was hold her hand, fingers tightly interlaced between hers.

About twenty people lounged around the pool deck, the night chill offset by several propane heat lamps. Mostly people from the entertainment industry—producers, directors, and their surgically enhanced trophy wives. Immediately she felt the familiar self-consciousness she experienced whenever she went home to southern California. That feeling of being too big, too bulky, ungroomed, and unkempt. Most of the time she was satisfied with her strong, athletic figure. She was toned and fit, and her body could do just about any athletic undertaking she asked of it. But somehow, around her parent's crowd, she suddenly felt like she should stop taking up so much goddamn space.

She snuck a glance at Tony, who was taking in the scene. She could only imagine how this must look to him, the beautiful people gathered around the exquisite infinity pool that seemed to drop into the ocean below. She could only pray that Tony could keep his prowling instinct at bay enough to convince her family he was truly into her. So far he didn't look particularly interested in any of the female guests. But tomorrow would be worse, and Lauren had no doubt the guests would include any number of hot young things who had worked with Lauren's father.

Mark MacLean presided at the bar—a big redhead with a jovial smile that hid a cunningly sharp creative mind. When he saw Lauren, a wide smile creased his tan, freckled face and his blue eyes nearly disappeared in a sea of laugh lines. He came out from behind the bar and swept her up into a big bear hug. She buried her face in his chest and inhaled the familiar, comforting scents of Irish spring soap and salty air.

"Look at you! You look like a girl," he said bluntly, his words softened by the admiration in his gaze. "I tell you, I could cast you for commercials."

Lauren rolled her eyes.

"I mean it. I'm doing a shoot for a health club chain, and we need footage of someone strong, fit, and gorgeous."

"She's definitely all that," Tony said behind her and offered his hand to Mark.

Lauren made a quick introduction and fought a grin as her father pinned Tony with an assessing stare. It was the age-old way fathers had of intimidating anyone who tried to get into their daughter's pants. To his credit, Tony maintained his pleasant smile and said, "You have a lovely home, sir."

That's right, she thought, lay on that Eddie Haskell act, the one that no doubt fooled dozens of fathers over the years.

Mark ignored the compliment. "So you and Lauren work together."

"Yes sir, for about the past seven months."

"And how long have you been seeing each other?"

"Four months," he said at the exact same moment Lauren said, "Two months."

"Well, which is it?"

Tony smiled conspiratorially at Mark and said, "For a couple of months there, what she considered hanging, I considered dates." He slipped his arm around her shoulders and she allowed herself the luxury of leaning into his solid warmth.

Mark chuckled, his face relaxing as he was convinced of Tony's affection. "Sounds like Lauren. She always had guy friends, but never realized they wanted to do more than watch football, if you know what I mean."

She shook her head as they shared a knowing laugh. If only what her dad said was true. She'd never told her parents about that humiliating incident with Brandon, the one time she'd been stupid enough to try to push the boundaries of friendship.

"Hey, don't pout," Tony leaned in and stole a quick peck. The brief contact was enough to startle her from her musings. But almost immediately, grim thoughts intruded. Once again, she lusted after her best friend. Only this time she had the added bonus of being tormented by touches and kisses that would lead absolutely nowhere.

"I'm not pouting," she said, pulling away slightly. "I'm just tired from the drive."

"Just one drink, sweetie, and then we'll let you go." Carly's heels clacked across the terra-cotta stone terrace and she thrust icy glasses into their hands. "I hope you like mojitos, Tony," Carly said with a wink. "That's the official drink of the evening."

Tony took a tentative sip and nodded in satisfaction. *Damn, he's good,* Lauren thought as she took a hefty sip of her own drink. She knew for a fact that Tony hated hard liquor in any form, and was strictly a beer and wine guy. But as he politely sipped his drink and made small talk with Lauren's parents, his face showed no evidence of his distaste. Unless, like Lauren, one had spent several hours a day for over six months watching and studying every gorgeous line of his face. Even then it was hard to spot, but Lauren could see the faint twist of his lips with every sip, the slight flare of his nostrils as the bite of the liquor hit his throat.

And they say women fake it.

Lauren quickly polished off her drink, eager to escape her parents' inspection and the pleasure-pain of Tony's delicious loverlike touches that meant absolutely nothing.

She stretched her jaw in an exaggerated yawn. "I'm beat. Mom, should we put our stuff in my room?"

"Oh, no, dear," Carly said with her tinkling, charming little laugh. "I booked you a room at the Balboa Bay Club." She winked conspiratorially at Tony. "I wouldn't want you to feel inhibited by sleeping in the same house as your parents."

"Carly," Mark said warningly.

"Oh Mark, don't be such an old stiffie." Even the usually cool Tony couldn't smother a laugh at Carly's interesting choice of words. Mark just rolled his eyes in exaggerated affection.

"Now, you two go on, and we'll see you tomorrow." Wild curls and the scent of gardenia enveloped Lauren as her mother pulled her close. "But not too early," she whispered, loud enough for Tony to hear.

3

Not too early turned out to be about six-thirty AM for Tony. Even that was a test of his endurance. For a man not big on self-restraint, spending even one *platonic* night in the same bed as Lauren was enough to send him over the edge. Now, as the morning sun turned the ocean from dark blue to marine, he ran down the sandy stretch, ignoring the burning of his calf muscles as they dug into the soft sand.

With limited privacy in the room, a run was the best way he could think of to eradicate the truly spectacular (if he did say so himself) display of morning wood he'd woken up with this morning.

He'd known he was up shit's creek the minute they entered the room at the Balboa Bay Club. All the suites were taken, Carly had explained, so they would have to make do with a regular ocean-view room.

It was still the nicest hotel room Tony had ever been in. Expensively furnished and beautifully decorated in shades of sage green, the room had every amenity a man could ask for. From the fully stocked wet bar, state of the art entertainment system, and private balcony that offered an unimpeded view of the Pacific, the room epitomized luxury.

It had only one glaring flaw.

Only one bed.

Lauren had shot him a wary glance as the bellman placed their bags on the luggage tray. As soon as the bellman left, Tony had indicated the overstuffed sofa. "I'll sleep there."

"No way," Lauren had protested. "You're doing me the favor, so if anyone sleeps on the couch, it should be me." She'd studied the bed, frowning. "Or we could always share the bed," she'd offered tentatively.

That stymied him. On the one hand, he knew a night in the same bed as Lauren, listening to her soft breath, knowing her sleepy warmth was just inches away, was guaranteed torture. On the other hand, some heretofore undiscovered masochistic side of him wanted nothing more than to sleep beside her.

And she looked so worried, biting that succulent lower lip that he knew would taste like tart lime and rum, how could he hurt her feelings by refusing?

"Okay," he'd agreed. "Damn thing is so big it practically has two zip codes."

With that settled, the brewing tension had eased somewhat, helped along by a couple of beers from the minibar.

Until Tony had discovered some additional nonstandard amenities in the room. The basket looked innocent enough, large and brown, made of woven wood. It even had a bouquet of flowers. The fact that they were those tropical flowers that looked like they had penises should have tipped him off.

But the contents were anything but innocent. Sipping idly at his beer as Lauren channel surfed in search of the Giants score, he'd started rummaging through the contents. He pulled out the first item and dropped it as though it were a rattlesnake.

"What the hell?" The pink rubber dildo bounced as it hit the carpet. Along with it were a pair of velvet-lined handcuffs, cherry-flavored massage oil, and a pair of panties with some sort of battery hookup.

The image of Lauren handcuffed to the bed as he sucked cherry essence off her nipples was enough to make his cock jerk in immediate and violent interest.

"What is it?"

He carefully kept his back to her as she came up behind him. She gasped, startled, when she saw the unnaturally bright penis on the floor. "Oh, no."

She shoved him aside and dug through the basket, muttering and shaking her head. A few seconds later, she triumphantly held up a card and tore it open, mumbling, "I knew it."

"Dear Lauren," she read, her voice ringing with exasperated disbelief, "I hope you enjoy the toys. I wasn't sure what flavor Tony liked, so I picked cherry. It seems to be a universal favorite. Love, Mom."

"I don't believe her," Lauren moaned, sinking onto the bed, face flaming. Her mouth gaped and her eyes got wide, as though she were on the verge of hysterical laughter or hysterical tears.

Humor was the only way out of this. Picking up the rubbery latex dildo, he shook it in Lauren's face. "I think I may be insulted. Is your mom implying I can't get the job done?"

Lauren shrieked and fell back, giggling as she tried to escape the fake penis waving snakelike next to her nose. "Gross!" She snatched it from him, shrieking again when she realized she held a ten-inch—and but for the color—very realistic-looking replica of an erect penis. "This is ridiculous! I mean, it's so big it has to be a joke."

Tony looked pointedly at his fly and back to the dildo. "I dunno. Length-wise, I'd say it's about a match, but girth-wise I think I have it beat."

Laughter fled from her eyes and her eyes got dark and speculative. But a nanosecond later the humor was back and she just rolled her eyes. "Yeah, I'll bet."

"Just say the word and I'll show you the proof," he waggled his eyebrows, eliciting another laugh, and sat down on the edge of the bed next to her.

"She is so inappropriate," Lauren said incredulously. "What mother buys her daughter—and a boyfriend she's never met—a full array of sex toys?"

He had no answer for that, and sensed she wasn't really seeking one. He looked down and saw that, in her frustration, Lauren was twisting the rubbery shaft rather violently. "It hurts me to watch you do that," he said, gently removing it from her grip.

She looked down, and realizing what she was doing, dropped the rubbery phallus with a muffled curse.

"With technique like that, no wonder she worries about your sex life," Tony chuckled.

Hurt embarrassment flooded her eyes then, and he knew he'd hit a particularly raw nerve. "Hey, I was just kidding," he said quickly, "you know that."

She wouldn't meet his eyes. "Some of us aren't natural contenders for the bedroom Olympics," she said and disappeared into the bathroom.

He hated that she made him feel like an asshole, especially when he had no way of knowing he'd poked a sore spot. By the time Lauren emerged from the bathroom fifteen minutes later, he'd worked up a decent level of irritation.

But then she sat down on the bed next to him, face scrubbed clean of makeup and looking so earnest as she laid a palm on his thigh. "I'm sorry I overreacted. Don't be mad, okay?"

He laid his hand over hers, feeling like even more of dick. "It's my fault. Sometimes I don't know what's off-limits."

She smiled in consternation. "Usually I can take it, as you well know. But my love life—or lack thereof—is a sensitive subject."

One she hadn't been willing to discuss any further, and by

mutual agreement the subject was dropped. The dildo went back into the basket, which was shoved as far back in the closet as possible.

Now as he pounded back up the beach to the hotel, he wondered what had happened to Lauren to make her so self-conscious about her own sexuality. She wasn't uptight and was rarely offended by his often vulgar sense of humor, but now that he thought about it, she never talked about her own sex life. And it wasn't just the pressures of having a porn star for a mom, although he imagined that was enough to give any woman a complex.

All the more reason to stay far, far away from her. Tony made it a point to give women with sexual baggage a wide berth, as they were more likely to put a high value on sex, often confusing it with commitment or love, and the last thing he wanted was to hurt Lauren further. But how a woman as beautiful and sexy as she could be so shy when it came to sex, he didn't understand. Then again, he didn't understand 99.9% about women and their hang-ups.

Lauren spent most of her hour-long run psyching herself up for the evening to come. Tony had already been up and out by the time she woke up for the second time. The first time had been at about four AM and she'd been plastered against Tony, her breasts nestled against the unyielding muscles of his back, her leg hooked over his. Through the fabric of her tank top and his T-shirt she felt the heat of his skin, the subtle shift of muscle and sinew as he breathed deep in sleep.

In some part of her sleep-fogged mind, she tried to dismiss the urge to cuddle as the result of overpowered air conditioning. But the need for warmth didn't explain why her nipples were beaded into hard knots or why her pussy throbbed and ached against the firm muscles of his ass.

Even in sleep, her body had sensed and submitted to Tony's sexual magnetism.

Thank God she'd managed to scoot away without him being any the wiser. Like it wasn't embarrassing enough that her mother had sent them a basket of sex toys. She couldn't bear to seal her humiliation by actually hitting on him, even it if it was in her sleep.

At the very least, she thought, as she rode the elevator up to their room, she would have no difficulty convincing her parents and their friends of her attraction. And Tony had already proven his ability to convincingly fake it.

She slid the card key in the door and wiped her sweaty face with the hem of her T-shirt. She pushed open the door and her heart rate immediately spiked at the sight that greeted her.

Tony stood in the middle of the room clad only in a towel, evidently having just stepped from the shower. Beads of water slid down the silky dark skin of his chest, disappearing into the towel wrapped around his waist. His forearm flexed as he flipped through channels on the remote, and Lauren was mesmerized by the play of muscle under flesh from such a ridiculously ordinary motion.

Unconsciously, she licked her lips as another bead slid from his damp, slicked-back hair, pausing on his neck before traveling down the slope of shoulder.

"Are you okay? You look flushed."

Her gaze snapped to his face and he greeted her with a friendly smile, as though there was nothing unusual about being in a room together with him practically naked but for a strategically placed swath of terry cloth.

"It's already hot out," she said, hoping that would be adequate explanation for her undoubtedly beet-red face. Of course this was normal, she thought sullenly, trying to cool her body's overheated reaction. Tony saw her as just one of the guys, right? No doubt he felt no more uncomfortable than he would in the men's locker room at the gym.

She twisted open a bottle of water and stomped onto the balcony so she wouldn't have to look at and lust after his nearly perfect form. What was the big deal, anyway? It wasn't as though she'd never seen Tony with his shirt off. Hell, she'd even seen him in a bathing suit when they'd gone out to the lake over the summer.

And every time, lust had raged, but not like this. Somehow this was more intimate. There was actually a bed not ten feet from her. If she were the sort of woman to make the first move, she might strip off his towel with a smooth flick of her wrist, push him back on the bed and climb on for the ride of her life.

Instead she gulped the icy spring water and contemplated shoving the bottle between her thighs.

Tony followed her outside, bearing a cup of coffee. She snuck a sidelong glance, noting that he still hadn't dressed. Mimicking his casual demeanor, she took the cup and sipped, nodding in approval as she tasted just the right amount of milk and sugar. The reminder of familiarity grounded her and she managed not to gape or drool when she turned to face him.

He leaned back against the railing, arms crossed over his naked chest. His hair was nearly dry, faintly curling around his ears and sweeping off his forehead in that cowlick she so loved. She could smell the scent of soap and his skin, heated from the morning sun, and it took everything she had not to bury her nose in his chest and kiss a path down the soft line of hair bisecting his abdomen.

But, while he smelled intoxicating, she knew she didn't. Even though she and Tony had worked out together dozens of time, she was suddenly embarrassed by the sweaty, smelly mess she presented. She quickly finished her coffee and said, "I'm going to shower and we can go get breakfast." She prayed he'd be dressed by the time she got out of the shower.

* * *

They were entering dangerous territory.

Tony couldn't ignore the flash of lust in Lauren's eyes, and he knew her flush came from more than the morning heat. There'd been no disguising the interest in her eyes, the heat of her gaze as it slid over every inch of his bare skin. He'd hoped to be dressed by the time she got back, but it would have been weird if he'd scrambled for his clothes the second she came in. So he'd played it off as no big deal, praying she couldn't see his burgeoning erection threatening to tent out the front of his towel.

But now he knew, with one-hundred-percent certainty, that Lauren wasn't indifferent to him at all. That her indifference was just an act, and that underneath her friendly façade, she wanted him as much as he wanted her.

He quickly pulled on his clothes as erotic images flooded his brain. His mouth watered at the thought of stripping her naked, sucking those gorgeous tits into his mouth. Were her nipples pink or mocha brown? Large and soft or hard, tight buds?

From the bathroom came sounds of the shower running. He could find out right now. His cock swelled against his fly as he imagined water sluicing over her skin, cascading over the firm juicy swell of her ass, gathering and beading in the wiry curls between her thighs.

His hand was reaching for the doorknob when he was jerked back to reality by the sound of the faucet shutting off. What the hell was he thinking? Did he want to ruin everything?

He squeezed his eyes shut, taking a few deep breaths in an effort to quell the urge to barge into the bathroom and lick her dry. Every nerve hummed in anticipation as he listened to the muffled sounds from the bathroom. He imagined her rubbing her fresh, sweet-smelling lotion on her damp skin. He'd discovered it earlier when he showered and had nearly come when he'd recognized the soft, subtle scent that always emanated from her skin. He'd rubbed a bit on his palm, stroked it down his shaft and jerked himself to a quick, hard release. He'd spurted against the shower wall as his head filled with the scent of Lauren and the imagined feel of her wet, exquisitely tight pussy milking him as she came.

Christ, he needed to stop thinking about her or he was going to need to rub another one out just to keep from jumping her when she exited the bathroom.

Somehow Lauren managed to keep her wits about her as she and Tony spent the morning running last-minute errands for her mother and picking up the anniversary gift she'd had made for her parents. She'd special-ordered a framed collage full of old photos of their family throughout the years.

Tony was his usual entertaining and charming self, and for a little while Lauren allowed herself to fantasize about what it would be like if they were a couple. Really nice, she decided as they walked hand in hand along the boardwalk. He'd escalated his usual friendly touches, holding her hand and dropping the occasional kiss on her cheek.

At first, she'd stiffened at the contact, unsure of what to make of it. Tony had scolded her, reminding her of his purpose there this weekend. "You need to stop jumping like a scalded cat every time I touch you," he'd said. "If you want people to believe we're lovers, you have to give the impression that you're used to my hands on you."

"You stuck your tongue down my throat in front of everyone last night," Lauren snapped. "I thought that was pretty convincing."

Tony shook his head. "Lovers share a level of intimacy, a familiarity with one another's bodies that's conveyed almost unconsciously." He moved purposely closer, until the scent of soap and light masculine sweat hit her nostrils. "They get in each other's space."

"You're always in my space," she muttered.

"But now you notice, where you didn't before."

Oh, she had always noticed.

"You're self-conscious about it, now that you actually have to *pretend* you're attracted to me," he said. His dark eyes and darker voice hypnotized her as he leaned closer. "See, you're stiffening up," he kneaded her shoulders for emphasis and her knees went gummy. "You need to relax, act as though you're used to having me touch you all the time," he leaned and his hot breath tickled her earlobe, "used to having me touch you everywhere."

Oh, she was toast. He could have stripped off her shorts and fucked her right there on the sidewalk if he'd wanted. Instead he'd tucked her hand in his and Lauren spent the rest of the day indulging herself in his loverlike caresses, twining her fingers in his, leaning into his wall of a chest when he slipped an arm around her waist, even nuzzling her nose into the heated dip in his throat.

Of course, none of this meant anything, she reminded herself firmly during her fleeting moments of sanity.

But hey, if he wanted to bulk up on rehearsal time, who was she to complain?

By the time she showered and got ready for the party, every nerve hummed with sexual anticipation. All the more frustrating because she knew it would go unsatisfied. Oh well. At the very least it distracted her from being nervous.

She combed the styling product Karen had given her into her damp hair, marveling again at how the slippery stuff turned her mop of frizz into smooth, bouncy curls. Then, following Karen's instructions, she pulled the heavy mass into a twist, allowing a few tendrils to curl around her face and neck.

She studied her makeup with a critical eye. Karen had supplied her with a palette of neutral tones, assuring Lauren that anyone with opposable thumbs could do an acceptable makeup job. "You can't overapply any of this," she'd sworn. "As long as you don't streak mascara down your cheek, you'll be just fine."

Lauren wasn't a complete moron with makeup, but it had been ages since she'd worn more than sunscreen, mascara, and lipstick. She slicked on one last coat of peach gloss, noting that the color almost matched the flowers on her dress.

Now the dress, that really freaked her out. She stepped back a few feet, wishing the dressing area had a full-length mirror. In the vanity she could only see herself from the waist up, and she wondered for at least the dozenth time why she'd allowed Karen to talk her into buying this.

Not that the creamy floral print didn't flatter her smooth, tan complexion and reddish hair, but it left her so . . . bare. The crisscross bodice put her breasts at the center of attention, plumping them up until they remained covered only by a miracle of fashion engineering. The spaghetti straps showed her toned arms and shoulders, and, while Karen claimed she looked strong and sexy, Lauren feared she bore a more than passing resemblance to a linebacker. The bias cut skimmed her ample curves and the hem settled just above her knee. At least she'd keep cool in the unseasonably hot weather.

The shoes, she conceded, were semireasonable, although she would have much preferred buying them in a practical color like beige or even cream. But Karen had insisted the peach leather kitten-heel slides were the perfect complement to the dress. Thank God Karen hadn't pushed her into buying stilettos. The dress was precarious enough—any extra tottering or wobbling would have immediately resulted in a wardrobe malfunction.

Steeling herself, she straightened her shoulders and twirled a curl around her finger until it coiled just so. As she exited the dressing area, she saw Tony sitting in the overstuffed armchair near the sliding glass door of the balcony, looking hotter than sin. His wheat-colored button-down shirt emphasized the rich color of his skin and hair, while his tobacco-colored trousers molded to his defined thighs as he sat with his ankle propped on his knee. He had a funny half smile on his face as he read . . . her copy of *The Stealthy Rogue.*

"You really get off on this," he laughed, not looking up from the book. *"His hand caressed her plump mounds, seeking the hard berry tips pressing against her bodice."* He skimmed farther, choking on a laugh as he read, *"His thick shaft sprang from its curly nest!* Curly nest? Do women actually get off on this kind of shit?"

Lauren flew across the room and snatched the paperback from his grasp. "Shut up! I like the story." She stuffed the book in her suitcase.

She spun around, hands on hips to find Tony staring at her with what could only be classified as a stunned expression. His eyes raked her from curls to toe polish. One word, one crack, and she would clock him . . .

His gaze made a return trip up her legs, over her midsection and hung right about chest level. "Speaking of plump mounds . . ."

She picked up a pillow and threw it at him.

"You look . . ." he shook his head, searching for words. Had she actually rendered Tony Donovan, king of glib, speechless? "Unfuckingbelievable. I mean it, Lauren, you're on fire."

A wave of pleasure hit her as she saw the truth in his eyes. His expression reflected open admiration and maybe the barest hint of sexual interest in his dark chocolate eyes.

He picked up the car keys and steered her toward the door. "Let's go. I can't wait to show everyone the hottie I scored."

4

If that little punk didn't stop gaping at Lauren's tits, Tony was going to kick his ass so hard he'd taste it in the back of his throat.

He'd smelled trouble the second Lauren spotted him across the pool, noted the way he'd stared at Lauren as her parents renewed their vows. After dinner was served, Carly brought the douche bag's presence to Lauren's attention. "Look sweetie, Brandon's here. You haven't seen him in ages."

While Lauren had been well aware of Brandon's presence all along, as soon as her mother motioned him over, Lauren's arms had tensed. She immediately, unconsciously, started preening, straightening her shoulders, subtly sticking her chest out until Tony was afraid her breasts were going to spill out of the wispy fabric of her dress. Feigning casualness, Lauren waved at the guy who stood by the bar at the far side of the pool. Tony immediately resented the way she smiled with nervous anticipation, like she couldn't wait to get reacquainted and catch up on old times. "Who's Braden?" he'd asked, deliberately mispronouncing the name.

Lauren tracked the other man's progress, playing it cool, letting him come to her. "Brandon," she corrected, "was my best friend all through junior high and high school."

Best friend, my ass, he thought as he noted the nervous flutter of her pulse against her throat. He hated Brandon on sight, with his pretty-boy good looks and hundred-dollar haircut. He carried his lean frame with a grace that reeked of years spent on exclusive golf courses and sailing expensive yachts.

Lauren quickly introduced them and Tony firmly shook the other man's hand, mentally scoffing at its manicured smoothness.

As Lauren and Brandon began reminiscing about old times, Tony absently regarded his own oversize workman's hands. If Brandon even knew how to hold a hammer, Tony would dress up in a tutu and dance Swan Lake.

But none of that seemed to matter to Lauren, who had cozied right up to long-lost lover boy.

"Don't worry about Brandon," Carly whispered to his left.

He took a fortifying sip of beer. "Who's worried?"

Her laugh tinkled over the disco tune the DJ played. "Believe me, I know that look. I put it on Mark's face often enough. Lauren only has eyes for you. She just wants her little taste of revenge."

"For what?"

She waved her hand evasively. "She thinks I don't know about it but . . . well, she should be the one to tell you. Let's just say Brandon didn't appreciate what he had right in front of him."

Tony's eyes narrowed. If Brandon was any more appreciative of Lauren's bountiful charms, he would be dipping his tongue into her cleavage.

"So how long have you been dating *him?*" Tony heard Brandon ask. Tony's hand white-knuckled around his beer bottle at the other man's derisive tone. *Him,* as though Tony wasn't standing less than a yard away, as though he was some poor piece of trash she'd brought into their fancy little world.

He nearly shattered the bottle at Lauren's reply. "Not long. It's nothing very serious."

Translation: you could still have me if you want me.

Clearly, Lauren hadn't told him the whole story. This weekend wasn't about getting Mommy dearest to remove her nose from Lauren's love life; it was about making sure douche bag here saw what he'd been missing.

He grinned at that. If she wanted to make Brandon jealous, Tony would be only too happy to oblige. As long as neither Lauren nor Brandon had any illusions about whom Lauren would be spending the night with.

A voice warned him he was about to cross a line, and once he did, there would be no going back. But right now, he didn't care. He was sick of watching Lauren flirt with another man, sick of denying himself when he knew damn well she wanted it as bad as he did. Unfamiliar jealousy curdled in his gut as Lauren laughed huskily at something Brandon said.

His hand settled on the curve of her hip. Playtime was over. It was time to make his move.

Lauren started as Tony wrapped a possessive arm around her waist and pressed his warm, moist mouth against the tender skin of her throat. She shuddered as his hot breath caressed her ear.

"Now honey, I know you want to let him down gently, but when it comes to you and your sexy body, I'm very serious."

She couldn't see Tony's expression but she could tell from the subtle tension on Brandon's patrician features that Tony was giving him his patented "Don't fuck with me" stare. The same one he used when someone was stupid enough to think Tony's charming, affable surface hid either a lack of intelligence or a weak will.

Obligingly, Lauren lifted her arm behind her and wove her fingers into the waves at the back of Tony's neck. Brandon's lips pursed, and she nearly ruined the effect by giggling.

Poor Brandon. She was a jerk to mess with him this way, but she couldn't help herself. But seeing him again after all this time, she couldn't for the life of her figure out what she'd seen in him, as a friend or a lover. He was handsome, she supposed, in a bland, vanilla rich-boy sort of way. And now that she had years to reflect on the friendship they had shared, she saw how incredibly one-sided it had been.

Brandon was the kind of guy who wanted her around when he needed a designated driver, or someone to write an English paper he'd blown off until the last minute. But ask him for a favor and he acted like you were asking for the Hope diamond.

She couldn't help the feminine thrill that had zinged through her when he had noticed—and obviously appreciated—her temporary makeover.

Leer all you want, she thought as he gazed at her cleavage, made even more pronounced by Tony's arm pressing her breasts up from beneath. *You had your chance at this a long time ago, and you didn't give a shit.*

Playing it up, she leaned back against Tony and sighed, "Is it just my body you care about?" She tilted her head up and met Tony's very convincing amorous gaze. So convincing that for a moment she forgot her performance. Where Brandon was blandly pretty, Tony was all smoldering, hot, dark beauty, the embodiment of twisted sheets and hot sweaty sex.

Tony traced a seductive finger over her bottom lip. "You know better than that."

Brandon muttered something about refreshing his drink. Neither noticed when he left. Slowly Lauren turned in his arms, felt his hands slide from the bare skin of her shoulders down to her waist. His head bent slowly, almost tentatively, until finally his mouth met hers.

Heat coiled and exploded in her belly at that first gentle touch. Somehow, she knew this kiss was different. This was no act to convince her parents or Brandon or anyone else who might be watching that they were lovers. This was a slow slide, the inquisitive taste of a man asking a question and begging for a yes.

Lauren didn't care who saw them. She coiled her arms around Tony's neck and slid her tongue between his lips. He met it with a hot, slippery slide of his own, tasting hot and musky and so sexy she wanted to push him down on the patio and crawl all over him. Cupping her cheek, he tilted her head to the side, adjusting the angle of their kiss until he could fully explore every slick inch of her tongue and inner cheeks.

She almost burst into tears when he lifted his mouth. He looked around, dark eyes hooded and slightly dazed and said, "Well, I guess we reminded Brandon who you came with."

An icy knot gripped her intestines. How could she have been so stupid! Of course it was still an act to him, of course he was trying to put on a good show. Any genuine passion she'd imagined had only been a reflection of her own overstimulated hormones.

Then he gazed down at her with those sinful dark eyes. "How soon can we leave?"

"Anytime, I suppose. Why?"

He bent his head until his forehead rested against hers and he answered in a low whisper. "Because I want to take you back to the hotel and fuck you until we're both too tired to move." He emphasized this with a subtle shift of his hips, until she could feel the hard press of his cock against her belly. Even through the fabric of their clothing she could feel the heat, the throbbing tension barely contained by the fly of his trousers.

Every nerve ending went on high alert as creamy wetness gushed between her thighs. There began a steady pulsebeat, matched in the hollow of her throat and the hard points of her nipple.

"I'll get my purse."

The second they stepped into the hotel room, a kernel of unease formed in the back of Lauren's head. What if this ruined everything? He was her best friend, and if she lost that closeness, she didn't know what she'd do. Worse, she'd have to watch him—or at least hear about him—and his other women. She had no illusions about Tony and his capacity for commitment, and knew that once he slept with a woman a handful of times, he quickly moved on to the next hot thing.

She was half in love with him and jealous of him as it was. Having sex could only make it worse.

Tony's dark gaze tracked her patiently, deliberately, as though he had all night to coax her out of her skittishness. She opened the sliding glass door and stepped out onto the balcony, hoping the sound of the waves and the cool, salty breeze would calm her roiling confusion.

Tony stepped out behind her and she gripped the railing, bracing herself as his big hands settled firmly on her hips. "Don't be nervous." His hot, open mouth suckled deliciously at the juncture of her shoulder, awakening nerves that seemed to have a direct line of communication with her pussy.

"I'm afraid this will—" she choked on a gasp as his hand came up to tease the underside of her breast through the thin fabric of her dress. "It will ruin everything, our," oh God, his thumb was rasping across her nipple, "our friendship."

"Not if we don't let it." He sounded like he was convincing himself as much as he was her. His other hand came up to join the first, and now he was gently kneading and cupping her breasts in his massive palms.

She made one last stab at sanity as her womb clenched and

her pussy throbbed and bloomed. "I don't know if this is a good idea."

His chuckle was almost menacing. "Can you feel how hard I am?" He ground his granite hard erection against the curve of her ass for emphasis. "I haven't had a hard-on like this since high school." The undercurrent of wonder in his voice sent a warm thrill down her spine. His hand slid down her belly, pressing her back against him until his cock snuggled firmly into the curve of her ass. She tilted her head back and he caught her mouth in a wild, tongue-thrusting kiss. The firm, pumping thrust of his tongue sent her inner muscles quivering as she anticipated the similar thrusting of his cock deep inside her.

"And," he continued, "you want me so much you're shaking with it, aren't you? I bet you're already so wet I could slide in you right now and I haven't even gotten your dress off."

Heat flamed in her cheeks as she quivered against him, too embarrassed to answer. No man—not that she had much comparison—had ever talked to her like this. Uneasiness returned as she felt suddenly very out of her league.

If Tony noticed her apprehension, he chose to ignore it. "If you're not going to answer me, I'll just have to find out for myself."

She bit her lip in anticipation as he pushed her skirt up her thigh and slid his fingers into the leg of her lace panties. He pressed his fingers into her creamy slit, groaning in satisfaction. "You're so hot I can smell it," he breathed, and she thought she'd die of embarrassment when the rich, briny scent of her arousal hit her nostrils. She struggled to pull away, but he kept her there with the firm pressure of his fingers slowly circling her clit.

Another rush of moisture oozed out, and he spread the creamy wetness generously over her throbbing flesh. "Do you know how many times I thought of touching you like this?"

His tongue snaked out and flicked her earlobe as his fingers spread, imprisoning her plump clit from either side.

A strangled sound was her only reply.

To her vast disappointment, his hand slid from her panties. Her dress pulled tight, then loosened as he slid the zipper open to her hips. Impatiently he pushed it down until the fabric puddled around her ankles, and she shivered as the cool night breeze teased her overheated skin.

"Someone might see," she whispered, pressing back against him and feeling all the more naked as the soft cotton of his shirt and the wool of his trousers rasped against her bare back and thighs.

He stifled her protests with a hard, carnal kiss and hefted the full weight of her breasts in his big hands. Callused thumbs circled and flicked at her nipples, and soon she didn't care if the whole world watched, as long as he kept touching her. She groaned at the hot slide of his lips and tongue across her shoulders, arched her back as he traced a fiery wet trail down her spine to the small of her back.

"This is better than I ever imagined," he breathed into the sensitive skin above the lace edge of her panties. "Your skin is smoother, your mouth is sweeter." He groaned again as he pushed her panties down her hips to join her dress. "And this," he slid his fingers into her hot core from behind, working one thick finger into her throbbing channel. Between sucking kisses on her thighs and ass cheeks he murmured, "Your pussy is so perfect. Wet and tight . . . I'm afraid I'm gonna come the second I get inside you."

Lauren moaned, inching her legs apart, urging him to work that digit even deeper. "I've been dreaming of getting inside you for so long I don't know if I can wait, but there's something else I've been wanting since I first laid eyes on you."

His finger withdrew and at the urging of his hands on her

hips she turned around, hands braced on the wrought iron railing for support. Her mind could barely get itself around the vision they presented: her standing, naked but for her silly little sandals, breasts swollen and achy, legs slightly parted. Him, still fully clothed, kneeling before her with demonic lust radiating from his eyes.

Her legs started to shake, the skin of her belly quivered. Dear God, this was really happening. She was really going to do this. And after tonight nothing would ever be the same.

He leaned in, close enough for her to feel his hot breath parting the neatly trimmed patch of curls. "I know you're going to taste so good . . ." His thumbs spread her pussy lips wide and she threw her head back, eyes closing as his lips closed over her clit. "Mmmmm," his satisfied groan vibrated through her, and a low harsh sound she'd never heard erupted from her throat.

He ravished her with hot, lavish strokes of his tongue, searing sucks of his lips. She'd never had a lover do this to her and now she knew what the fuss was about. The moist pull of his lips, the firm thrusts and flicks of his tongue were beyond anything she'd ever imagined, even in her hottest fantasies.

The tip of his tongue circled her clit once, twice, then furrowed into her slit, licking firmly up and down before thrusting inside. She squirmed to get closer. The soft hard penetration was at once mind-blowing and maddeningly unfulfilling. She needed something harder, thicker, driving inside.

As though he read her mind, he slipped his tongue from her snug canal and again fastened his lips around the pulsing bud of her clit. One finger, then another, stretched her wide and the combined pressure was enough to make her shout. His low murmurs of pleasure and the soft, sucking sounds of his loving sent flashes of heat radiating from her clit to every nerve ending in her body.

Pleasure coiled like a spring low in her pelvis, and she

rocked against his mouth, urging him to suck her harder, to fuck her deeper with those skilled fingers. Her orgasm hit her in an explosion of color and light, gold and red bursts firing behind her eyelids. She had a fleeting hope that she wouldn't launch herself backward over the railing.

Luckily Tony was there, sliding up her body and wrapping his arms around her. The cool, crisp fabric of his shirt rasped against her heated skin and she shuddered as he devoured her mouth. Her own musky scent clung to his lips, mingling with the scent of his lime shaving cream.

He sucked and bit at her lips, pulling her hands up to the front of his shirt. Obligingly she worked her way down the row of buttons, eager to get him as naked as she. He rained hot kisses on her cheeks, ears, and neck as she spread his shirt open with a satisfied murmur. He leaned in and she gasped at the first contact of skin on skin. The wiry hairs dusting his chest teased her oversensitized nipples and she pressed closer, rubbing against him like a cat in heat.

He ducked his head and tongued her nipples in teasing flicks. His hand closed over her wrist and he slid her palm against his erection, pressing fervently against the fly of his trousers. "Feel how hard you make me? I bet I could punch this through drywall."

Frustrated by the barrier of clothing, she impatiently unbuckled his belt and unfastened the trousers. Her hand shoved inside the waistband of his boxers and now her palm overflowed with red hot silky smooth skin. She traced her fingers over the head, slid lower so she could grip him. Her mouth went dry.

"Oh my."

"What?" His whisper was choked.

She hadn't realized she'd said anything. "You weren't kidding?"

"About what?" She could barely see his face in the moonlight, but his gaze had gone so dark and vague she would have been surprised if he knew his own name.

She slid her fist down his shaft in a measuring glide. "The dildo." Her thumb traced the impressive breadth of the head, dipping in the little slit at the tip to capture a thick pearl of fluid. "I think you are thicker."

He groaned and closed his fist over hers, thrusting his hips and guiding her motion, showing her how to pump him until he was rigid and throbbing and all but pulsing out of his skin.

"There's a condom in my pocket," he growled. "Get it out."

Were they going to do it out here?

"Now."

The harsh, demanding tone was one she'd never heard from Tony. It brooked no argument. It sent a fresh spurt of moisture to ease the way of that maddeningly thick cock. She reached in his front pocket and fumbled around a bit, finally extracting the small foil packet.

"Feeling pretty sure of yourself, were you?"

"Sometimes it pays to be optimistic. Now put it on me."

She did, so thrilled by the idea that he'd premeditated sex with her that she didn't even flinch at his domineering tone.

The second the condom was on, he cupped her face in a gentle, sensuous kiss that belied his barely contained sexual aggression. "I've been waiting a long time for this, Lauren."

Gently he turned her around and placed her hands on the rail. He pressed close until his chest was sealed against her back, the tip of his cock teasing the plump folds of her pussy. She groaned in anticipation as his fingers dipped down between her legs, spreading her open.

He probed, bending his knees a little and then, oh Jesus, he was sliding inside. She bent forward, tipping her ass up to give him better access, as the slide and stretch traced the thin edge between pleasure and pain.

"You're so tight," he murmured, a hand coming up to play

with her breasts. "I don't want to hurt you," he eased back, then slid forward again, going deeper this time, "but it's so hard to hold back when all I want to do is fuck you hard and fast."

She clenched and jerked around him, her body attempting to suck him deeper, even though it wasn't quite ready. He rocked against her, easing his way in until finally he was buried to the hilt. She shifted and squirmed against him, trying to adjust to the sensation of being so thoroughly penetrated. With every move, the tip of his cock nudged against nerve endings she never knew she had, outside and in, until finally she began working her way back and forth, in tiny little strokes.

His hands seemed everywhere; on her breasts, on her ass, fingers sliding into the juicy folds of her pussy to tease her clit. She shuddered as a puff of warm, moist air tickled her ear and his tongue snaked out to lick her earlobe.

He settled into a slow, easy rhythm punctuated by strums of her clit and hot wet kisses on her neck, shoulders, cheeks, lips. His breath sawed in and out of his chest, mingling with the distant crashing of the waves and the rush of the night breeze.

"No!" she let out a frustrated cry when he suddenly pulled out. Her pussy throbbed in protest, angry to be denied the orgasm that had hovered so near.

"I want to watch you when you come. I want to see your face." He pulled her through the sliding glass doors and shoved her back on the bed so hard she bounced. She lay there, legs sprawled. The bedside lamps were on, and suddenly a wave of embarrassment threatened to eradicate all thoughts of pleasure. The few lovers she'd had were strictly the lights-out-under-the-covers sort, and they never seemed inclined to study her with the intensity Tony exhibited.

She reached for the bedspread folded at the end of the bed.

"Don't you dare." The lusty growl stopped her dead. "Don't you have any idea how gorgeous you are?"

He slowly peeled back his shirt and her self-consciousness

fled as she focused on the unbearably delicious picture he presented. Thick, ropy muscles banded his chest and arms, broad shoulders tapered into firm, rippling abs that epitomized the term "six-pack."

And lower . . . lower was the most impressive erection she'd ever seen, in person or in porn, shiny, wet, and straining toward her like it couldn't wait to get back inside her.

Impatiently, she scrambled to her knees and helped him shove his boxers and pants the rest of the way down, laughing at his curse when he had to pause and take off his socks and shoes.

Then he was climbing on top of her, pausing to remove her sandals as he hooked one, then the other leg around his hips. "Put me in," he whispered, guiding her fingers down between their bodies. She gripped his shaft, guiding him forward until the tip of his cock brushed against her sex. She slid him back and forth, bathing him in her juices until neither of them could stand to wait any longer.

This time his penetration was strong and smooth, and they both groaned as he sank all the way to the hilt. He hooked an elbow under her knee and gripped the headboard as he began to thrust—heavy firm strokes that went beyond anything Lauren had ever experienced.

She thrashed and squirmed under him, fingers digging into the silky flesh of his back as each thrust sent a bolt of electricity sizzling through her. The bed frame groaned and so did he as she ground against him with every stroke, seeking the firm pressure of his pubic bone against her clit.

His brow furrowed in fierce determination, his eyes gleaming as he struggled to hold back his release. His arms shook with the effort, fingers trembling as they traced the curve of her cheek.

"Lauren," he whispered, voice breaking as he plunged deep.

"I can't wait." His lips pressed into a thin line as he fought for control. "*Shit.*"

His cock jerked and throbbed and he held himself deep inside her, gripping her hips so tight she knew she'd have bruises. His unmistakable loss of control hurled her over the edge, and with a sharp, high cry, she came, clenching and milking him as she sought to drain him of every last drop of come.

He collapsed on top of her, resting a minute before capturing her mouth in a long, lazy kiss. "Damn it," he murmured, licking his lips as though savoring her taste, "I didn't get to watch you." He waggled his brows suggestively. "Next time."

5

*N*ext time.

He'd just come so hard he'd nearly blacked out, and already he was thinking about the next time.

He gently eased himself from her body, his cock making a halfhearted attempt at revival as her slick tissues tugged at him. Flopping over on his back, he pulled her close until her head rested on his chest, trying to quell the anxiety swirling through his brain.

Jesus, he couldn't remember the last time he'd so completely lost control. But everything about her drove him insane, from the way she looked naked, to the way she tasted, to the sexy sounds she made as she came. His heart still pounded and his hand shook as he played with the soft ringlets piled on top of her head.

This intense reaction meant nothing, he told himself firmly. This bone-deep satisfaction, and his eagerness to experience it all over again, was to be expected, after his longer than usual dry spell.

Right. And that was why he simultaneously wanted to flee

and curl himself around her and never let her go. This had been a mistake. But as he looked down and met her uncertain gaze, he knew he'd slit his own wrists before letting on that he regretted sleeping with her.

She smiled awkwardly as she twined her fingers in the mat of hair dusting his chest. "Did we really just do that?"

Determined to keep the mood light, he replied, "We sure as shit did." She nuzzled her lips against his neck as he gently removed the clip holding her hair up and his fingers burrowed in to massage her scalp. After a moment, he tilted her chin up, forcing her to meet his gaze. "And it was about a million times better than I ever imagined."

She flushed, looking embarrassed and pleased. "So I was okay?" She winced and blushed redder. "You don't have to answer that."

"You were amazing."

She turned her face into his chest. "Oh, like you'd really tell me the truth if I sucked."

"No, you didn't suck, not that time, anyway," he laughed, relaxing as they settled into their usual banter. This was good. They weren't getting too deep or too analytical about what was happening here. "But I'm hoping you'll get around to that." That earned him a glare. "That part when I was trying to drill you into the mattress, you felt that, right?" he teased.

She nodded begrudgingly.

"I think it's safe to assume I'm not lying," he teased.

She curled back into his chest and threw a leg over his. Never a big fan of postsex cuddling, he found himself savoring the feel of her silky curves pressed against him. He couldn't stop his fingers from tracing ticklish patterns down her spine, over her ass, and up around the smooth skin of her shoulders. Languor set in and he almost felt as though he could sleep, until she whispered the question he'd been dreading.

"What happens now?"

He jerked his hand from her back, then reminded himself to play it cool. Hoping she hadn't noticed his startled reaction, he continued the soothing caress and tried to put her off. "Well, I'm going to rest up a little bit, get some more condoms from the bathroom, and go for round two?"

She propped her forearms on his chest and gave him an admonishing look. "You know what I mean."

He met her look warily. "What do you want to have happen?"

Lauren rolled her eyes. Typical guy, twist it around so she had to make all the decisions. Like she could tell him the truth.

Well Tony, I hope this means I'm your serious girlfriend and that you're falling in love with me. When we get back to Donner Lake, maybe I should just pack up my stuff and move into your house.

Yeah, like that would go over well.

Instead she settled for the most sanity-saving, least heartbreaking option.

"I'd like to be able to go back to the way we were before. You know, friends."

"Friends who fuck?" he asked with all the eagerness of an eight-year-old wheedling for an X-Box.

She slid her gaze from his face. If she stared at him too long she was likely to give him anything. And now that she knew what she'd be missing, she wondered if she was crazy not to enjoy his amazing bedroom prowess as long as he was interested. "I'm not really good at that sort of thing," she admitted. "Despite all my mom's advice over the years, sex tends to make me get attached. So I think we should view this weekend as an isolated incident, and go back to friendship as usual at home."

"So this is like a weekend pass, then everything goes back to normal?" His palms spread on her ass cheeks and squeezed.

Her back arched. "Exactly. What happens on the road stays on the road."

"So I have until midnight tomorrow?" He pulled her up his chest until he could nuzzle his face between her breasts.

"Yes," she sighed. Her stomach suddenly reminded her she'd barely eaten at her parents' party. She started to push off him but he stilled her with a firm grip on her hips.

"Where are you going? I only have twenty-four hours left."

She laughed, an unfamiliar, girlish giggle. Huh. Maybe Tony's wonder dick had tapped into some previously undiscovered reserve of femininity inside her. "I'm hungry. I'm going to order some food." She pushed harder, playfully wrestling as he tumbled her over on her back, pinning her.

He ground himself against her belly, the bulge of his penis half hard and stirring. "Just give me like, thirty seconds," he whispered, leaning down to nip at the soft inner curve of her breast, "and I'll have a nice, thick sausage for you to chew on."

She laughed in delight, marveling at how good it felt to be with him like this, laughing and joking as always, but with the added bonus of postcoital bliss.

She was so screwed.

Once her giggles stopped, Tony obligingly rolled aside and let her leave the bed. He figured she needed nourishment to keep her strength up. And then there was the added bonus of getting to watch Lauren walk across the room naked to fetch a robe from the closet.

Uh huh, he had a big, fat salami for her all right. In the light cast from the bedside lamps, he could make out the subtle play of muscle in her legs as she walked, the flex of her arms and shoulders as she donned the thick terry-cloth robe. Not to mention the soft jiggle of her truly world-class tits and the firm plumpness of her ass.

He had a sinking feeling that there was no way would this weekend be enough. It would take weeks, possibly even months of round-the-clock fucking for him to get his fill of her strong sexy body. He couldn't ignore the twinge of regret at the thought that this wouldn't go any further than this weekend. But he trusted what she said about getting attached. He knew Lauren wasn't the kind of woman who could have an ongoing sexual relationship with someone without wanting commitment.

All the more reason to make every single minute he had count.

She hung up the phone and settled back down on the bed, curled against his side. Snatching the remote from the bed stand, she flicked on the TV and turned to ESPN.

He grinned. Talk about a dream woman.

Pretending to focus on the highlights from the Giants game, he nonchalantly slid his hand under her robe, up her thigh, until it rested just beside the cinnamon-colored curls of her bush. She grabbed his wrist to halt his progress. "Room service will be here soon," she whispered through clenched teeth, even though there was no one to overhear.

He leaned over her, his other hand coming up to tug at the right lapel of her robe until her full breast was bared. She tried to slap his hand away. "Cut it out. I'm trying to watch this."

But he heard the catch in her breath, saw the telltale flush creeping up from her throat to her cheeks, saw how that delicious brownish pink nipple hardened before his eyes, begging to be sucked and licked. He was only too happy to oblige.

"Okay, then." He ducked his head and tongued the stiff peak, groaning himself at the sweet salty taste of her. "You watch, and I'm just going to suck on your tits and play with your pussy until the food gets here." He slid his fingers between her clenched thighs. A soft, shuddery sigh escaped her, as she tried to maintain her composure.

Her thighs parted infinitesimally at the insistent probing of his fingers. He turned his face, nuzzling the other side of her robe over to reveal her other breast. He nipped the other nipple and was rewarded by a fresh wash of cream over his fingers. He didn't think he'd ever felt a woman get so wet, so drenched and ready for his cock. Good thing too, considering how small she was inside. He sucked her nipple hard and groaned at the remembered tightness. She'd gripped him like a fist, so tight at first he almost couldn't move, even with all her natural lube.

His thumb circled the plump kernel of her clitoris as his fingers sought the hot, clinging tightness of her vagina. Both slid in more easily now, now that she was soft and stretched from his cock. Her gaze was still fixed on the TV, but she arched her hips forward and spread her legs wider, inviting him to delve deep. Tiny muscles fluttered and clenched, clinging to his fingers as he slid them in and out. His thumb pressed more firmly on her clit, eliciting a soft gasp and another gush of moisture.

Sexy little moans erupted from her throat, and she gave up all pretense of watching television. Tony watched her beautiful whiskey eyes go all blurry and unfocused, saw her mouth go soft and slack, as she twisted and squirmed against his hand. His cock throbbed against the smooth skin of her thigh as he unconsciously rubbed back and forth.

He wanted to sink inside the dripping heat of her pussy, but something compelled him toward unselfishness. This time was just for her. He wanted to revel in her pleasure, show her how much he loved to make her come. Somehow he suspected few in her past had. She was the sexiest, most responsive lover he'd ever had, and he wanted to make sure she knew it.

"That's it, come for me. I love to see you. You're so hot and wet against my hand." He pressed and circled her clit, so tempted to put his mouth on her and suck up her delicious juice, but he was riveted by her face and didn't want to miss a second.

And then she was coming, her orgasm clenching around his

fingers in firm ripples that made his cock jerk in envy. Her brow furrowed, her teeth caught her lip and her eyes started to drift closed.

"Open your eyes," he ordered, wondering where the primitive, domineering urge came from. He'd never felt it with anyone but her. "I want you to look at me. I want you to know who's making you come." Her sharp cry echoed through the room as she spasmed and shuddered, shaking the bed with the force of her climax.

"Oh, God, you are so beautiful when you do that," his hand pressed against her mound, sending aftershocks through her limbs. He rained kisses on her flushed face, not sure what he loved more: the sweet startled look on her face as she came, or the vague, immensely satisfied expression that immediately followed.

A sharp knock interrupted his musings. Lauren's eyes went wide. "The food!"

Tony stole one last kiss and slipped from the bed. "You get the door while I go clean up. Although," he paused, bringing his hands up to his face, and made an exaggerated sniffing sound. "I don't know if I ever want to wash my hands again."

"Gross!" she shrieked and beaned him with a throw pillow on her way to the door.

By the time he got out of the bathroom wrapped in his own robe, she had set the tray bearing a fruit and cheese plate, shrimp cocktail, and an enormous chocolate sundae on the coffee table. He snagged a bottle of red wine from the minibar and snuggled down next to her on the sofa. She smiled up him uncertainly, and he knew she was having a hard time taking this all in stride.

He poured them each a glass of wine and held his up for a toast. "Cheers." He watched her sip her wine and leaned in for a kiss. "I'm really glad I came with you this weekend, Lauren."

"I'm glad, too," she murmured, then sat back, face flushed with color as though worried she'd admitted too much.

They ate and watched TV, and thankfully she loosened up after the first glass of wine. He poured her another and asked the question that had nagged him before he got completely distracted by sex.

"So what's the deal with you and Brandon?"

Her glass paused halfway to her mouth as she turned to look at him. He watched as she deliberated whether or not to tell him.

"Do you really want to hear this?" she asked, buying time.

"I wouldn't ask if I didn't."

"I may not have your experience, but even I know not to discuss old lovers with new ones right after you've had sex."

Bingo. "So you *were* lovers." Jealousy, uncomfortable and unfamiliar, gnawed at his belly. As a rule, he didn't care who his lovers had slept with and who they were going to sleep with, but the thought of Brandon running his perfectly manicured metrosexual hands all over Lauren made him physically ill.

She grimaced, realizing what she had revealed. She took a fortifying sip of wine and sat back on the couch with a derisive snort. "As if you could call it that. Brandon was my first. It was uncomfortable, it was awkward, and it was over in about two minutes."

"On behalf of all men, let me offer my apologies."

She smiled at that, but her eyes were a little sad. "It was my fault, really. I crossed a line I shouldn't have."

His confusion must have shown because she continued. "Brandon was my best friend in junior high and high school. As you can imagine, with everyone knowing about my mom, I didn't exactly play up my femininity."

"You didn't want everyone to think you were like her."

"Right," she grimaced. "So I became a total tomboy. I was big and tough anyway—"

"You're not nearly as big as you seem to think," he interjected.

"In high school I was, comparatively, but that's not the point. Point is, guys just saw me as one of them, and I liked it that way."

"Until?"

"Senior year. I decided I was in love with Brandon. I think it was more that everyone around me was having sex and dating and I felt left out. Anyway, I actually bought a skirt and a tight tank top, borrowed my mom's makeup and went over to Brandon's and seduced him." She threw her head back with a wry laugh. "Poor guy. He thought I'd been kidnapped by aliens. Anyway, we did it and it was awful, but I thought, okay, we can improve, now that he's my boyfriend."

Her hands twisted in her lap and she looked down, shoulders hunched protectively. Obviously the memory still stung. "Afterward he told me he didn't feel *that way* about me." Though she tried to conceal it, he could hear a watery sniffle. "When I asked him why he had done it, he told me he was curious to see if I had any of my mom's skills. He told me if I wanted to keep a guy's interest, I'd have to do more than lie there."

His heart ached at the thought of Lauren, with her generous heart and wide, laughing smile, being shot down so brutally. At the same time he wanted to pound Brandon's face into the concrete for scarring her to the point where she couldn't recognize her own beauty and sensuality.

She looked up at him then, long, dark brown lashes a little damp around her glassy eyes. "I didn't know he was going to be there tonight, and it wasn't my plan to use you to make him jealous," she said earnestly. Her smile was sheepish. "But I couldn't help rubbing his nose in it a little."

"If I'd known he was that much of an asshole I would have smashed his perfect white-boy nose."

She laughed at that. "He'd just take the pussy way out and sue you for assault or something. It was enough that he knew I vastly preferred you over him."

"Blue-collar over country-club, huh?" he said without rancor.

She placed her wine glass on the table and turned fully toward him. Her eyes had a saucy, seductive glint as she slid her hand under his robe. "Mm, I'd say it's more like, spicy Italian sausage over turkey on white." Her fingers traced up his inner thigh and he groaned as her tongue teased at his neck.

"You want to know something really depressing?"

He could barely focus on her question as her fingertips feathered against his aching balls. "What's that?" He turned his head so he could nuzzle into her neck. God, she smelled so good, like sex and spice and the fresh scented lotion he loved.

She cupped him now, gently rolling his testicles around in her fingers. "Out there, on the balcony? That's the first time I ever had an orgasm . . . with someone else in the room."

She lifted her head to watch his reaction, but thankfully didn't stop playing with his balls. She looked uncertain, as though her lack of experience might turn him off. He untied his robe and spread his knees, encouraging her explorations. Then he untied her robe so he could fill his hands with her glorious tits.

He cupped one hand around the back of her head, pulling her down to his mouth. He slid his tongue into her mouth, trying to show her in that one kiss how sexy she was, how much she turned him on.

As if it wasn't obvious enough from the hard-on angling up to his belly button. He reached his hand down, interlacing her tentative fingers in his and drawing them up to his shaft. "So your other lovers weren't very . . . attentive?" he asked between darting thrusts of his tongue.

She fed him soft kisses, exploring his mouth, exploring his

cock, like they were newfound treasures. "No. I very quickly realized I was better off . . . in my own hands."

He thrust against the firm grip of her palm. "You do have good hands." She hummed a sound of pleasure into his mouth and traced the head of his cock, her thumb spreading thick beads of precome all over the silky skin.

He squeezed his eyes shut. If she didn't quit, he was going to bust all over her. "Honey, you need to quit, or I'm gonna lose it," he growled.

"I love that I can drive you crazy," she murmured, stroking her hand faster. "I can feel how much you want me, and somehow that's more of a turn-on than anything."

He groaned and tried to still her hand. If she only knew how much he wanted her . . . He couldn't remember the last time he'd been this hard, especially after coming less than an hour ago. But already he was rock hard, aching like a hormonal fifteen-year-old. His head fell back against the back of the couch as Lauren slid off the couch and knelt between his thighs. He nearly hit the ceiling at the first puff of breath on his aching cock, his toes curling at the first tentative flick of her tongue.

"Is this okay?" she whispered, big eyes questioning as her plump pink lips slid just around the head.

"Jesus, yesss," he hissed, "but I can't promise I'll last long so if you don't want—" his protest melted into a groan as she sucked him into her mouth. Her head moved back and forth in tentative strokes, all the more arousing for their lack of skill.

She sucked him deep and released him, occasionally pausing and smiling at his erection as though admiring her handiwork, before swallowing him as deep as her throat could take. He'd never been with a woman so into going down on him. Her tongue swirled around the head, the pointed tip flicking along the tiny slit at the tip. "Fuck, Lauren, if you don't want me to come in your mouth—"

She uttered a muffled cry of delight that vibrated down his

shaft and wrapped her hand around his cock, pumping him hard as she sucked at the tip. He fisted his hands into the couch cushions to keep himself from grabbing her head and forcing his cock down her throat.

The familiar tingling intensified at the base of his spine and then it burst into a thousand sparks as jets of liquid heat shot into her mouth. She sucked him all the way through, pumping and squeezing him until she'd swallowed every drop.

She pushed herself up and climbed on his lap. Her lips were swollen and shiny and she looked so pleased with herself that his dick made a futile effort to raise its exhausted head.

What the fuck? He was as horny as the next guy, probably even more so, but something about Lauren made him nuts. He was barely finished coming and he couldn't wait to fuck her again. Usually about now would be the time he'd plan his escape, but instead he felt profoundly relieved that neither of them was going anywhere for at least the next twelve hours.

He did some mental calculations and decided he couldn't waste time on sleep.

Hooking her legs around his waist, he pushed her robe off her shoulders and stood up, bracing her weight with his palms on her ass.

She squirmed. "What are you doing? I'm way too heavy for this."

"Bullshit," he replied, carrying her easily over to the side of the bed, but refusing to release her.

"I mean it. You'll hurt yourself or something, and how will you explain that to Mike. 'Lauren and I were fooling around and you know how big she is—' "

His tongue in her mouth effectively shut her up. "I easily have at least sixty pounds on you. As far as I'm concerned, you're downright dainty." He laid her gently across the bed as though she weighed nothing and stroked her curls back from her face. "I love that you're tall enough that I don't have to hunch my back when we kiss. And I love watching you work and seeing how strong you are under all this soft skin." He trailed his fingers up the firm outer edge of her quadriceps, evident even in relaxation. His other hand held her breast up so he could tongue her nipple. She closed her eyes on a soft hum. "I love watching your tits bounce when you run on your gorgeous, strong legs." He turned his attention to her other breast, dropping kisses on the baby-soft skin of the underside, working his way to the large pinkish brown aureola. "You're like the perfect combination of strong and sexy, and I get hard every time I look at you."

She pulled his face up and kissed him, and when he pulled away, her eyes were slightly glazed. Her mouth trembled a little, and there was something in her eyes—gratitude, tenderness, and a touch of wariness that made his gut clench.

He had the strangest urge to kiss that wariness into oblivion, when he knew damn well she shouldn't trust him with her heart. Or should she?

"You should write romance novels," she said, shaking him from his all-too-frightening train of thought.

"Oh, really," he grinned, seizing on the opportunity to lighten the mood. "Let's see," he reached over her head to where her paperback lay on the nightstand.

She rolled over and jumped on his back. "Don't! You're just going to make fun of me."

"No I'm not. I'm looking for ideas."

She rolled off him and onto her back, covering her eyes with her forearm. "Trust me, you don't need any ideas."

"But how else will I learn to please you, Lady Lauren?" He thumbed through the pages until he found an interesting scene, noticing the creases where the page had been folded down. "And look, this scene is even bookmarked."

"I bought it used."

"Oh, yeah, this is good," he murmured as he scanned. Who

knew there were so many words for tits? "Shall I start by caressing the fragrant skin of your thighs?"

She rolled her eyes.

"Or perhaps trace the soft curves of your peachlike breasts?" He frowned in mock concentration and cupped her breast in his free hand. "But to be fair, yours are more like melons than peaches."

She laughed at that and peeked at him through her fingers.

"Oh, I know what I want to do." He placed the book facedown and knelt over her, knees bracketing her hips. "I want to bury my head against your bosom and lick their hard tips."

She giggled and gasped, twining her fingers in his hair.

"Want to run your fingers through my curly nest?"

She laughed harder and tugged on his hair in punishment. "How about if you probe my silky folds," she taunted, then groaned when he followed her suggestion.

"Should I tell you how your womanly dew feels silky against my fingers?" His fingers slipped and slid against her creamy slit. Her back arched, pressing her breasts against his face. "Or how I'm aching to slide inside your welcoming depths?"

A half laugh, half groan gurgled from her throat. "You got all that from one scene?"

"You think I don't snoop when you leave your books lying around?"

"I suppose you think I'm a desperate, horny woman?"

"Desperate? No. Horny? Hell, yes and hallelujah."

Her low, hearty laugh washed through him, inviting his own. He'd never had sex like this, sexy and playful, full of laughter and fun. But he realized Lauren always made him happy; just being around her made him want to laugh.

Again, it occurred to him that he might be in big trouble.

She wrapped her hand around his cock and rubbed the head against her wet core. "I think it may be time to sheathe your manly rod."

"One last taste of your sweet, pert lips," he murmured and caught her mouth in a carnal, tongue-sucking kiss. He hurried to the bathroom and grabbed the box of condoms from his toiletry kit. He extracted a foil packet and tossed the box somewhere near the foot of the bed, sheathing himself in record time.

She eagerly pulled him on top of her, parting her legs so he could kneel between.

"How should we describe this part?" He leaned down to kiss her as he teased her clit with the head of his cock.

She smiled in delight and wriggled closer. "You're going to impale me on your shaft?"

He slid inside, just a fraction of an inch. He loved the way her eyelids lowered and her lips parted, still smiling up at him. " 'Impale' sounds so violent. How about, 'slide inside your honeyed depths?' "

"Ooh, I like that."

He wasn't sure if she referred to the phrasing or his slow, steady penetration. She arched her hips with a sly smile, coaxing him deeper, hands tracing down his back until her palms were flat against his ass.

His teeth gritted at the almost unbearable sensation of her hot clinging flesh around his cock. He slid deep, all the way to the base. Her smile faded and pure pleasure suffused her face. His breath caught at the sight of her, eyes dark with need, hair spread in a curly tumble around her head, silky skin tanned golden, sprinkled randomly with little freckles.

At that moment she was so beautiful it nearly hurt. Something burst free in his chest, pouring warmth through his limbs, diffusing into a choked feeling somewhere around his throat.

"Lauren," he leaned down to kiss her, needing to feel the press of her body against him everywhere, not just his cock in her pussy. He rolled them over until she lay on top, holding her pressed tight against him. "Lauren," he whispered against her mouth, sliding his tongue in her mouth, luxuriating in her unique taste, absorbing every facet of this amazing woman.

He knew nothing could ever be the same.

Lauren writhed against him, reveling in the ticklish rasp of his chest hair, the slick sweaty slide of his skin against hers, the heavy thickness of his cock buried to her very core.

He chanted her name like a curse or a prayer. "Lauren."

Each utterance made her breath catch, her heart clutch. She threaded her fingers through the slippery silk of his hair, burying her mouth against his, needing to feel him everywhere.

His hands closed on her hips, stilling her rhythm. For long moments he held her still, kissing her, caressing her skin with long strokes up her back, down her legs, even skimming his thumbs over the soles of her feet where they rested alongside his legs.

She'd never felt so close to another human being, never experienced this urge to absorb a man into her body, into her soul. Sharp tears stung her eyes as she realized this had spun far beyond her control. She'd been an idiot ever to think she could go back to their easy friendship after experiencing this. She kissed him hard, as a moan of mingled pleasure and despair rose from deep in her chest.

She loved him. God, she loved him so much. And she could never tell him.

Frustrated, almost angry now, she squirmed against his hold, needing to feel him thrusting hard and deep. Needing the physical release of orgasm to ameliorate the pain of her heart cracking open.

She pushed up until she sat astride him, leaning back until she could watch his throbbing, blue-veined cock sink eagerly in and out. She rode him like a wild woman, like a warrior maiden taking vengeance on her captive. Any lingering doubts of her sexual abilities disappeared as she became a sex goddess, taking her pleasure from this poor mortal male who happened to fall into her clutches.

"That's it, Lauren, ride me hard." He braced his feet against the mattress and shoved deeper.

She cried out, high and sharp as the head of his cock bumped a bundle of nerves hidden deep within. She increased her rhythm, moving faster and faster and felt him swell even bigger. She bent her head to watch, her gaze riveted on the sight of his cock squeezing in and out of her pussy, gleaming wet from her juices.

She looked up at his face. He watched her, watching them, his eyes dark slits, jaw clenched as he fought against his own climax. His hand came up to pinch at her nipple, sliding down until it rested at the top of her mound. Her clit was exposed, ruby red and throbbing, begging for the rasp of his callused thumb.

"Come on, baby, I want you to come with me." His thumb circled her clit, and she flinched and moaned as her body clenched around him.

She didn't want to come yet. She wanted this to last forever. This savage giving and taking of pleasure, feeling every nerve in her body sizzle with delight, knowing that he fought and strained for it as much as she.

Then his thumb made one, two, three slippery forays around her clit, up and down the sides, sliding against it in the same rhythm of her thrusts, and she was gone. Heat burst from her womb, down her limbs, with such intensity that even the tips of her toes and the top of her scalp tingled.

Tony came at the exact same moment, until his orgasm became hers, and hers his, and they both shuddered under the relentless waves.

For several moments, neither one could move, much less speak. Lauren huddled against his chest, shaking, listening to his heart thundering like a jackhammer under her cheek. Sweat and tears streaked down her face, mingling and dripping onto his chest.

His hands shook a little as they rubbed up and down her back. She felt a modicum of relief when she realized she wasn't the only one who felt a little ransacked after that.

Eventually he rose to get rid of the condom. A fresh wash of tears pricked her eyes as she felt him slide from her body. How many more times would she get to feel that luscious sensation?

After tomorrow, everything had to go back to normal.

The mattress dipped under his weight and he slipped under the covers with her. His arm fastened around her waist and he pulled her firmly back against his chest. The heavy weight of his penis nestled against her ass, and his palm flattened between her breasts. She drifted to sleep, wishing he'd never let go.

6

_____

"I don't know about you, but after last night's _excitement_ I could have stayed in bed all day." Carly MacLean made this pronouncement over eggs benedict and mimosas.

Lauren tried to ignore her mother's all-too-perceptive gaze. From the moment she and Tony had arrived, her mother had been sliding her those knowing glances and making little comments until finally Lauren wanted to stand up and shout "Yes, we fucked! A lot! And so good we could probably get a gold medal in the Olympics of fucking. So you can stop worrying about your poor, frigid, potentially lesbian daughter."

But she said none of this, simply moved her eggs around her plate, tracing designs in her hollandaise. Her characteristically healthy appetite seemed to have abandoned her somewhere in the night.

She couldn't decide if it was the postorgasmic euphoria, the deliciously distracting feel of Tony's hand on her thigh under the table, or perhaps the sick, choking feeling she got when she imagined what would happen when they got back home.

Nothing. Because she couldn't do this indefinite casual sex

thing, and Tony made no bones about his desire—or rather, lack thereof—to settle down.

"Sweetheart, you're not eating," Carly commented around her own delicate bite of eggs. "That is so unlike you." A wicked glint appeared in her eyes. "You must be so *tired.*" She slanted a sly look at Tony, who smiled blandly as if not understanding her mother's innuendo.

Bless him.

"I know when I'm *tired,*" Carly continued, "my appetite absolutely fails me. Isn't that right, dear?"

Lauren's father shot Carly a censorious look and didn't reply.

"How long do you think it will take you to get home?" Mark asked Tony in a completely unsubtle change of subject.

Tony wiped his mouth before replying. "Without traffic, eight hours or so." He leaned back in his chair and slid his arm around Lauren's shoulders.

A shiver raced down her spine at the lovely feel of his fingers coiling themselves in her hair, the warmth of his palm on her bare shoulder.

He had touched her this way a thousand times in the past, casual, friendly touches. But now everything was infused with an undercurrent of sexual promise that she feared she'd never be able to suppress.

"The time went by too quickly," Tony continued. "I would do just about anything to have this weekend last a bit longer." He was looking right at Lauren when he said this.

The crack in her heart widened a little bit. *A bit longer.* That's all he wanted. Not forever.

Just a couple more fucks until the novelty wore off and he found himself once again in need of variety without entanglements.

She had a sudden, awful sensation that she was about to burst into tears. "Excuse me," Lauren said abruptly, and mustered up any last shred of composure she possessed. She made it across the pool deck without tripping or crying and found refuge in the pool house.

The luxurious bathroom, which doubled as a changing room, was dominated by a large padded bench in the center of the room. Lauren sank down on it. "What the hell am I going to do?" she moaned to herself. Once again, she'd fallen in love with a friend. At least this time she was confident that Tony, unlike Brandon, was actually attracted to her.

That was what made it so much more dangerous. Brandon had crushed her in one swift blow, but at least he had ended it quickly. No ambiguity there, and with the added dose of humiliation to keep Lauren away, she'd gone off quietly to lick her wounds without having to see him all the time.

But Tony . . . It would be so easy to continue sleeping with Tony when they got home. Yet, while she would just fall deeper in love, he would merely be taking the edge off.

The click of the latch startled her from her thoughts and she heaved a frustrated sigh as her mother entered the bathroom. *Great. Just what I need, my mother pressing me for a play-by-play.* Did other mothers show this unusual fascination with their daughters' sex lives?

"So you two finally did it," Carly said without preamble as she sank down on the bench next to Lauren.

"What do you mean, finally?"

"Oh, you can tell when a couple has finally slept together," she replied with great authority. "I could tell you hadn't yet, yesterday—the way you circled around each other. And the way Tony looked at you," she shuddered a little for effect, "like he wanted to lay you out on the buffet table and eat you up."

Whatever attraction Tony genuinely felt, he had obviously amped it up for the benefit of their audience. She supposed she should be grateful.

Her mother was still chattering about sexual dynamics and

body language. "And this morning, he's more territorial, the way he keeps touching, his hand on your neck, on your thigh. And he looks at you like he finally knows exactly what you taste like."

"Mother! Gross!" Lauren shot up off the bench. *You'd think that after she delivered a dildo to my room, I wouldn't be shocked by anything.*

"What?"

"Why do you have to say things like that? You're my mother, for Christ's sake."

Carly held her hands up in front of her, palms out. "Sweetie, I just want you to feel comfortable about sex. You've always seemed a little uptight about it and—"

"What do you expect?" All the resentment born of growing up a porn queen's daughter came rushing out. "By the time I was thirteen years old, practically everyone in my class had seen your movies. And even if they didn't, they knew about them!"

Carly's cheeks flushed and her mouth set in a tight line. "I'm not ashamed of my past."

Lauren fisted her hands in her hair and paced. Her mother, for all her faults, was a wonderful, good-hearted woman, and the last thing Lauren wanted was to hurt her. But still . . . "Mom, I'm not saying you should be ashamed. But you have to understand, when other kids saw that, they expected me to . . . to . . . be like you. To do that stuff."

"That's why you stopped wearing makeup," Carly said, the dawn of enlightenment cresting her face. "You were always such a girly girl, stealing my makeup and trying on dresses. And then . . ."

Then, Lauren remembered, she'd stopped all of that altogether, and done her damnedest to make everyone forget there was anything feminine about her. Until the fiasco with Brandon, of course.

"The last thing I wanted was for anyone to see me sexually, and then you—" she remembered her mother's frank talk when she was younger, all but encouraging her to have sex when she wanted with whomever she wanted, and not to forget the stash of condoms Carly always kept in the upstairs guest bathroom. "You made me feel like a freak because I wasn't having sex."

Tears welled in Carly's eyes, trailing in fat droplets down her cheeks. "Lauren, I never meant to make you feel like a freak. Why didn't you ever say anything?"

Lauren shrugged. "I was a teenager, and I suppose I hoped you would drop it if I kept ignoring you."

"I was afraid of what would happen when you found out about my past," Carly said between sniffles, "and I hoped that if you felt as I did, that sex was nothing to be ashamed of, you would be better prepared to deal with whatever anyone said." She smiled wanly. "I suppose I went a bit overboard."

Lauren sighed. "I'm not ashamed of sex, or of you. It's more that I'm insecure about it." She smiled ruefully. "It took me awhile to get up the nerve to do it, and when I did . . ."

"Brandon," her mother said tightly.

"How did you know?"

"Like I said. You can tell when people have had sex. Plus, you used to spend almost every afternoon after school and most weekends with him, and you suddenly stopped." She rolled her eyes. "I can only imagine what a disaster that was."

Lauren chuckled. "You have no idea."

Carly's delicate nose wrinkled. "He must be awful in bed. You can tell by looking at him."

Lauren didn't bother to defend him. "He was only eighteen. His technique has probably improved."

Carly shook her head emphatically. "No, you can see it in his face, that self-satisfied, narcissistic look. It's all about him, all the time." She paused, slid Lauren a glance. "Tony, on the other hand, truly appreciates women. Am I right?"

Lauren's cheeks caught fire. "Mom, in case I haven't made it abundantly clear, I'm not comfortable discussing sex with you."

She was mildly chastened. "Okay, okay, I won't bother you for details, but it's nice to know you've found a man who really knows how to put a smile on your face."

"Don't read too much into it, Mom," Lauren replied glumly, sinking back down on the bench. "I don't think it's really headed anywhere."

"Oh, I wouldn't be so sure."

Typical parent, attempting to give hope when there was none. "Trust me. Tony's not about to settle down, especially with someone like me."

Carly snorted. "I'm not even going to acknowledge the pity party about to start." She paused, and Lauren could tell she was pondering her next words very carefully. "Listen to me, honey. Sex can mean nothing, and sex can mean everything. And I can just tell, whatever you and Tony are doing, it's not the nothing kind."

"It is on his part."

"I wouldn't be so sure."

Lauren rolled her eyes and stood. If her mom wanted the last word, she would cede it. She wanted nothing more than for her mother to be right, but knew better than to get carried away by false hopes.

Her mother caught her hands just as they were exiting the bathroom. "I'm sorry if my prying has made you uncomfortable, honey. I just want you to be happy, and find someone who can give you the kind of love your father has given me."

Lauren grabbed her in a hug. Carly was tiny, nearly a foot shorter than Lauren, yet somehow Lauren still felt like a little girl taking refuge in her mother's embrace.

They returned to the table, and both Tony and her father

looked up expectantly, relief crossing both faces as they noted the women's amicably joined hands.

She sat down and Tony immediately tipped her face up for a soft kiss. She decided she might as well enjoy the last few minutes of their pretend relationship.

"We thought maybe you'd fallen in and your mom was lost trying to rescue you," Tony grinned.

Her mother quirked a meaningful eyebrow at Lauren, looking pointedly at his hand where it rested on her shoulder. "Girl talk."

Her dad looked a little worried. He was plenty familiar with the inappropriate turns his wife's girl talk was capable of taking.

The housekeeper cleared their breakfast plates and Tony sighed, sounding convincingly regretful. "Well, I suppose we better get on the road, since my slave driver of a brother wants us at work by eight tomorrow."

A sharp pain hit somewhere near Lauren's ribs at the reminder of reality. Or maybe it was just indigestion, she thought, ignoring the fact she'd barely touched her food.

Within minutes they were off, amid tears and kisses and threats to rent a house in Squaw Valley over Thanksgiving.

"I like your parents," Tony said as he negotiated his way through weekend beach traffic back to the highway.

Lauren braced herself for one of his patented inappropriate comments, perhaps something about her mom.

When she didn't respond, he elaborated. "A lot of times, when you meet people like that, with that kind of money, they're really snobby." He looked at her carefully. "Lots of parents in your folks' position wouldn't like their daughter dating a guy like me."

Her brow furrowed in confusion. "A guy like you?"

"You know, blue-collar. When you could have the king of the country club."

She snorted. "Yeah, right. Like a former adult film actress and a former porn director can afford to be snotty." And just as she started feeling all warm and fuzzy that he liked her parents, she remembered that this was all just a game of let's pretend. "I don't see why it matters anyway. I only invited you to convince my mom I was finally getting laid, and I think we accomplished that. Whether they like you or not doesn't matter."

Tony's jaw clenched, both at her uncharacteristically snippy tone, as well as her comment.

True, he had come with her to Newport Beach under the guise of pretending to be her lover.

And now that they weren't pretending anymore, he'd be damned if he'd let her just brush it off. "I'll see them again when they come visit."

She made a scoffing sound.

"What?"

"Tony, we don't need to do this indefinitely."

"Do what?"

"I don't need you to keep pretending to be my boyfriend. Trust me, if I were in the market for one, you'd be the last guy I'd pick."

"Why?" The question flew out of his mouth, before he could remind himself that he should be relieved.

She turned to him, brow furrowed. "Are you kidding? Tony, it's obvious you have no interest in commitment, and I'm not even sure you could if you tried. A woman would have to be a moron or a masochist to ever attempt a relationship with you."

Ouch. Not that he was looking for a girlfriend, either, but she didn't have to be so vehement.

She had a point, though. His longest relationship to date had been a month, back in high school. And it had only lasted because it took him that long to get in her pants.

After that, he stuck with girls who didn't say no, and if they did, he moved on, always confident that someone just as good or better would be willing. And once they had done it once, maybe twice, he got out before she started getting any ideas.

But he couldn't cut Lauren out of his life so easily, and once again he mentally punched himself for sleeping with such a close friend. He couldn't imagine not having Lauren in his life, but after such a small sampling of her heretofore untapped sexual prowess, he didn't know how he was going to be able to be near her without trying to fuck her senseless most of the time. And just to make everything totally confusing, a whole slew of unfamiliar, intense emotions twisted around in his gut every time she so much as smiled at him.

Lauren was silent, curled up and in the passenger seat. He reached over and casually rested his hand on her knee, unable to keep from touching her, even as he knew he should back off for both their sakes. But he couldn't stop himself from touching her, not when she was so close. And in a few short hours they'd be home, and he was supposed to put all of this behind him. Forget how she looked, straddling his hips, lips parted as she moaned. Forget how she felt, hot, slick, and tight, clenching around his cock as he came.

The semierection he'd had all day lengthened and thickened until he was pressing urgently against the zipper of his jeans. How could everything possibly go back to normal when he wanted her this much? A sudden fantasy sprang to mind, one of waking Lauren up in the morning by sliding inside her, and rocking her to sleep at night the same way. Of looking at her over coffee in the morning, knowing that moments before he'd had her howling up at the ceiling. Of working beside her every day, knowing she was his.

He nearly laughed at the irony as it hit him. For the first time in his life, he could imagine committing to one woman. And based on her earlier comments, Lauren wanted nothing to do with it.

She jumped as his hand tightened involuntarily on her thigh, then covered his hand with her own. Lust exploded in his gut, more desperate now as he realized there could never be anything more than this. He still had until midnight, and the least he could do was give them both something to remember.

Lauren started and shot a questioning glance at Tony as he abruptly pulled off the highway. She leaned over, looking frantically at the dash, convinced she'd find a warning light beaming. "What's wrong?"

"Nothing," he said in that low, silky voice that brought to mind vivid images of sweat-slicked skin and twisted sheets. "I just want a little snack."

She licked her lips nervously. "There aren't any services off this exit." The two-lane county road stretched through acres and acres of farmland, with nothing but almond trees on both sides as far as the eye could see.

After a couple of miles, Tony turned down a smaller side road and pulled the suburban off into a turnout. He cut the ignition and turned to face her, dark chocolate eyes glinting with a look she'd become very familiar with during the night. "Everything I want to eat is right here."

Just those words, in that husky rumble, were enough to soak her panties through. She squirmed in her seat, clenching her thighs together as though that could possibly slow the pulse pounding between them. "Tony, we can't." God, her voice sounded feeble and childish. She tried again. "We agreed, this was just for the weekend, and after that, back to business as usual."

He unbuckled his seat belt and slid across the bench seat. Twisting to face her, he slung one arm over the back of her headrest and propped the other hand against the window. "The weekend isn't over yet, and, as far as I'm concerned, I have until tonight at midnight."

She pressed back until the door handle dug into her back. "But we have a long drive and it's getting late . . ." Her fingers dug into the leather upholstery, resisting the craving to shove their way under his shirt and into his pants.

He leaned closer, and she moaned at the hot brush of his open mouth against her throat. "Just a little detour. I'm betting this won't take long."

"What if someone comes?

His hand slid up under her stretchy blouse and squeezed her breast as he licked a hot trail up her neck. "That's the idea."

With a tortured groan, she threaded her fingers into his hair and tugged his mouth down to hers. One last time, one for the road. What could it hurt?

Yes. He sucked her tongue into his mouth, kissing her so hard the back of her head ground against the headrest. Reaching down, he pressed the button to shift the seat back as far as it could go, then flicked the reclining lever. Lauren emitted a startled giggle as she found herself abruptly prone.

"Gotta hand it to Chevy," Tony murmured against her lips. "They give a man plenty of space to work."

His hand went back to her breasts, palm sliding inside the flimsy cup until all he could feel was soft, scented skin and beaded, pinkish brown nipples urging his fingers to pinch and twist.

His hand slid lower, into the vee of her tightly clenched thighs, which parted slightly at his urging. Her breath came in hot pants and he could feel the heat and dampness of her right through her jeans. He groaned against the silky skin of her throat, needing to taste her so badly his mouth watered.

He unfastened her jeans, shoving them, along with her panties, down her hips. She kicked off her sandals and he tugged at the cuffs, pulling her pants completely off. He shifted until he knelt in the cramped space between the dash and the seat. His mouth came down on the silky smooth skin of her belly, right above the damp curly hair of her bush. He sucked and licked at her skin, and when he lifted his mouth he saw he'd left a little love bite.

He liked the idea of Lauren waking up, going to work and trying to pretend everything was back to normal, when all the time his mark would be on her baby-soft skin.

She nearly jumped off the seat at the first flick of his tongue, and he caught her knees and pushed them up and back until her feet rested on the dashboard.

He trailed his fingers along the insides of her legs, his tongue and lips following, pausing to lick and taste the adorable freckles sprinkled along her inner thighs.

His thumbs traced her labia, spread her gorgeous pink pussy wide. He took just a second to admire, then hummed in satisfaction as his lips settled over her juicy clit.

As a rule, he enjoyed going down on a woman, if only because it was the easiest way to get her off. He may have been ruled by his dick, but he was always polite enough to make sure his partner came, too.

With Lauren, though, he was starving for her unique taste, craving her unique scent, until he thought he might go out of his mind if he didn't get his face in her lap.

And, oh, Christ, he loved the sounds she made when he flicked his tongue over and around her engorged bud. Soft whimpers, escalating to warbles, and then a deep, chesty groan when he slid his fingers inside her dripping sex.

Her slick walls shuddered and clamped over his fingers, and his cock twitched in envy. "You're so gorgeous down here," he murmured. "I think you have about the most gorgeous pussy I've ever tasted. Mmmm." He feasted on her, lapping up the slick fluid that flowed onto his tongue, thrusting and twisting his fingers until he filled her from every angle and her hips arched uncontrollably against his hands and mouth.

"Tony," she whimpered, and his name on her lips was the most perfect sound he'd ever heard. "Tony!"

Her feet dropped from the dash and her thighs closed around his head as she jerked and bucked, shuddering and twitching.

He gently pressed her thighs open and shifted up, and in about two seconds his jeans were unzipped and a condom was on.

He shifted her so she faced away from him, elbows braced against the reclined seat back. Her smooth, round, perfectly muscled ass tipped up, the lush pink folds of that perfect pussy peeking at him between her thighs.

He loved the way his hands looked palming her cheeks. Dark and big against pale, silky skin as they spread her wide to accept the invasion of his cock.

They groaned in perfect unison as he sank deep and began thrusting without restraint. "You make me so fucking hard," he panted, pounding against her as the sound of flesh coming together filled the close interior of the car. "And you're pussy's so tight and slippery, it makes me want to fuck you forever, but I know I can't last."

He surged impossibly deep and held himself still, leaning down over her until his face was next to hers against the leather upholstery. He caught her chin, turned her face to the side and took her mouth. He slowly began the steady, pounding rhythm, twisting and tangling his tongue with hers, tasting her strained moans as she worked herself frantically against his cock.

His balls tightened, signaling his impending climax and he reared up, settling his hands on her ass, watching as her eager pussy swallowed every inch of him.

The windows fogged, the sounds of sex sounded unnaturally loud in the enclosed space, and every bit of it was more arousing than anything Tony had ever experienced. He wanted her so fucking much, and every time he touched her, she responded just as fiercely.

At the first flutter of her climax he lost it, thrusting hard and fast, not stopping until they were both utterly drained. He came so hard his arms buckled, and he collapsed against Lauren's back, burying his nose in the mass of soft red curls spread against the seat.

The afterglow was short-lived. Lauren shifted pointedly underneath him, reminding him that he was probably mashing her into the seat in an unnaturally arched position.

Reluctantly he pushed himself up and slid out, undeniably shaken. What had started as a way of reminding her how much *she* wanted *him,* instead proved to him that, out of all the women he had ever known, only she incited the kind of craving that made him come so hard he nearly passed out.

He slid over to his side of the seat and cleaned himself up as best he could while she did the same. He felt like he should say something, but feared if he opened his mouth something ridiculously sappy—and completely unlike him—might slip out. So instead he leaned over and kissed her, tracing his thumb along the strong curve of her jaw and the clean line of her cheekbone. Then he held her close, the thought that this might be the last time he held her twisting in his guts.

He buried his face in her hair, wondering if there was anything he could do to change her mind, and prove to her that he was exactly the kind of man she needed.

7

Lauren did her best to keep their conversation light, meaningless, and utterly without depth for the rest of the ride back to Donner Lake.

Not easy when her brain practically screamed at her to hash out this thing between them, once and for all. What exactly had happened, anyway? Had he simply wanted to get laid, or was there even a teeny, tiny chance that he might actually consider a relationship with her?

Only the fact that, deep in her bones, she knew the answer to that question kept her from bringing it up.

Tony was Tony, and many of the things she loved about him—his charm, his laid-back attitude, his easy laugh and often immature sense of humor—were the very things that kept him from even entertaining the idea of settling down with one woman.

But dammit, she hated being in this gray area. For most of her adult life, her relationships with guys had remained firmly in the friends arena. No bleeding over into romantic territory for her—she was usually smart enough keep everything strictly platonic.

But not this time. And really, when she thought about it, there was no middle ground here, either. She had only one choice, and that was to stick with her original plan and, after they got home tonight, pretend none of this had happened.

They'd simply slip back into their regular routine, having a few beers, watching the game, working out.

Your usual guy stuff, she thought ruefully.

And she had no doubt that, within a couple of days—by Wednesday, at the latest, she'd be able to move without feeling twinges and pulls deep inside her.

But as she listened to the low rumble of his voice, saw the flash of his smile as he laughed at something she said, she wondered how long it would take before she could look at him without getting this awful crushing sensation in her throat and chest.

It was late by the time they crested Donner Summit, but she could see the lake below, shimmering silver, illuminated by the nearly full moon.

She'd loved this view from the first moment she'd seen it as a little girl, driving with her parents on their annual ski vacation. Now that she lived here, the view never failed to pervade her with a sense of peace, a gut-deep conviction that she had come home.

But not tonight. Tonight she took in the granite cliffs and dark water as they drove by on Highway 80, and she feared at any second she would burst into tears. The weekend was really over now. She would go back to being Tony's friend, and he would go back to the throngs of women only too eager to satisfy his overactive appetites.

"Well, this is it," he said as they pulled up to her walkway. He unbuckled his seat belt and got out as she did the same, and unloaded her suitcase from the back of the Suburban.

"So I'll see you tomorrow, bright and early," she said, and

grabbed the handle of her wheelie bag. To her surprise, he took the handle from her. "You don't have to walk me up."

He ignored her and followed her up the short path, propping one arm against the doorjamb as she searched for her keys.

"I don't know why women carry these things," she grumbled as she dug through her purse. "You can never find anything in them." Finally, she extracted her key, and with a hand that shook only a little bit, unlocked the front door. "Okay, well, good night, then." Her voice sounded breathless and strained. *Leave,* she thought, *please just leave and make this easier on both of us.*

To her dismay, he reached up and cupped her jaw in his big hand and gave her that heavy-lidded look that made her knees weak and her panties wet.

She gripped the doorknob in one hand and her suitcase handle in the other, having no doubt that if she let go of either she'd immediately claw his clothes off, right there on her front stoop.

He leaned down until his mouth barely touched hers. "Let me come up," he breathed over her parted lips, then gently, oh, so delicately, sucked her bottom lip between his teeth.

"No," she whispered, and her pussy silently pulsed to the rhythm of *you bitch, you bitch!* But she had to stay strong. She swallowed and somehow managed to back away one step.

He stood up straight and gaped at her, as if he couldn't believe he heard her right. "What?"

She flattened her palm against his chest, then yanked it away as the delicious warmth of his skin seeped through the soft cotton of his shirt. "This was just for the weekend, remember? Back home, back to normal. Buddies, just like always, right?"

A flash of irritation wrinkled his brow, but disappeared so quickly she thought maybe she'd imagined it. "Right. That's cool." He wrapped her in a quick hug, one of friendly affection, just like he'd done a hundred times before they ever even considered having sex.

And because it was just like every other hug, there was nothing wrong with her wrapping her arms around his neck and returning the embrace. But when she buried her nose against the patch of skin left bare by his open collar and inhaled as though his scent were life-giving oxygen, she knew it was time to retreat.

She mumbled something, a garbled combination of "good night," and "see ya" that came out "goodseeya" and practically staggered into her entryway.

Back to normal, my ass.

Even though he hadn't gotten laid again last night, Tony had woken up in a ridiculously good mood. He'd bounded out of bed, raced through his run, eager to get to work and see Lauren.

Come to think of it, he mused as he installed a set of cabinets for the kitchen remodel they were handling, he couldn't remember a day in the last seven months that he hadn't been excited to get to work. To see Lauren.

He'd always enjoyed his job, but having her around made him especially eager to get out of bed and spend the day working beside her.

Too bad she'd spent most of the morning trying to avoid him. He snuck a glance at her across the room where she was busy ripping up linoleum. She glanced up, quickly lowering her gaze as soon as she met his. Disappointment settled like a boulder in his stomach. Clearly, despite what she'd said, Lauren was having as hard a time as he was at letting things get back to normal after what they'd shared. She was trying not to show it, but after months of close friendship, she couldn't hide her obvious discomfort. She wouldn't make eye contact, and every time he got close to her she stiffened tighter than a guitar string.

Not for the first time today, he wondered if he should have kept his hands off. This whole thing was playing out just as he'd feared, with Lauren acting weird and uncomfortable, making him edgy and unsure of how to proceed.

On the other hand, the sex they'd had was truly amazing, and he honestly couldn't bring himself to regret it. And more than that, he uneasily acknowledged, the connection between them was more powerful than anything he'd ever experienced, and impossible to ignore.

Later that afternoon when Lauren oh-so-casually ducked away when Tony tried to put his arm around her shoulders as he'd done a thousand times before, he tried to convince himself it was a good sign. Despite what she'd said, she obviously wasn't able to let go of what happened between them and go back to being mere friends. She might think of him as crappy boyfriend material, but if he was honest and told her he wanted to be more than bang buddies, maybe she'd give him a chance.

His spirits buoyed by the thought, Tony fought the urge to confront her right there and then. But right now, with all the other guys around, was definitely not the time to have a "state of the relationship" talk. He glanced at his watch. Today was Monday, and if Lauren really wanted to keep things normal, she'd show up on his front porch at five-thirty, just in time to watch Monday night football on his wide-screen. He grinned, mentally rubbing his hands with glee. He only had to be patient for two more hours, and then he could get to work convincing Lauren that he would have no problem settling down with just one woman, as long as that woman was Lauren.

Tony sullenly glared at his watch. Nine-thirty. The game had ended half an hour ago, and Lauren hadn't shown, hadn't called, nothing. He had nearly picked up the phone a half dozen times, always stopping short of dialing her number. If she needed a little space, fine. He wasn't going to chase her down.

8

"Why didn't you show up last night?"

Tony's voice in her ear sent a hot pulse through her core. *That's why.* Lauren straightened and turned, taking the paper cup he offered. She took a sip of the hot latte, sweetened with half a sugar packet, exactly the way she liked it. Her heart squeezed and she wondered how on earth she was going to maintain her distance from a man who not only made her come so hard she saw stars, but also brought her coffee fixed perfectly to her taste. Which brought her right back to why she hadn't, as had been her habit over the past several months, gone over to Tony's to watch whatever major sporting event was being televised. "I had some stuff to do," she said lamely, looking away from his dark, penetrating gaze. Truth was, she'd known damn well that if she'd gone over to Tony's she wouldn't have made it past kickoff before throwing him down on the couch and tearing his pants off. So she'd stayed home and watched the game on her crappy twenty-two-inch screen, eating stale tortilla chips for dinner, unwilling to leave the house for fear that if she got behind the wheel, her body would overrule her brain and drive her right over to Tony's.

But it was so hard to stay away from him when every cell in her body cried out for just one more taste, one more touch. Every time he looked at her, it took every ounce of willpower not to open her mouth and beg him to take her to bed, to confess that she'd settle for anything he wanted to give, even if it was a few quick fucks between friends.

If she did that, she knew, she'd only end up hurt, her heart bruised and maybe broken, hating herself for being stupid enough to want more than he was capable of giving. So for now she needed to maintain a little distance and hope this awkwardness would pass.

To her dismay, as the week went on, it only got worse. Every time she looked at Tony, her brain overflowed with images of him naked, over her, under her, behind her. Of his dark head buried between her thighs as he licked his tongue up inside her. Her body responded accordingly, making it nearly impossible for her to have a normal conversation with him.

Worse, with every day her irritation and hurt grew as he proved himself more than able to go right back to being friends. Clearly the fact that they'd had sex multiple times in a twenty-four-hour period didn't even register as a blip on his radar, much less wreak any sort of emotional havoc.

Still, he wasn't indifferent to her efforts to avoid him. Whereas before they'd taken it as a given that she would show up at his house several nights a week, every day he'd been sure to issue explicit invitations. All of which she'd turned down with one lame excuse or another.

Friday was no different. "Let's go for a run tomorrow," he said, catching her as she was climbing into her truck. His hand rested on her thigh, burning through the fabric of her heavy-duty canvas work pants.

Oh, I can think of a better way to exercise. She licked her lips and did her best to banish the lusty images from her head. "I don't—"

He jumped in before she could refuse. "This might be the last weekend we can run all the way up to Horseshoe Lake before it snows. We haven't gone in ages."

A vehement "Yes" was on the tip of her tongue. She loved running the trails with Tony, always enjoying their banter as he challenged her with a quick pace. Yet she didn't think she was up to the torture of watching his hard, muscled body move fluidly up the mountain, knowing that she had no business touching him, no business imagining him naked. "I can't," she said softly. "I made plans with Karen."

His full lips tightened, his nostrils flaring at his irritated inhalation. "This isn't fair, Lauren. Last weekend, we agreed when we got home, everything would go back to normal. What we've been doing this week, this isn't normal. I'm doing my part."

Tears stung her eyes, and she swallowed hard. "I'm trying," she said, her voice tight. "But I," her voice trailed off as his fingers pressed into the flesh of her thigh. Unable to focus with even that small contact, she jerked away.

Tony drew his hand back as though burned, then threw his hands up in impatience. "Fuck this," he said angrily. "I'm tired of pussyfooting around this, getting blown off by you every time I turn around. Why don't you give me a call when you get over it?"

Call me when you get over it. Tony's words echoed in Lauren's brain all day Saturday as she ached to call him and take him up on his invitation for a run. It was a beautiful, crystal-clear fall day, the kind where the rugged mountains stood out in stark relief against the near painfully bright blue of the sky. Yet she resisted, as every time their conversation replayed in her brain, a stabbing sensation throbbed in her chest.

He wanted her to get over it, because obviously he had. So

instead of joining Tony for a run, she spent all day doing anything and everything in an effort to distract herself. First she
went on a ten-mile run on her own, then scrubbed her apartment from top to bottom. By the time she collapsed onto the
couch in front of *Saturday Night Live,* her entire kitchen was
organized and alphabetized.

By Sunday afternoon she couldn't take it any more. Used to
spending the better part of her free time with Tony, she found
she missed him desperately. After nearly a week of barely
speaking to him, she ached to simply sit on the couch next to
him as they watched TV. She took a deep breath, bolstering her
resolve. If Tony wanted her to get over it, to go back to the easy
friendship they'd shared, she would do it. She'd known better
all along than to expect anything more, and had even made it
clear to Tony that this was exactly what she wanted.

Toughen up, she told herself. Time to put her money where
her mouth was, and put their wild weekend firmly behind her.
Hadn't she spent the past seven plus months ignoring her wild
attraction to Tony? Surely she could do it again.

*But now you know exactly how he looks naked, how he
tastes, how his cock feels moving hard inside you . . .*

Ruthlessly silencing the mischievous voice, Lauren quickly
showered and dressed. The Oakland Raiders game was on in
forty-five minutes, giving her just enough time to pick up a
peace offering of pizza and beer to take over to Tony.

9

The Raiders had just kicked off to the Broncos when a knock sounded at the door. He quickly hit pause on his DVR, his heart picking up a few beats. It could only be Lauren, ready to make peace and watch the game. His stomach clenched at the implication. If she was over here, it meant she was able to move on from what had happened last weekend, and ready to settle back into their old, familiar friendship. But Tony had had a lot of time to think over the past few days. A lot of time to miss her. And in missing her, he realized his feelings had progressed far beyond friendship a long time ago. If he wasn't in love with her, he was damn close.

Now he just had to convince her to give them a chance.

He took a deep breath and self-consciously smoothed his hair, wondering when he'd become such a coward. But his stomach was in knots and his hand actually shook a little as he went to answer the door, steeling himself to confess to Lauren the true depth of his feelings.

"Hi Tony."

Disappointment flooded his chest as he recognized the woman standing on his doorstep. "Erin?"

Her green eyes raked him up and down, her dimples flashing as she grinned. "Can I come in?"

Without waiting for an answer, she pushed by him into the entryway. "Nice place," she said on a low whistle, sauntering down the hall to the kitchen, hips deliberately swaying in her tight jeans.

Objectively, Tony had to admit Erin was attractive, even beautiful. She had a great little body, showcased nicely by a black turtleneck and dark washed jeans that appeared to have been shrink wrapped on her. Her dark brown hair hung in a silky fall almost to her waist, and she had pretty green eyes and a full red mouth that he knew she knew how to use. When he'd met her several months ago in a little bar in Tahoe City, she'd sparked his interest and he'd taken her up on her invitation back to her hotel room.

Now, as she leaned back against the breakfast bar and stuck her chest out in a not-so-subtle invitation, he felt nothing but the desire to get her to leave so he could go over to Lauren's and get this whole mess straightened out.

He tucked his hands in the back pockets of his jeans, searching for a polite way to ask her to leave.

Oblivious, she reached out and grasped the fabric of his black T-shirt and used it to tug him toward her. "How did you find my house?" he asked.

"Looked it up in the phone book," she said, in a sing-songy voice that someone down the line must have told her was cute.

His brow furrowed. "But I'm not listed." And as far as he remembered, they hadn't even exchanged last names. A stab of regret hit him hard. No wonder Lauren saw him as nothing but a male slut.

As though reading his mind, Erin laughed and said, "Okay, you got me. That night, when you went to the bathroom, I looked through your wallet." She bit her lip and raised her eyebrows, "Clever of me, wasn't it?"

Or creepy, depending on how you look at it.

"Anyway," she continued, walking her fingers up his chest and moving close enough that their thighs brushed, "I came up to visit my parents and thought I'd look you up. We had so much fun last time, I figured, why not?"

Tony leaned as far back as he could, as her arms settled around his waist. "That's really nice Erin, but—"

Before he got another word out, she grabbed the neckline of his shirt and yanked his head down to hers. He thought he might have tasted blood as her lips mashed his against his teeth, her tongue snaking around for entry. Somehow she turned them so his back was up against the breakfast bar, effectively boxing him in. Vaguely he heard the sound of a door slamming, and he put his hands on her hips to shove her away.

Lauren felt as though a giant fist had just nailed her right in the chest. Her breath froze in her lungs as she stupidly stared at the scene in front of her. At Tony, leaning against the breakfast bar that separated his dining room from his kitchen, kissing another woman. His hands were on her narrow hips, her arms were wrapped around his neck as she strained on tiptoe to reach his mouth.

Every nerve in her body told her to flee the scene before they realized she was there, but her feet were rooted to the floor. How could he do this? How could he be with someone so soon? She must have made some sound because Tony's head snapped up. His dark brown eyes closed guiltily as he met her stunned gaze, and he gently pushed the other woman away.

She carefully set down the large pizza box and the six-pack of beer on the kitchen table. "I'm really sorry," she mumbled, making a feeble attempt at a smile. "I didn't realize you had plans and thought I'd come over to watch the game." Tears seared the back of her eyes, and she turned and hurried to the door before she made an even bigger ass of herself by crying over a guy who changed bed partners like he changed his underwear.

"Lauren, wait!" he shouted as she flew out the front door and made a beeline for her jeep.

Ice coursed through her veins, making her hands shake as she tried to shove the key into the lock. Before she could get into the truck, Tony grabbed her by the arm and spun her around. Taking a deep breath, she hung on to the last fragile threads of her composure and shook him off.

"Lauren, this isn't what you think. I didn't even invite her over."

She fought to keep her expression nonchalant. "Don't worry Tony, it's not my business what you do, or who you sleep with, as long as it isn't me."

She turned away and somehow managed to open the door of the truck. He wrapped one big hand around her biceps, his touch burning through the thin fabric of her shirt. "Please, don't leave."

She looked over his shoulder, meeting the beautiful, petite brunette's inquisitive green gaze, and did her best to muster up a sarcastic smile. "I don't know what your other girlfriends are into, but in my world, three's a crowd."

Pulling away, she slammed the door of the jeep and drove away in a haze. She made it to the end of Tony's road and turned the corner before the sick humiliation overwhelmed her. Her stomach knotted painfully as she thought of how carefully she'd dressed, how she'd actually taken the time to put on makeup and style her hair, even as she'd tried to tell herself it didn't matter if Tony found her attractive.

What kind of an idiot was she, thinking she could go back to being his friend after what they'd shared? Thinking she could handle the sight of him with another woman when even the mere thought made her want to vomit? She thought she could deal with it, thought she'd be ready for it. But she hadn't thought it would be so soon, and didn't think it would hurt so much. Idiot. What did she expect? She was in love with a man who was going to be with other women. Of course it hurt.

All these months, she'd been able to suppress her true feelings, convince herself that she was only infatuated. Not in love. In the last week the dam had broken, and she realized with cold, stunning clarity, that there was no way in hell she could go on acting like her feelings went no further than friendship. And today proved beyond a doubt that he didn't feel the same.

Her cell phone rang obnoxiously, and a fresh wave of tears spilled as she recognized Tony's number. She turned it off, knowing there was no explanation he could offer that would make her feel better. Knowing she didn't deserve an explanation at all, and had gotten exactly what she deserved for pushing the boundaries of friendship yet again.

Scrubbing her eyes with the heels of her hands, she started up the truck. Clearly, she couldn't keep working with Donovan Brothers, or even living in the tiny town of Donner Lake, for that matter. Her heart pinched at the prospect of not seeing or talking to Tony anymore. But seeing him every day, forced to work beside him, would eat away at her bit by bit. It was wimpy, it was cowardly, but she saw no option but to leave. Even though she knew this sharp, devastating pain would fade with time, she wasn't enough of a masochist to put herself through it.

Swallowing back a sob, she turned into Mike Donovan's driveway.

Tony slammed the heel of his hand into his steering wheel as he saw the empty parking space in front of Lauren's apartment building. Even though her jeep was gone, he tried calling her apartment. No answer, as expected. He called her cell for what seemed the fiftieth time, only to be dumped immediately into voice mail.

Goddamn her! For the first time in his sorry life, he was in love, and the woman wouldn't even take his calls. How was he supposed to convince her she'd misread the situation if she wouldn't even take his calls?

He waited in front of her house for a full hour. Unwilling to give up, he drove down all two blocks of the town's Main Street, hoping for a glimpse of her truck. Screw her, he thought. Damned if he was going to spend all night driving around looking for her. He would see her tomorrow at work anyway, and by God, he was going to get her alone and make her listen. Make her understand that he loved her, and no matter what she thought she saw, there was no one for him but her.

The next morning, he barely got out of the truck before he found himself body slammed, hard, up against the truck. The door handle dug into his kidney and his breath whooshed out as 230 pounds of powerfully built older brother smashed into him.

"Great fucking job, Tony!" Mike shouted, punctuating it with a shove that nearly unbalanced him. "Just couldn't keep your fucking dick in your pants, could you?"

Tony shook his head, tried to regain his equilibrium. "What are you talking about?" As though he didn't know.

"Well, thanks to some 'personal issues,' involving you, Lauren quit last night. She says she'll stay until I can find someone to fill in, but with about a month to go before we're severely limited by weather, I'm stuck trying to find a new carpenter."

"Shit."

"Yeah, shit. Worse, Lauren's my friend, my wife's friend, and I have to watch her get fucked over by my oversexed little brother."

"It's not like that."

"You mean you didn't have sex with Lauren last weekend

and she didn't find you at your house last night with someone else?" Mike thumped him in the chest.

"It wasn't what it looked like," Tony said with an angry shove back. "Look this is between me and Lauren. This isn't any of your business."

Mike grabbed his arm in a vice grip. "Not my business? I'd say it's my business if your overactive libido costs me a key employee. And I'd say it's my business when my good friend shows up at my door crying, telling me she can't work with you anymore. Lauren's not like your other women, Tony. You can't just fuck around with her and dump her when you get bored."

"I love her," Tony yelled, slightly gratified as Mike's jaw dropped in obvious shock. Come to think of it, Tony himself was a little surprised to hear himself say it out loud. But it felt good. Surprisingly right. So he said it again, this time more quietly. "I love her."

Mike relaxed his grip on Tony's arm. "Are you sure?" he asked, staring at Tony as though he expected a little green man to jump out and reveal he'd taken control of Tony's brain.

Tony smiled. "I'm sure. Now if I can just convince her . . ."

"She's at home. I told her to take the day off."

Tony's stomach clenched at that. She must have been really upset for a hard-ass like Mike to offer the day off.

Five minutes later, Tony pulled into Lauren's parking lot and sprinted up the stairs to her door. He rapped hard on the door, tapping his booted foot impatiently as he waited for her to answer. The door opened slowly, revealing Lauren in tantalizing bits. Her hair was still wet from her shower, making dark spots on the shoulders of her robe. Her face, scrubbed clean of makeup, bore little evidence that she'd been crying. But when he looked more closely he could see her eyes were slightly puffy. If he had anything to do with it, she'd never again shed a single tear because of him.

"Can I come in?"

She nodded and stepped aside. Moving into her apartment's tiny kitchen, she grabbed a cup of coffee from the counter and stirred in a spoonful of sugar. "So I guess you talked to Mike," she said quietly.

"Lauren, please don't quit, not because of me."

"If you came to talk me out of quitting—"

"That's not why I'm here. I came to talk to you about what happened last night."

She held up a hand to silence him, and the sleeve of her robe slid back to reveal the smooth, tan skin of her forearm. "I already told you, you don't owe me an explanation. It's not your fault I couldn't keep my feelings out of it." She stared at the ugly blue and green flecked linoleum, refusing to meet his gaze.

He moved closer, unable to stop himself from reaching out and stroking the baby-soft skin of her inner arm. She jumped at his touch and tried to pull away, but Tony reached out with his other hand and tipped her face up to his. Her tongue stole out nervously over her plump, soft mouth, an invitation he couldn't resist. His lips closed over hers in a soft, searching kiss. Her lips parted, a soft moan escaping her throat before she shoved him away.

"Please don't do this," she said shakily. "Please don't make this any harder than it is." She tried to move around him, but Tony backed her against the counter, settling his hands on either side of her hips.

"Listen to me, please," he said. "I want more than a casual affair with you, Lauren. I want to be with you—"

"Ha!" She flung her head back, eyes shining with tears and anger. "You want to be with me? Is that why you had what's her name over last night? You want to 'be' with her one night and me the next? No thanks!" She shoved hard at his shoulders, but he held firm.

"I didn't invite her over," he practically shouted. "Why can't you believe me? Yes, I knew her before, yes, I slept with her, but I never thought I'd see her again and I didn't invite her to my house."

She snorted and folded her arms. "I'm supposed to believe that?"

He leaned in so close his forehead nearly rested against hers and he could feel the press of her breasts against his chest. "When have I ever lied to you? Yes, I've been with lots of women. Yes, I was a complete and total horndog for most of my adult life, but I've never lied to a woman just to get her into bed, and I don't say things I don't mean."

She turned her head to the side, jaw clenched. He put his mouth right next to her ear and whispered. "I love you, Lauren. And I mean it."

Lauren's entire body froze in shock. "What?"

"I love you," he said. His hand came up to rest against her cheek and gently forced her to meet his gaze.

He was so close she could see every individual lash, feel the hot puff of his breath against her mouth. His hands shook a little as his thumb traced her bottom lip. "Lauren, every morning for the past seven months, I wake up and I can't wait to get to work. I can't wait to see you and talk to you. And even when we don't talk I like knowing you're there, working beside me."

The tiny kernel of hope in her belly sprouted a tentative shoot.

"I've wanted you for so long, but I kept my hands to myself because I didn't want to mess up our friendship. But after we made love, I knew I could never go back to the way it was."

Made love. She tried not to read too much into that.

His dark eyes were suspiciously bright. With tears? Was that actually possible? Lauren felt the familiar sting in her own eyes.

"I love you, Lauren," he said. "I think I have for a long time, but I was too stupid to figure it out."

She sucked in a breath and leaned back abruptly. "Tony, I—"

Part of her was terrified to say it back, to take the incredible risk of actually having a relationship with him. What if he woke up tomorrow and resented the confinement of monogamy?

As though reading her mind, he pulled her close, burying his nose in her hair and taking a deep inhale. "Believe me, Lauren. There's never been anyone like you for me. There will never be anyone like you."

It felt so good, to be held by him, to bury her nose in his shirt and smell the warm scent that had driven her crazy from the first moment she'd met him. She could feel the faint tremors in his arms, hear the slight catch of his breath. He was as nervous and unsure as she. The realization broke down the last barrier holding her back. Even a lifelong player like Tony could get his heart broken, but no way was she going to be the woman to do it.

Wrapping her arms tight around his shoulders, she tipped her head back and pressed a sprinkling of kisses to his neck, his jaw, wherever her lips could reach. "I love you, too," she said, half-laughing, half-crying between pecks. "All that stuff you said about being happy every day because you knew you would see me," he clutched her harder, "it's the same for me. And I quit because I couldn't stand the idea of being with you every day, knowing I couldn't have you."

"Oh you can have me," he said, his voice lowering an octave as he pressed his hips firmly against hers. The satin of her robe did nothing to hide the firm bulge in his jeans, pressing into the notch of her thighs. "You can have me any time, any way you want," he paused, the teasing glint fading from his dark eyes. "For as long as you want me."

"How about forever?" She asked, trying to keep her tone light and failing miserably.

He lifted her up onto the counter and slid his hands under the lapels of her robe. Streaks of heat emanated from every place he touched. "That sounds like a good start." Her head fell back, eyes drifting shut as his mouth traced a hot wet trail down her neck. She wrapped her legs around his hips, pulling him tight against her.

His big hand closed over her breast, a low, satisfied sound rumbling from his chest as he cupped the heavy flesh. "I was hoping you were naked under here." He quickly undid the knot at her waist and pushed the silky material down her shoulders. "I've missed you so much this past week," he murmured. His fingers traced her curves slowly, almost reverently.

Heat pulsed between her thighs, along with a surge of power at the thought that this man who could have any woman he wanted, was shaking with need for her. Her fingers flew over buttons and zippers until Tony's clothes lay in a heap on her kitchen floor. Somehow they found themselves on her rickety old bed that squeaked and groaned as they rolled across it. Somehow he managed to slip on a condom without taking his hands and mouth off of her. He slid his cock along her folds, drawing out thick moisture and teasing her until she grasped his hips like she meant business. "I love a woman who takes what she wants," he teased. With one long, smooth stroke he was inside her, his dark eyes shining as he smiled down at her. "But most of all, Lauren, I love you."

Hot Wired

VALERIE MARTINEZ

With special thanks to C.M.

1

There was a note stuck to the cactus. I stood for a moment in the kitchen as solitary and still as the only two objects that inhabited the room: the cactus and the rickety table upon which it sat. Staring at the cactus, with the clownish yellow post-it attached to its pallid midriff, I felt lonely in my new apartment. I had slept there the past three nights, but it still felt unfamiliar, like a stranger's bed.

I hurried to the note. It was from my cousin, Verónica, of course.

She had brought home the cactus the day I moved in. Three days ago.

"It's to remind you of home," she'd said, placing the plant smack in the middle of the kitchen table, which we had hauled in from its rotting place on the street the night before. "In case you get homesick for Tucson."

I smiled politely at her hospitable gesture. Droplets of drizzle from outside were caught in the unbrushed fur that covered the cactus. I had never seen a cactus quite so *hairy* before. Not in Arizona. Despite its furry appearance, this was not a plant you wanted to pet. Its hair was wiry and white like a crazy old man's, and its needles sharp and brittle as a bone. Yet, to my horror, my cousin was quite literally, and lovingly, stroking our new living addition to the apartment from head to base and back again. Not only was this *loco* because the damn thing was sharp, but also because, well, the cactus was fairly phallic. I mean, *really* phallic. A prickly prick, and a well-endowed thirteen inches at that. It even had a nicely shaped head to top it off.

As I watched my cousin jerk off a cactus in our dingy kitchen, her vampy nails clicking as they ran up and down the spines, I panicked. I had moved hundreds of miles from home, where rent was free, living with my parents, and where a twenty-four-hour bus line didn't stop right outside my bedroom window, and into this dank, basement apartment with my hypersexual cousin. I had to remind myself it had been my idea to move to San Francisco and in with my cousin for the summer.

But over the past three days of cohabitation, I had come to see the cactus as benign. Like a gay, male roommate whom I was glad to see waiting for me when I came home damp and disheveled from carrying groceries.

I set down my grocery bags—mostly cleaning supplies for the moldy apartment—on the kitchen table and carefully peeled off the post-it.

There was an address. The three-letter word BAR. And a stick figure drawing of two girls drinking from bottles labeled childishly with skulls and crossbones. By the curly doodles of hair on one of the girls and the prominently penned *chi chi's* on the other, it was immediately apparent that the illustration was of me (*chi chi's*) and Verónica (hair) getting drunk.

It was four o'clock in the afternoon.

The wooden number 9 on the otherwise unmarked door of the bar had swung upside down from its loose screw so that I mistook it for a 6.

I paced up and down the sidewalk, pockmarked by blackened gum and cigarette butts, searching in vain for number 229. I peered into brightly painted *taquerías* that exhaled their rich aromas to lick at my taste buds. I passed storefronts lit up by twinkling gold crucifixes and paused in front of markets selling rain-specked orange and yellow fruit. It had started to drizzle, and I pulled the fake fur–lined hood of my jacket over my head.

Summer in San Francisco was not quite what I had expected. The sky seemed permanently drained from blue to an anemic grey.

A man in a baggy jacket walked by me and slung soft-spoken Spanish my way. Just as I decided it was time to give up and head back to the empty apartment, a door behind me burst open.

A young man stumbled out onto the cold sidewalk. He wore a thin, white undershirt but didn't appear cold. His jet black hair was curiously slicked back like Elvis and his jeans were cuffed up at the ankles. He was white, but his eyes were dark like a Mexican's, heavily fringed with black lashes. They flashed at me with indiscriminating drunken desire.

I shivered for him. The sight of his tattooed biceps exposed so nakedly to the wet and the cold gave me a strange maternal desire to cover his bare arms. He stared back at me blankly, answering my private yearning with indifference, and smoothed the front of his jeans to straighten himself out. Then, without a single glance back, he walked away and turned the corner out of sight. The smell of beer and cigarettes in his wake drenched me like an aphrodisiac. I had found the bar.

Tequila makes me slippery. Shot glasses slip through my fingers. One shatters to the ground but only scares the bar dogs that trace the floor like shadows. My tongue moves in and out from English to Spanish. I can talk to anyone when I'm drunk: Verónica's friends with their hair coiffed in bizarre 50s hairdos and streaked with cartoonish colors. They crowd a large table with their unisex, tattooed arms. Their shiny quarters fill the jukebox with rockabilly tunes. I ask the boys about their ink, boldly touching the saturated skin, and shyly admire the girls' arms flowering with color that blushes up to their collarbones.

My father always warned my brothers not to get tattoos where a judge could see them. Unbeknownst to him, my oldest brother, Tito (coincidently, the name of this bar) had CHI-CANO tattooed in old English letters across his stomach.

Verónica had immediately spotted me in the doorway where I stood squinting through thick, bar air for the sole face I knew in this town. As she pulled me into a booth close to the door, strands of her black hair stuck to my lipstick. She tugged me close to her in a drunken embrace until I nearly ended up sprawled on top of her.

"This is *mi prima!*" she announced, struggling back up to a seated position. I was squeezed between her and a boy with a closely shaved head.

"I'm Nacho." He immediately handed me a fresh beer from the table stockpiled with shot glasses and bottles. Out of all the boys at the table, Nacho was the only one who reminded me of the boys I knew back home. Low-riding khaki pants, button-up plaid shirt, small gold-framed picture of Jesus dangling around his neck, and dangerous eyes that knew how to give a girl their full attention.

"Lola. Thanks for the beer." I felt the girls at the table watching me, their eyes turned up at the corners with a sharp curve of eyeliner shaped like a hawk's beak. They knew, and I knew, that, before the night was over, Nacho and I would be hooking up.

"Verónica tells me you're from Tucson." He spoke to me politely, his voice softly accented with a *cholo* incantation. This was the type I fell for despite my better judgment, and a muscle in my heart instinctively tightened against him. Everything about him was crisp: his ironed clothes, the edges of his flushed lips, his square jaw, his attentive manner of speaking to me. His cheeks were freshly shaven and radiated a scented afterglow. His mustache and goatee were neatly trimmed.

"Yeah, I'm just here for the summer."

"Well, maybe I can convince you to stay longer than that." He winked at me with all the charm of the devil.

"Lola! Lola!" My cousin was screaming in my ear.

"You have to meet my best friend! Teresa, this is my cousin Lola."

I had never seen a Chicana get her hair so blonde. It was practically white, with Marilyn Monroe waves and a rack to match.

I immediately wanted to be her and momentarily forgot macho Nacho at my side.

"Nice to meet you." She wore a black-and-white checkered pencil skirt that made her waist look tiny, like a wrist you could encircle with one hand.

Teresa sat down next to two heavyset girls in shrunken cardigans. She seemed bored talking to them, but they eagerly leaned in to hear whatever she was saying, their bouffants bobbing slightly as they nodded agreeably.

"Lola, here!" Verónica had only been paying attention to getting drunk. She handed me a double shot of tequila and stuck a lime in my mouth.

Tequila makes me slippery. Veronica and I slipped around on the dull vinyl seats as we laughed about things that we immediately forgot or never understood in the first place. We have the same laugh. We always have, which used to confuse our parents to no end. I had thought maybe our vocal chords had outgrown each other after all these years, but I was wrong.

"What are you, twins or something?" Nacho only made us laugh harder. We fell into each other, wasted. Verónica's face was too close to mine, and the scent of her hair spray made me dizzy. She looked like a gypsy with her curly masses of black hair. Night to my day, she was as pale as the moon, whereas I was the color of sun-baked earth.

A warm hand slid beneath the hugging waistband of my jeans. It didn't surprise me. It touched the softest skin of my belly before slipping out again. I felt Nacho's breath dampen the back of my neck. I tried to ignore him and echo Verónica's laughter, but she had turned to talk to a boy wearing Buddy Holly glasses.

Watching my cousin flirt had always commanded my awe and admiration. It was like watching a rodeo and realizing that roping a cow really does require a large amount of skill and raw talent. My cousin could turn any raging bull into a big, dumb cow that would buckle to its knees as if slaughtered. It didn't matter that she made eyes with every man in the room—she had a way of making each man feel special, and their cocks undoubtedly twitched with the quickening beat of their hearts. It made me proud to be her cousin, except for that fact that she had left me stranded for a guy who was, in my opinion, more oaf than *umph*. I had no choice but to turn and meet Nacho's gleaming eyes. And when a man looks at you like that, there's no turning back.

Nacho followed me to the bathroom. My ass twitched like tackle at the end of a fishing rod. The seam of my jean's tight crotch pressed into the private grove of my body, rubbing me pleasurably as I headed, tailed by Nacho, to the back of the bar.

There were two separate bathrooms, a single toilet in each, and Nacho and I had the privacy of our own room. It was tiny and painted a bordello red. There was something momentarily sobering about the audibly leaking toilet and the bare bulb dangling from a ceiling so low that it looked as if a child had scrawled graffiti across it. I studied the back of Nacho's broad shoulders as he bolted the door behind us. Something about those expansive shoulders made me feel that he was twice my size even though we were about the same height. I stepped forward as he turned around. Our bodies decisively crashed into each other, shortly followed by our lips.

By the way his hands firmly grabbed my waist, I wouldn't have guessed him to kiss me so gingerly. I squeezed the warm back of his neck, emboldening him to kiss me deeper. He did. Immediately, his open mouth was all over my neck, feeding. My body stiffened, catlike in its desire to be rubbed all over, but Nacho only gripped my jutting hipbones tighter to hold me in place, where he wanted me.

With his head at my neck, I luxuriously ran my hands over the soft bristles of his buzzed hair. They rose underneath my fingertips like goose bumps, *tiny erections of the skin.* My hands circled the crown of his head where the forgiving lightbulb had cast a faint halo. When my hands got dizzy from running laps around his head, they fell, exhausted, to his shoulders, which stretched out in opposite directions like a shoreline. I let his tongue pick up the rhythm of the race up and down my neck.

Pleasure knocked my head back against the door. Nacho was on his knees, gnawing the shy flesh of my stomach. I looked down and my pleasure doubled, seeing a man like that on his knees, eyes closed, lost in the creases of my skin. I was desperate for him to get in deep, for his lips to make out with the swollen lips of my pussy. I hurried to undo the top of my jeans.

Nacho glanced up at me a bit surprised as if he had read my dirty thoughts. He teased me by rubbing his hand up and down the fold of fabric that securely covered my zipper. Nonetheless, I felt a surge in my pussy as the heel of his hand pressed into my clit, still heavily concealed by denim. The roughness of the fabric and the firm push of his palm started getting me off. Nacho stood up to thrust his tongue back into my mouth.

I knew how wet a tough boy like this could get me, and I wondered if he could feel me seeping through my jeans. He had me pinned against the door with one hand pushing into my crotch and the other cradling and deliciously squeezing the bottom of my ass. I writhed hard against his broad palm, increasing the friction against my cloaked clit, wanting nothing more than for him to fuck me against the door painted such a permissive red.

"You want this, don't you, *chica?*" Nacho slammed his hand between my legs with such pointed deliberation that I thought I'd come on the spot. I moaned yes, and his crotch responded by pushing into mine. I felt his hardness struggling against the crisp material of his work pants.

There was a banging on the door that wasn't from us.

"Lola? Lola?!? Are you in there?" *Verónica, not now.*

"I have to piss. And we got to go! You have your first day of work tomorrow."

If there's anything that'll kill the mood, it's the word *work.* Nacho was still dry-humping me, ignoring my cousin's rapping. I pushed him away reluctantly.

"I got to go. My new job starts in the morning." His tongue tried to silence me. I succumbed to it, then spit it out.

"Really, Nacho, I got to go." This time, I really pushed him back. He looked at me in disbelief as I unbolted the door. The slapping bass of old time rock'n'roll hit me hard as I emerged. Only the fat girls in their little sweaters were left at the table tittering over mixed drinks.

Verónica had me by the wrist and was dragging me out the front door. Dogs scattered like ashes at our feet. It was dark outside. It could have been nine at night or two in the morning—I had no idea. I was too drunk to remember to turn around and smile at Nacho, whom I had left in the bathroom alone to contemplate his hard-on.

2

"Lola, your dad's on the phone!"

I groaned. I had just collapsed onto my futon, not even bothering to take off my mustard-stained uniform. My first day as a waitress was exhausting, my nurse-white sneakers in a constant, shuffled conga line as I trailed my cousin with a pitcher of burnt coffee. Verónica had been working at the mock drive-in diner for over a year and had gotten me the job for the summer, the summer before starting my *real* career, as my father no doubt wanted to remind me on the phone.

I stretched out my hand for the cordless, still facedown in my comforter. Verónica handed me the phone after saying a sugary good-bye to her *tío*.

"Hey, Papá."

"How was your first day at work?"

"Good, I guess. Surprisingly tiring." I left out the part about being so hungover that Verónica had to stand outside the bathroom door on the lookout for our manager, Louis, with his twitchy mustache, as I prayed with my head hung in the toilet bowl that the septic fumes would induce vomiting. *Give me vomit or give me death.* But God granted me neither, and I had to suffer my own form of purgatory with the diner's oldies on loop bebopping my splitting headache.

"That's good, but remember, you're young now. Imagine how hard it would be to waitress when you're older or if you had your mother's bad legs." As if his constant peering over my shoulder as I studied all those years hadn't made certain that his *hija*, the daughter of a car mechanic, would make it out of the *barrio.*

"It's just for the summer, Papá. I'll be back in the fall to start my teaching job. Nothing is going to keep me from that." I didn't add that the job meant I could finally move out of my parents' house into a place all of my own, although I imagined it would be close by so I could still help out my mom around the house when her diabetes got bad. Living here with Verónica was just a taste of things to come when I would have my own apartment in Tucson. For one, I could have boys spend the night.

"I know, Lolita. I just know how exciting your cousin's lifestyle is to you, but just remember she—"

"Dad, hold on. I've got call waiting. One sec, okay? Don't hang up." I clicked over. "Hello?"

"Verónica?"

"Uh, no, this is her cousin Lola."

"God, you two sound the same. I was calling for you, anyway."

"*Nacho?*" I sat up, erect, in the bed.

"Nice, you recognized my voice . . . even though we didn't get to talk much last night." I felt myself blush in sudden heat, remembering Nacho on his knees sucking the sensitive flesh of my stomach.

"Um, how'd you get my number?" This was so unexpected. Our bathroom tryst in the dive bar I thought was just that, a bathroom tryst in a dive bar.

"Well, I figured you lived with your cousin, so I thought I'd call and see if you want to hang out sometime. Go for a ride in my car or something."

"You got a nice ride?" I perked up. The daughter of a mechanic, an appreciation for cars was in *mi sangre*.

"You bet. And I got more than that." I laughed nervously and felt a hot surge between my legs. How fast that easy, cocky tone of his voice got me excited.

"So when are you going to take me for a ride?" I spoke through the breathy mask of my bedroom voice.

"How about I pick you up Thursday night. Around eight?" That was in three days. I needed him here now to lift the short hem of my polyester waitressing dress, flip me over, and yank down my cotton panties. I was about to ask him what he was wearing (imagining him in a wife-beater and no pants) when I remembered my father on the other line.

"Shit, Nacho. I gotta go. See you at eight. Thursday. You know where we live?"

"I do. See you at eight, *chica.*"

Flustered, I clicked back to the other line.

"Dad?" The dial tone admonished me with its nasal drone. I sighed and sank back into the billowy folds of my comforter. I knew I should call my dad back, but I closed my eyes instead. The fantasy of Nacho's square hands rubbing me down after a long day on my feet relaxed me. Before I knew it, I was fast asleep.

3
_____

I saw Nacho before Thursday. It was Wednesday, the day before our supposed date, and Verónica and I had gotten off work just in time to make it to Tito's for happy hour. Our pockets were crammed with small bills, hard-earned tips to blow on hard alcohol. When I saw Nacho, he was sitting in the same booth in the same bar with a girl (not me) who had lip liner permanently tattooed on her mouth. When she smiled, a closed-lipped smile, the lines of her mouth pulled taut like two red strings. She saw me staring at her and tossed a look of flying daggers. I meekly returned the look with a smattering of butter knives.

"Lola, that girl is *basura*." Verónica had a way of hissing words in Spanish to hide the fact that she couldn't speak it fluently. She quickly shuttled me to a stool at the bar, and we sat with our backs to Nacho and Tattoo Mouth. They were keeping company with a bunch of *cholos* whose precisely folded bandannas half-hooded their eyes and made them look sleepy.

Verónica ordered us two margaritas.

Chile pepper lights, like the ones my mom strung around

our Christmas tree each year, blinked above a long mirror behind the bar. I checked it frequently like a rearview mirror and watched Nacho move into the fast lane. I felt as if I were being rear-ended.

"I think I'm going to go for a walk." I stood up abruptly, upending my bar stool.

"But you haven't even tried your margarita!" True, but it was already watery. I hated watery margaritas. I liked them blended thick like milk shakes.

"I just wanna get some air. I'll be right back."

"Do you want me to come with you?" Verónica peered into the hurt expression that glazed my eyes.

"Don't worry, I'm fine. I'll be right back."

I had no intention of returning.

I looked up and down the grey street for a pay phone. I felt lost in condensation. A thick fog had enveloped the city like a wartime gas. It infected my head and made it impossible to clear my thoughts.

I spotted the mock shelter of a pay phone two blocks away. As I approached, the bundle of wet newspapers next to the phone turned out to be a sodden, homeless man. He was passed out cold, and his arms were wrapped around the phone's trunk like a thirsty man who has crawled through the desert only to die upon reaching a palm-treed oasis.

Carefully, I sidestepped the prostrate body and dug into my purse for the unused calling card my father had handed to me at the airport. Using a penny to scratch off the pewter strip, I debated whether or not I was actually going to place the call. My fingers, that most impulsive body part, made the decision for me and tapped across a complex code of buttons.

My ex-boyfriend's voice mail picked up. I hung up without leaving a message. He would never know that I called.

Now what?

I looked around me. The streetlights flickered on and reflected themselves in the iridescent oil slicks of the street. Suddenly, it was Friday night all around me, swirling like a carnival ride. Crackheads pushed their shopping carts into oncoming traffic, maniacally assuming the right of way. Valets jumped to the curb at attention as tanklike SUVs pulled up in front of swank restaurants. Hipsters with dyed black hair that sat on their heads like helmets ducked behind the grimy windows of cafes and bars. A mariachi band paraded from taquería to taquería serenading first dates and immigrant families.

An old Mexican woman with an androgynous, wrinkled face stopped me. She was selling homemade tamales out of a teal-colored cooler. She couldn't have been more than five feet tall.

"*¿Cuanto cuestan, abuelita?*"

Her smile was toothless and sweet, as if she had eaten too much candy over a lifetime. I bought two tamales and gave her an extra dollar. She patted my arm before rushing off to accost a pedestrian with tribal tattoos twisting like vines around his face.

I ate the tamales as I walked on, warmed by their company. Curiosity and the wanderlust of loneliness led me through quiet alleys that let out suddenly onto estuaries of populated street.

Pausing in front of a huge mural that covered a community center, I used my teeth to scrape the pasty remnants off the corn husk. The mural glowed with an eerie green light. The scene was of a field being sprayed with pesticides by a low-flying plane as Mexican migrant workers toiled below. One of the field hands was pregnant and her peacefully sleeping fetus was bathed in toxic green effulgence. I started in on the second tamale and noticed some gang graffiti bordering the edges of the mural. As I leaned in for a closer inspection of the cryptic lettering, which appeared to be a combination of roman numerals and chicken scratch, the loud backfire of an engine interrupted my thoughtful chewing. I jumped, but it didn't scare me. I could long tell the difference between gunfire and backfire.

On the opposite side of the street, the rear end of an old pickup truck, rumbling with constipation, jutted out from an open garage. The warm fluorescence of the garage held a womblike pull for me. My earliest memories were of my father's auto shop; the mechanical whirring could lull me to sleep better than any lullaby, and often my mother had to take me there to get me to sleep at night.

I approached the garage with the timid stealth of a deer. Love at first sight hit me with the voluptuous curve of the shiny, red hood of a '51 Chevy pickup. It was the kind of hood that you wanted to get fucked against: the slick, hard metal slope matching up perfectly with the lumbar curve of your spine. And that impossibly red color! Like the perfect shade of nail polish or a hard cherry candy that it takes forever to suck into oblivion.

I must have been about eleven years old when I first laid eyes on this model Chevy. My second cousin Cristina's boyfriend drove his '51 pickup, an electric blue, into my dad's garage to get its rattling muffler fixed. He let me sit in the passenger seat and even turned on the radio for me. The interior had the musty aroma of horse blankets. I remember thinking *this is what it feels like to be grown up* as I looked over at him adjusting the radio. His slender features—one might even have called them delicate, if not for the thuggish-looking man-boy fuzz above his upper lip—appealed to my girlishness. I imagined I was Cristina and he, my boyfriend, was driving me around town with the windows rolled down.

A leg in a navy-blue coverall dangled like a cigarette from the gaping mouth of the driver's-side door. Whoever was sitting inside cut the engine. The night sputtered into stillness. I was afraid to move, to be discovered leering. I was standing dead center in front of the garage. The man got out of the truck with a sigh so heavy that I would never have expected him to be any younger than one of my *tíos* who worked at my dad's shop.

Dark eyes, heavily fringed with black lashes, caught me like a pair of headlights. I could only brace myself against the impact.

He also froze in his tracks when he saw me. We looked at each other perplexed, like animals of two different species trying to recognize what the other was, unable to communicate, curious but apprehensive. His skin was as smooth as that of a teenage boy in an electric blue Chevy. And now I was old enough. Twenty-three. He looked only a couple years older.

He ended the staring contest with a blink. As he reached down to pick up a wrench from the grease-soiled floor, my eyes quickly frisked his body. The arms of his coveralls were rolled up past his elbows revealing a tapestry of tattoos like a second sleeve etched eternally onto his skin. He had the loose movements of an exceedingly tall person, yet without the awkwardness that usually accompanies such height. His shoulders were a bit narrow for his muscular arms.

I had seen him before. The first time I went to Tito's. His drunken exit from the bar had unwittingly showed me its entryway. The white boy with Mexican eyes and Elvis hair.

I couldn't just keep standing there. When he looked back up, I was gone.

"Lola, *chica*, where have you been? We've been worried about you!" Verónica opened the gate to our apartment to let me in. I had forgotten my keys.

"*We?*" My gaze skipped past her shoulder and skimmed the bristly top of a shaved head in the kitchen behind.

"What's Nacho doing here?" I pulled Verónica out onto the sidewalk. She was wearing a black miniskirt with leggings, no socks. My boozy cousin swayed on a purple pair of thrift-store pumps.

"Don't worry, that *basura* was his ex-girlfriend. He dumped her in the trash, where she came from, months ago. She just showed up at Tito's like some psycho-bitch."

I was skeptical, but a big part of me didn't even care. My teeth were chattering from an excitement I dared not name.

"When you left like that, he totally ditched her and kept bugging me about you, wondering where you went." She shrugged as if reenacting her answer to his inquiries, and a loose strap of her tank top slipped off her shoulder. The hollow of her exposed collarbone was slightly blue, but she didn't appear to be cold. Her breath formed warm tequila clouds.

My whole body was shivering, but I wasn't cold, either. I was afraid my teeth would shake loose and leave my nerve endings exposed from my gums. I covertly pinched the flesh of my forearms in an effort to stop my incessant quaking. It was of no use. My thoughts would only backflip to the shiny, red pickup and those dark eyes that teased me of things I wanted to know, and my bones would set off rattling all over again. Just imagine all the places you could fuck on a truck like that! Not just on the engorged hood. Up against a sun-heated dashboard. Lying back on the creaky floorboards of the truck *bed!*

"Lola. *Hey, Lola!*"

I had felt his eyes penetrate mine, but maybe I had just imagined that. Maybe my gawking had forced him to return the gaze.

"Lola, c'mon! He's been waiting for you to get home." Gypsy eyes implored me. I followed Verónica into the apartment like a sleepwalker led by a dream.

I didn't want Nacho, but I could have him. I had a flame I needed him to feed, afraid if someone didn't, it would extinguish and I would be at a loss how to light it, left holding just a flint and stone in my bare hands.

Verónica disappeared into her room. From the heavy rustling

muffled behind her closed door, I judged she too had a male suitor.

I approached Nacho from behind. He sat patiently at the kitchen table like a schoolboy waiting for his lesson. The table was smoking with cigarette butts half-extinguished in empty beer bottles.

As if I was reading Braille, my fingers traced the prickly dots of hair that faded into the nape of his neck. He didn't turn around. My nails sunk into his neck, almost in a choke hold. His head only turned when my fingers started to squeeze into the collapsing cartilage of his esophagus.

"Damn, *chica*." But he liked it. I shimmied between him and the kitchen table. My crotch was at the dangerous level of his undressing eyes. He immediately pulled me onto his lap.

"Damn, *chica*." Apparently, he didn't have anything else to say. Fine with me. I slipped my tongue in his mouth and he pushed his hard-on, tenting in his pants, between my legs. That I wanted. I grabbed onto the bulge like the horn of saddle to ride the rhythm of his hips. The boy was pumping into me like he had a drill in his pants that could screw through the layers of our clothing. I had to put an end to this dry humping business. Fast.

"C'mon, Nacho. I want to show you my room."

I switched on the only lamp in my small room and rotated its shade so that the tear in the muslin covering faced the wall. My room had the shameless appearance of a bachelor pad. In the dim light, Nacho tripped over empty take-out cartons and soda cans that surrounded the futon mattress barely raised off the floor by a low frame. My stereo was propped up on an overturned cardboard box, and I turned it on. The music was low and moody.

Nacho was already unbuttoning his shirt when I stumbled

back to him. My suitcase, overflowing with unfolded clothes, lay directly in my path. I had yet to acquire a set of drawers.

"Here, let me help you with that." My urgent fingers struggled with the tiny buttons. I wasn't prepared for the sight that met me. The seductive eyes of multiple women stared at me unapologetically, laying claim to Nacho's broad chest. I peeled off the rest of his shirt to get a better look at his tattooed harem.

Most of the faces were anonymous, wearing the vacant expression of strippers, but some dangled first names in looping cursive. The tattoos covered the entire region of his pecs, like the breastplate of a conquistador, and spared only his dusty rose nipples. A tattoo of the Virgin Mary guarded his not-so-virgin heart.

"Yolanda?" I poked an accusatory finger at the name in indelible black ink positioned under the exotic mouth of a long-haired beauty.

"My sister?" He shrugged sheepishly.

"Liar." I shoved him fiercer than I had intended, and he fell back onto the futon. He grabbed ahold of my calf and pulled me down on top of him.

I fumed with a desire hatched from a convoluted jealousy. As I stripped off my shirt, I wondered what it would take to become one of those girls permanently engraved into his skin. Nacho quickly distracted me by squeezing my hard nipples, which poked through the black lace of my bra. He then tugged at them with his teeth.

"*Don't tear my bra.*" He grinned, raising his devilish eyebrows. In one stroke, he pulled down the spindly material and cupped the naked fullness of my breasts.

His hands were large, large enough to completely cover my ample tits. His grip was crushing, and he just kept squeezing and squeezing until juice began to slip between my legs.

"*You like that, don't you?*"

I responded affirmatively by unzipping his pants. I searched frantically until I found the ultrasmooth head of his cock. He moaned when I touched that precious bead of precum and rubbed it around the tip, slowing working down his stout, slightly ridged cock.

But he didn't let me jerk him off.

"*I want to taste you, Lola.*" His words made my limbs tingle in anticipation as if I were about to have a stroke.

Nacho undid my jeans, and I slipped out of them silently while enjoying the cool slide of the denim. The air trembled slightly above my exposed legs. Nacho's teeth were immediately at my panty line, and he deftly used them to pull off my underwear. My discarded panties rolled up at my toes.

When his eager mouth returned, my hand was clamped over my curly mound like a shell. He tried to nudge it out of the way with his nose, but I only allowed a quick slip of his tongue through a crack in my fingers. Determined, his tongue tried once more to break through the seawall. Again, I teased him and let him just barely make contact with my pearly pinkness before clamming up again.

I started to laugh, enjoying this little game of mine, but Nacho shot me a look—his lips drawn into a serious, thin line—that meant business. Softly, my hand dropped away like a falling petal. His tongue provided the pistil to my denuded flower.

His tongue flickered in and out. Everything began to feel swollen: his tongue swelling inside my opening, the rim swelling to encompass the tongue. The tightness of all this engorged flesh was almost too much to bear, and I groaned. Providing momentary relief, Nacho moved up to my clit with cooling licks. But then his fingerlike tongue began to tickle my hyper-sensitive clit, and I began to giggle uncontrollably with girlish pleasure. Nacho responded by shoving a finger inside me, where it found a slick fit. This silenced my laughter, and now I gasped tight little gasps each time his finger poked that burning little bundle of nerves tucked up inside my pussy.

"*Nacho!*" My breathing quickened into a pant, though it was he who was licking me all over like a dog. His thirsty tongue lapped up pools of my naked body, which undulated from his finger-fucking.

"*I want to taste myself on your lips.*" I pulled his mouth to mine and attempted to suck away any lingering traces of my pungent taste. His cock, with its pestering hard-on, pushed into my thigh. I grabbed it; its powerful rigidity required a firm grip as I stroked the shaft. I had the reckless urge to stick it where his finger delved.

I wondered if he would want to. Fuck, that is. I sought his eyes, but they were closed in a grimace of pleasure. I slowed the rhythm of my hand so that he would open them. When he did, they glinted like narrow shards of glass.

His face was strange and mysterious to me in the hovering darkness. Heavy shadows hung to his cheekbones sculpting his face like a Mayan mask. Another hard shadow chiseled his jaw-line with masculine precision. His stone features were breathtaking in the menacing light, and I wanted his rock hardness to melt into my molten center.

"*Nacho, I need you to fuck me.*" The need felt like hot lava dripping down my body. Then I realized that Nacho had come on my ribs.

4

"Is this going to stain the tub?"

Verónica lowered my head over the rim of the bathtub to apply the remaining purple lather of black dye to the base of my hairline. We were going to a party in a few hours.

"I don't think it matters." With a gloved hand, Verónica turned my head toward the urinelike stain on the bottom of the tub.

I could never understand how she could take baths in our tub, allowing her dimpled flesh to lie against such a foul-looking and mysterious stain. When I showered under our weak, detachable showerhead, I did everything I could to keep my feet from touching that stain. This often involved a superstitious dance around it like children do to avoid the ubiquitous cracks in the sidewalk for fear of breaking their mothers' backs. My cousin, on the other hand, religiously took a bath once a week surrounded by votive candles lit to the Virgin of Guadalupe and fecund mounds of bubble bath voluptuously covering her naked parts. Often, she wanted company while she took her baths, and I would perch on the closed toilet seat and talk to her until the bubbles began to dissolve into clear water. At that point, I would discreetly excuse myself from the room.

Verónica had always been comfortable with her body, which undeniably had the sumptuous shape of a burlesque performer. When I was barely thirteen, I flew to San Diego to spend my spring break with my cousin. An hour after my plane landed, we were lying on the beach: Verónica in a tiny, lilac bikini that just covered her nubile teenage parts, and I, sheathed in a one-piece that forced me to suck my stomach in. Neither Verónica nor her mother, my tía Coral, who sat in a beach chair just within earshot and slathered with suntan oil that gave her the sheen of a roast turkey, seemed aware of the effect this pubescent display had on the male beach-farers around us. It was I alone who suffered the embarrassment from their shameless stares at young flesh ripening in the sun.

Nevertheless, lying on the silky, blond sand of that southern California beach, I experienced a new sensation of freedom from behind the criminal amount of makeup my aunt let me wear. Liquid eyeliner, which my cousin dexterously applied in the car speeding away from the airport, allowed me to deny with a hard crease of black any man's gaze. This look I had learned entirely from my cousin. It wasn't the sight of her Medusa masses of hair that turned, even at that age, that certain part of the male member to stone; rather, it was that subtle turning down of her eyelid, heavy with liner. Her iris would tuck in the outer corner of her eye just as she shuttered her lid and turned away. This left her subject with the bewitching impression of an ancient Egyptian fresco, kohl eyes following the tomb raider wherever he moved.

"You think Nacho will be at this party?" I sat on a low stool in front of Verónica's vintage vanity. Old photographs of pinup girls, curling with decades of being manhandled and stashed away in attics, were tucked into the frame of the vanity's mirror.

"I don't think so. This really isn't his scene." I was beginning to think this wasn't going to be my scene either. Verónica was styling the top of my long hair into a pompadour. A bobby pin scraped my scalp, raw from the harsh dye, to secure it in place. She had wanted to cut Bettie Page bangs, but I insisted that I felt enough like a harlot with my new raven locks. My hair shined like black shoe polish and radiated a chemical perfume that made my eyes water, but I liked the way it hollowed my cheeks and deepened my eyes. I felt ghostly, the way I imagined Verónica did with her porcelain skin. I stared into the mirror, enchanted by my phantom appearance.

"What happened between you and Nacho anyway? He's been calling you all week, and you haven't returned any of his phone calls." Finished fixing my hair, Verónica sloppily mixed herself another drink of vodka and cranberry juice. We were drinking from her retro set of martini glasses. An old record warbled on her player.

"Oh, nothing much. He passed out before anything really happened."

I thought of Nacho's back heaving in sleep. It was covered with memorial and gang tattoos. I wasn't sure which tattooed side of him—his wanton front or his felonious back—I preferred to stare at in my insomnia.

He had hugged me close and his drying cum stuck us together like paste. He told me he was from Hollenbeck. LA. Said he had seen things. His best friend shot dead right in front of him. I had heard these stories before, these midnight confessionals made in my thin arms from boys too macho to look at you straight in the daytime. These tragedies no longer impressed me. I had hardened to them many heartbreaks ago. Fortunately, Nacho passed out midslur before detecting my lack of sympathy.

"Sounds like Nacho. He's kind of *un borracho*." Verónica, I knew, had gotten laid that night. I had heard her guest's baritone grunting, followed by her feline whimpers, through the shoddily erected drywall that separated our two rooms. After they settled down, I lay twisted in my sheets, itching from insomnia and sexual frustration. The apartment was silent from those eased into sleep by their orgasms, and my carnal needs only grew louder. I put my finger on the pulse of my pussy, which throbbed with the beating of my heart. An almost forgotten image of penetrating eyes, dark like smoldering coals, flared in my mind. The tight grip of a hand on a wrench. I found quick release with a couple knowing jerks of my fingers.

"Are you into him?"

"Who?" I picked up Verónica's eyeliner from the cluttered vanity. I was thirteen again and painting my face in my cousin's image, trying to transform my small, brown eyes into large, gypsy ones.

"Well, Nacho, of course!"

"I don't know." I wanted to tell her about the boy with the truck, but what could I say? There was no story there, just fantasy. I did have a feeling, though, that Verónica knew him. After all, I had seen him leaving Tito's the first night I went there, and that was Verónica's main haunt.

"I think Teddy's going to be at the party tonight." Verónica changed subjects as fast as the flitting of her eyelashes.

"Who?" Maybe his name was Teddy. . . .

"The boy from last weekend." There had been a few in between as well, but as far as I knew, she had only slept with this one. Verónica went out almost every night, whereas I stayed home, exhausted from waiting tables, and asleep by ten.

Tonight, however, was Friday, and Verónica was zipping me up in her red bombshell dress with white polka dots. It was too small for her, but snugly fit my more subtle curves, while cutting dangerously low across my full tits. I tipped my head forward, feeling a bit like a rhinoceros with my styled hump of hair, to apply vermillion lipstick close to the mirror. Verónica slunk up behind me in the mirror and clung to my waist like a kitten trying out her claws. She smiled her vixen smile, and I matched it in the mirror. Our black hair tumbled together, indistinguishable, like shadows in the night. The night was young and so were we. And I knew that somewhere in this same city, a boy was driving a red pickup through streets filled with fog, thick like dreams.

Beer cans were sunk in a bathtub filled with ice like black-market organs. The tiny bathroom was the epicenter of the party. People were packed in like thirsty cattle at a trough. Verónica elbowed her way to the beer supply as I waited by the toilet. I watched her encounter a mosh pit of resistance until she found a narrowing crack between two skinheads, who looked about ready to brawl. She slipped out of sight. A guy with a heavy beard, and heavier bladder, burst through the crowd and began to piss right in front of me. He groaned as he released the stream of a racehorse. I pressed back awkwardly against the towel rack to avoid getting splattered. Luckily, Verónica immediately returned with two cans of beer.

"Gross, Gus!" She addressed the heaving urinator with a rough slap on the back. I winced; he was wearing a denim vest studded with blunt spikes, but, after all, this was a girl who fondled cacti.

"Hey, Verónica! You're just jealous 'cause you can't pee standing up. I believe they call that dick envy."

"It's *penis* envy, you dick. Way to impress my cousin here." I waved mutely.

"I'd shake your hand, but I've got to shake this first." Gus grinned beneath his beard, limp dick still in hand.

"Um, it's really okay." I shrank back farther into the mildewy towel that hung behind me.

Verónica rolled her eyes and handed me a tall can of Bud.

"Sorry, no Tecate." I didn't care. I loved any cheap beer.

"Let's get out of this piss pit!" Verónica grabbed me by the wrist. We wriggled through the pressing bodies like a tapeworm. I consumed everything I saw: clear-skinned boys with mohawks and gutter-stained clothes, tough chicks with mohawks wearing messy eyeliner and ripped fishnets, skinny boys also wearing eyeliner and fishnets, girls so glammed up they could be mistaken for drag queens, girls with such a smattering of facial hair and small chests that they could be mistaken for pubescent boys. This was nothing like parties I went to back in Tucson.

I touched all of them, indiscriminately brushing up against their flesh in my parasitic path of consummation. Their sweat, like the lubricating trail of a snail, helped me slide past. Excitement pricked my skin with live wires, and my nipples hardened with the heightened awareness that all these bodies were naked and warm underneath their clothing. The beer can in my hand was freezing, but I liked its weight—an anchor to keep me from rising to the ceiling with the coalescing voices and cigarette smoke and loud music.

They were all lined up for us, the boys with jeans cuffed up at the ankle and pomaded hair: the rebel look of an earlier day. They stood against a far wall as if waiting for a firing squad, indifferent, if not defiant, in their casual stances. I looked to my cousin. She was looking at them. Her eyes had hollowed into bullets, and gunpowder filled her heart.

"Shall we?" I gently touched her elbow as if inviting her to dance. She followed my lead.

"I call the one on the right." He had icy blue eyes. She could have him. I didn't trust eyes that blue, believing them to reveal a cold heart.

My arm slipped easily around her waist, which was elongated by a slim, black dress that gave way to nest of ruffles midthigh. I steered us on our wayward course, but nearly shipwrecked before reaching the wall. Emerging from the shaky light of the adjacent kitchen, the boy with Elvis hair appeared before me like an apparition of the King himself. His pompadour, so black it gleamed blue, was slightly messy, as if a girl had carelessly run her nails through it. He joined the pack of boys, and they greeted him with a subtle tinge of deference. Leaning against the door frame with ease, he raised an arm to hold on to the molding as he spoke to the boy with icy eyes. His bicep bulged like a python post–feeding frenzy, his tattoos providing colorful scales.

My knees began to wobble as if I had sea legs. I was so close now that I could reach out and put my hand through his pale skin, which was virtually translucent in the faulty light.

"What's up, Neil?" Verónica was touching his shoulder, which apparently was solid. The girl knew everybody.

His dark eyes passed over her like nightfall and dawned on me. He saw my tight bodice, bound in polka dots, that practically served him my tits on a platter. He saw my long, black hair that tickled my ribs and that only his surpassed in sheen. He saw my thin, exposed limbs flushed with the heat of the party.

My eyes were watery as if drunk on tears. We were practically eye-fucking right in front of Verónica. I think she noticed.

"Uh, Neil. This is my cousin Lola. She's visiting from Tucson."

"Hey, I'm Neil." His handshake was assertive. My hand fell limp, fainting in his grip.

"You look familiar. Have we met?" He asked this with teasing eyes that refused to reveal whether he remembered me from outside the garage.

"I don't think so. I'm Lola." I liked this shiny-eyed game of ours. It was dangerous, like playing Russian roulette with a well-greased gun. It would make me drink too much because I couldn't trust the feeling of being this alive.

Verónica intervened.

"Hey, Neil, have you seen Teresa?" He frowned slightly. I hated seeing those bee-stung lips turn down, even for a moment.

"Um, no, I haven't." Verónica looked around, distracted. His eyes began to wander the crowded room as well. I had to come up with something fast. I took a quick chug of beer and blurted out:

"Do you own that red '51 Chevy pickup?" Both he and Verónica turned to me in surprise.

"Yeah, I do." He looked amused, and it encouraged me to continue.

"I've seen it around the neighborhood. The '51 is one of my favorite old trucks."

"Really?" I had him snared. Now I only had to reel in my net.

"Yeah, totally. Do you still have its original six-cylinder motor with a four-speed transmission?" Not only could I walk the walk (twitching those slim, red-clad hips of mine), I could talk the talk.

"Actually," his voice had this deep frequency that began to vibrate something loose in me, "I've replaced it with a small block 350."

"So, do you have stick or automatic transmission?"

"Automatic, but I drive it like it's my stick." I giggled dumbly. I was tipsy. He was smiling a crooked smile that was more like a smirk. His teeth were straight and a little smallish. He seemed impressed by my basic mechanic knowledge.

"My dad owns an auto shop in Tucson. I grew up around a lot of lowriders," I explained.

"Cool." He was a man of few words, but our eyes continued their tireless foreplay, establishing all that needed to be said.

I finished my beer with a slight gasp for air. My whole body was thirsting.

"Can I get you another beer?" There is nothing more attractive than a man attentive to your needs.

"That would be great. Thanks, Neil." His top lip curled into that sultry, asymmetrical smile of his upon hearing his name.

"I'll be right back. Don't move."

I watched him enter the kitchen with a slight swagger in his square hips and a slight lurch in his square shoulders. Everything about his build was hard and long. I could detect the absolute firmness of his torso underneath his somewhat tight, black T-shirt, that kind of firmness some covet in a mattress but I covet in a man. That kind of firmness that doesn't give.

He really was impossibly tall. I noticed this again when he returned with a beer, held haphazardly at the level of his crotch, where my eyes didn't have to fall far to conduct their quick reconnaissance mission. Any movement was well cloaked by his stiff jeans.

"Here. It's from my personal stash in the fridge." He told me he was good friends with the hosts of the party. Did I know them?

"No, I don't really know anyone here. Or in this entire city, for that matter. Except for my cousin, of course." I didn't mention Nacho. Just then, I realized Verónica had disappeared. So had the icy-eyed boy who had been standing there.

"How do you know my cousin, anyway?"

"Oh, from around, I guess." I raised an eyebrow warily; it was perfectly arched with the cold precision of a pair of tweezers.

"I work down at that bar Tito's every Sunday afternoon. You've probably been there with Verónica. She's a pretty loyal patron."

"*You do?* I do—I mean, I have . . . been there." All of a sudden, I was flustered. I had been drinking too fast and those mixed drinks back at the apartment were catching up with me.

So was the realization that I was actually talking to the boy with the '51 Chevy. I began to swoon.

"Um, I'm sorry. I think I need to get some air."

Before I knew it, I was pushing my way through the teeming party, like a fish swimming upstream, gasping both air and water in its disorientation. If only I could find a way out of this pool of people before I drowned in intoxication, theirs and mine.

A heavy hand, almost pawlike in its weight upon my shoulder, tunneled me through the crowd and out the front door. It guided me down the front steps of the old Victorian house whose green shingles shuttered out any testimony of the rollicking party inside. Neil sat me down on one of the lower steps. He sat one step further down so that we were at the same level.

"Thanks," I murmured, somewhat embarrassed, now that the cool air, carrying the faint scent of ocean, sobered me up a bit.

"Hey, no problem." He touched my chin gently so that I would look at him. His lashes were thick with understanding.

"I'm kind of embarrassed. Sorry." As I looked down, his hand dropped from my chin and rested on my bare knee. I wasn't wearing any tights. A thick heat spread up and down my leg. I hoped I wouldn't have to stand up anytime soon because my leg had melted.

"It's okay. Really. Remember, I'm a bartender." *And I'm just a dumb, drunk girl who needs to be babysat.*

His hand moved back to my face to wipe away the mascara sweating underneath my eyes. His thumb was slightly clumsy. This time he held my gaze.

Was he going to kiss me? His lips looked absolutely deviant . . . yet sweet, like those of a naughty little boy. Lips I would never want to wean from my own.

"I should get you home." It wasn't a kiss, but a ride home was second-best.

"That would be great. Are you sure you don't mind?"

"Of course not, doll." He really was straight out of the '50s. Especially with that strong Marlon Brando nose of his.

"My truck's just around the corner."

This was an occasion I could rise to. I stood up. Verónica's tight red dress had shimmied up my thigh. As I tugged it down, I caught him looking. His blazing eyes burned me like the sun. We had to get to that fire-engine-red truck of his, fast.

We didn't talk much during the drive to my apartment. The truck's rumbling comfortably filled the silence. I liked watching Neil drive, the way he gave the road his full attention. He looked at ease behind the wheel, but I noticed the subtle tensing of his muscles as he took a turn. It was as if his brawn, and not the truck's engine, was powering the machine. I wondered what it would be like to be the object of such intense concentration, to be on the receiving end of those tight flexes of sinew. As if in reflex to my thoughts, I felt the muscles between my legs contract, drawing up and in as if receiving a member of his flesh. I crossed my legs, pressing my inner thighs closely together, to sustain the pleasure.

Neil sensed my shifting on the cushioned lap of the truck's front seat. He reached toward my knee, but it was the stereo he was aiming for. He switched it on and turned the volume low. A hillbilly singer was squawking like a chicken.

"How long are you in town for?" He was still staring straight ahead, even though we were stopped at a red light. Had I imagined his interest in the onslaught of eye contact back at the party? He sat slightly slouched behind the wheel with the impassive expression of a chauffeur.

"I'm here for the summer. I start a teaching job in the fall, back in Tucson."

Relief cracked his stony countenance.

"I thought you were just visiting for the weekend or something." His eyes lighted back on me, searing my previous doubt.

"So you're a teacher?" His interest seemed genuine. For some reason, it made me blush.

A car honked behind us. The light had turned green. Once again the road commanded his gaze.

"Well, not yet. I just got my teaching degree. I only graduated a month ago."

He nodded, and his hand tapped the seamless leather between us as if in reverie. I had the urge to slide across the smooth upholstery and tuck myself under his strong arm, have it drape over me securely like a seat belt.

"You know, I've always thought about being a teacher."

"*Really?*" I tried not to sound incredulous, but I just couldn't picture Neil, with all his tattoos and grease, reading a storybook to a classroom of third-graders.

"Yeah, *really*. I like reading and talking about books." He smirked at me in that sexy, cocky way of his. I had to admit, there were some things he could teach me. . . .

"What's your favorite book?" I challenged. His eyes narrowed as he took a sharp turn, and if I hadn't been wearing a seat belt, I would have been thrown into his lap.

"Lolita." He said it slowly with pointed deliberation, his smirk drawing out into a mischievous grin. He reached over and yanked a tendril of my loose hair.

"Ouch!" It didn't hurt, but rather inflamed me with an icy heat. There were a few things this Lolita could teach those cruel lips of his.

"Isn't this your street?" I hated him for changing the subject after he had charged me up so, but he was right. We were on my block.

"Yup. I'm up there on the right where that guy in the white T-shirt is standing."

The truck slowed and quieted to a low but anxious drone. My body was buzzing like a bee. He turned to me, the sexual tension between us thick like honey.

"Thanks for the ride." My seat belt was off, and I was free to go. Instead, I leaned toward him like a sapling braving the wind.

"Anytime, Lola." His arms reached for me like the thick branches of a tree. He uprooted me and pulled me toward that solid trunk of his body.

"Lolita," he exhaled into the single breath of air that was the only thing that separated us. I sucked in the tiny particles of moisture that lingered to the dissipating word. His hands on my shoulders squeezed past flesh, past nerve, to bare bone. I trembled for the inevitable crush of his lips to completely break me.

Instead, I screamed.

Something had smacked, hard, against the passenger-side window. I turned to a flurry of white that repeatedly crashed against the resilient glass like a moth mistaking a lightbulb for the moon. Before I could stop him, Neil had leapt out of the truck, yelling, *Whatthefuck?* I recognized the psychopath in the white T-shirt slamming his body against my door.

It was Nacho.

5

Neil had Nacho by the back of his neck and slammed him facedown onto the hood. Although both men were pretty built, Neil was twice Nacho's size. Nacho flailed foolishly under Neil's steady grip. Neil's face was masked with the stoic reserve he used while driving, even as dark blood spilled onto the shiny, candy-apple red hood of his truck. Nacho was able to lift up his bloody face up just enough to spit my name at the windshield, which protected me from the blows and blood and turned me into a spectator of this masculine sport.

"Lola, you *puta*!" His eyes were rimmed red, and the boy was obviously high. I hoped Neil didn't understand the Spanish slur, but he definitely seemed to understand the tone that defiled the name he so cherished. For that, he pummeled Nacho's shaved head back into the hood. Neil's eyes flashed at me with the recognition of what this fight was about. A split second later, Nacho threw Neil back.

They momentarily faced each other in the pool of headlights and then violently embraced like wrestlers, twisting and contorting for leverage. Neil broke them apart with a tight uppercut to Nacho's chin. In a last-ditch effort not to fall, Nacho grabbed on to Neil's shirt. The thin cotton of the black tee, threadbare in some areas, tore easily. Neil's barrel chest widened the gash of material. I gasped. The sight of his broad chest heaving aggressively was the manliest thing I had ever seen. Although his chest wasn't as tattooed as Nacho's, Neil was well armored with a tough-looking tat of a dagger over his heart. It had the jagged line of a jailor's, or sailor's, amateur hand. And it was large. A throbbing quickened between my thighs at the sight of its sharp tip, and I imagined it coolly pressed against my own breast. I sunk back into the seat and parted my legs. My hand snuck into a cauldron of heat. I gingerly stroked my damp panties, and watched Neil grab Nacho's shirt and rip it down the middle in divine retribution. They bared their chests and then literally smacked together, hard flesh against hard flesh. My hand dove underneath my panties. My finger jabbed at my clit but kept slipping from all the wetness that had pooled between my swollen folds. The boys were on the ground now: first Nacho on top, then Neil with his long body all stretched out and tense, grinding Nacho into the pavement. I had to lift up to see them now, and I propelled my finger inside my pussy to prop myself up. As Neil delivered tight punches with his massive right arm to Nacho's tiring body, I pumped my finger wildly inside and then added another for girth. With each blow that landed, I hit my G-spot with violent pleasure.

Suddenly, the blows ceased. Nacho was moaning on the ground, bloody from his nose to his chest. He rolled to his side in fetal position. Neil had eased off him and rose from the asphalt. Reluctantly, I slid my hand out from between my legs as Neil staggered back to the truck. I tugged down my dress—hoping the moisture between my legs wouldn't seep down past the hem and give me away—just as he heaved himself into the driver's seat.

"Shit, Neil, are you okay?!?" Blood stained his cheek like rouge, and he was breathing hard. He gripped onto the steering wheel, his knuckles dripping with blood.

"I think I cracked a rib." I could tell it hurt him to breathe, and he inhaled sharply with a grimace. There was a musty towel on the floor of the truck, and I hastily picked it up. Sidling up next to him, I gently blotted his knuckles until they were bone white. The blood wasn't his.

"I'm so sorry about *him*." I gestured to the body writhing in pain on the ground. I didn't know what else to say, and Neil just sat there brooding silently. Tentatively, I moved closer to wipe his cheek. There was a slight gash on his pronounced cheekbone, like a nick in sculpted marble. He winced from my breath on the broken skin.

"Sorry, does that hurt?"

"No, it's fine." His voice was brusque, but he let me press the towel against his cheek to stop the bleeding. I placed my other hand soothingly on his shoulder and began to gently knead the tight weaving of muscles. His breathing calmed and his eyes closed, doubling the thickness of his luscious lashes.

By instinct, I glanced down to his lap. The sight of a sizable bulge widened my eyes. I caught my breath and cautiously slid my hand between the open flaps of his ripped shirt. He breathed in deeply as my hand traveled down the dense plane of his torso. Solid muscle and bone indistinguishable, my fingers car-avanned over ridges of both.

"This won't hurt a bit," I promised low into his ear and ripped open the rest of his shirt down to his belt buckle. He moaned, his eyes still closed, and I continued to play nurse.

"I just need to check one thing here. Make sure everything's in working order." He bit his lip and nodded bravely, my pa-tient with the rocking hard-on. The dark hairs of his navel were slightly matted with perspiration, and the muscles of his lower abdomen contracted with pleasure under my touch. I was a hair away from examining that protruding organ of his when Nacho again ruined the moment.

"Shit, here he comes again!" Sure enough Nacho had risen from the dead and was stumbling toward us like a zombie. Neil was quick to react. He turned on the engine and threw the truck into reverse. Like a wounded beast, Nacho charged the truck, bellowing at the top of his lungs. As Neil made a sharp U-turn, almost sideswiping Nacho, I caught wind of Nacho's threats: *My boys are going to fuck you up, man! You better watch your back!*

As we safely sped away in the red Chevy, the white of Nacho's mangled shirt became the size of a louse egg in the rearview mirror. I wasn't sure where we were going, but Neil was sure driving there like a bat out of hell. But I didn't care if we were on the fast track to Nowhere because Neil finally had his strong arm around me and was squeezing me close.

6

"I don't think you should go back to your apartment for a while." Neil had finally pulled over into the abandoned lot of a decrepit, drive-in movie theater. The giant screen was torn and flapping in the wind. It reminded me of Nacho's T-shirt.

We were somewhere just south of San Francisco.

"This place is awesome, Neil. How'd you find it?" A half moon spilled its ghostly light onto silver tufts of grass and patches of gravel. The lot was like a cemetery to a bygone era.

"Let's just say it's my secret hideout. And now that I've shown it to you, you can never leave." His eyes glimmered, his teeth gleamed, and his hair glistened. I felt like I was seeing stars.

"Hey, Neil. I'm really sorry about that guy. I mean, I only hung out with him a couple times, and I thought he would've got the message when I didn't return his phone calls. . . ."

"Shush. I don't care." He took my face between his hands, pressing his broad fingertips into the slender bones of my cheeks and jaw. His lips looked just ripe for kissing. "I'm just glad you didn't go home alone to that creep waiting outside your place."

"Really, thanks for—" His mouth crushed the words back down my throat. His tongue was thick and skillful. So were his hands. They easily slipped up my dress and underneath my panties. He ran his fingers lightly between the swollen lips of my damp mound.

"Have you been like this the whole time?" He had stopped kissing me to withdraw his hand and admire the gleam from my pussy in the moonlight.

I nodded hungrily, eager for his hand to return to its proper resting place. Neil glanced around the deserted lot of the drive-in, which was shrouded from the road by trees. Effortlessly, he lifted me against the dashboard.

"Show me how you do it," he ordered, gesturing to my parted legs. The gruff tone of his command couldn't get me to pull down my panties fast enough. I tossed them around the rearview mirror for luck.

Balanced precariously with my bare ass against the dash, I spread my legs as wide as my dress permitted. Neil peered into my pussy as if it were a well, his eyes dipping thirstily into its depths.

I leaned forward to run my hand through his greased hair and rocked back so he could watch me rub my clit with the pomade's residue. Without taking his eyes off my prize, he stripped off what was left of his shirt and folded his arms behind his head. His arm muscles bulged, straining the ink of his tattoos, making me so hot that I plunged one of my fingers into my pearly pink as the other continued to finger my clit. I was dying for him to touch me—somewhere, anywhere—but he just sat back and watched the show, his dark eyes glinting in amusement. It was infuriating how worked up he was making me. My wetness was spreading down my inner thighs, well within his reach, but his beefy arms just rested lazily behind his head, refusing to take over my hand's licentious labor.

Finally, I couldn't take it anymore and pounced. But he was quicker. He rolled me beneath him, holding me lengthwise onto the seat in his powerful grasp. With his body stretched out on top of me, I experienced the raw weight that Nacho had struggled so futilely against. No one, I was sure, could beat Neil in a fight. Lucky for me, he was working me over with his mouth instead of his fists.

Our kisses were wet and messy and often missed their mark in the frenzy of open passion. In one swift motion, Neil pulled down the tight bodice of my dress and squeezed my full breasts, luminous in the pale light of the night, while his tongue flicked at my hard nipples with a reptilian furor.

"Fucking gorgeous," he murmured into my open mouth as I swallowed his words along with his firm, delicious tongue. My eyes rolled back in pleasure to the torn ceiling of the truck. *This was really happening.*

He peeled off the rest of my dress. His large hands tightly hugged my sides like a second pair of ribs as he stared in wonderment at my naked body. I had never wanted a man to look at me so starkly, to reveal everything to him through my own nudity. His volcanic eyes smoldered as they took in all of me.

"*Fuck*, Neil, I need you to touch me." He pressed the broad heel of his hand against my pussy, but he didn't finger me. Instead, the weight of his unforgiving palm sunk into my clit, pinning me down to the seat of the truck by the core of my body. The more I writhed against his hand, struggling for release, the more he increased the pressure, until shock waves of pleasure coursed up and down my inner thighs.

I counterattacked, aggressive with desire, and cupped the bulge in his jeans with a steadfast grab. Quickly, I unzipped his pants. He wasn't wearing any underwear, and his cock sprung eagerly into my hands.

The hot-rod truck was no phallic substitute for this bad boy.

Neil groaned as I worked his throttle with long strokes. In a joint effort, we shucked off his jeans without throwing off my grip on his massive hard-on. Skillfully, I pulled up on his cock, manipulating the smooth skin over the ridge of his head. His cock was absolutely peachy, both in color and in its soft but firm texture. Neil's clumsy fingers—his pleasure inhibited his motor skills—tried to find my slick opening, but I refused them entry by coyly clamping my thighs shut. I only wanted his cock in there. This, I let him know.

"Do you have a condom?"

"Are you sure?" His eyes were gentle and searching.

"Unless, you don't want to. . . ." Maybe he didn't. That would be a first.

"No, of course, I do," he smiled a bit bashfully. "I've wanted you since I first saw you outside Tito's."

My body tingled hotly with a thousand pinpricks.

"You remembered that?" I whispered in disbelief.

He nodded.

"Yeah, and I wanted to talk to you so badly when I saw you outside the garage, but you ran away before I had the chance."

I felt a wave of heat wash over me, knocking me senseless. Desire clung to us like humidity, and I felt as though I would suffocate if we didn't consummate it.

"Get a condom." My voice was shaky but determined. Neil sprung into action, plunging his arm deep into the glove department. I heard the clanking of tools (a tire iron, perhaps?) as he rummaged around until he found a condom.

I insisted on gloving his cock, eager to run my hands down its length again as I rolled on the snug latex. As soon as I did, Neil grabbed me by the waist and pushed me up hard against the steering wheel so that I faced him.

"I want you this way, so I can watch your expression as I drive into you."

"Fuck me however you want, as long as you fuck me," I panted, locking my arms behind and around the steering wheel. I barely had time to brace myself before his cock hit my bull's-eye dead-on. With the first powerful thrust, I fell into him, but he just propped me back up against the wheel, his arm fully extended between my breasts.

"I need to see you," he repeated sternly and pumped his piston back into me. My throat opened up with a guttural noise that rose from a place deep within me that only Neil's cock could reach. I let go of everything, inside and out, including the steering wheel, and let him bang into me, his full force the only thing holding me up. My spine kept hitting the flat circle of the horn, and short blasts spurted into the still lot.

Neil's hands flew to my hip bones, anchoring my moist center as he eased me down into his gyrating lap. I began to buck wildly now, his cock hitting my G-spot with unnerving precision, and I shuttered in climax. Neil let out a low, long growl, forewarning his own orgasm. I brought my mouth close to his snarling lips and grabbed the back of his neck, my fingers grasping impossibly thick, black hair. My pussy tensed around his stiff cock in an almost painful moment of anticipation. Then, as Neil roared with his own release, the flash flood of my own orgasm broke through.

"Jesus, now I really can't let you go back to your apartment." I was sitting on Neil's lap, naked, staring at the moon that was definitely half-full and not half-empty. His burly arms were wrapped around me and provided all the warmth and comfort I needed in the silent world in front of us.

"Why not?" I shifted on his lap, making his sleepy cock twitch in arousal. Neil bit playfully into the tendons of my neck and then rubbed his nose against the fading teeth marks.

"Because, Lolita." I smiled at his lascivious nickname for me. "You are just as amazing as I had fantasized."

"Excuse me?" I spun around in his lap so I was facing him, or more like straddling him. His hand immediately stroked the tended patch of curls between my legs and found the slippery moisture that still clung between my nether lips. He petted me gently, soothing away any soreness from our rough ride.

"You were my mystery girl. I even told a couple of my friends about you, this beautiful woman who appeared mysteriously before my bar and then again at my garage."

"And you fantasized about me?" My voice grew husky.

"Yeah," he admitted sheepishly, suddenly shy of the subject. I reached between his legs and tenderly stroked his balls. I liked the tight little sac, almost silky to the touch.

"Was this a part of your fantasy?"

"Um, not exactly, but I think I'm going to work it in next time." He rested his head back and his lips parted slightly. I leaned forward to take his pillowy lower lip between my own and sucked on it softly as I cupped the twin orbs of his scrotum, juggling them in my palm like a sack of marbles.

"So you thought about me when you jerked off?" *My favorite form of flattery.*

He bit that delectable lower lip of his as he nodded.

"And what were you doing to me, perve?" His chest heaved, the tattooed dagger expanding to swordlike dimensions. I ran my finger down the hard crevice between his pecs.

"Well, first, I pushed you up against the hood of my truck when I discovered you in front of my garage. Then, I pulled down the gate so that only the really curious who heard your moans would peep through the strip of grating." His cock started to stir in his lap, and I urged it into lengthening with the gentle pull of my hand.

"Then, I yanked down your jeans and slid your bare ass up the hood, spreading your legs so that your pussy opened up like a goddamn flower."

"Then what?" My voice was barely audible, constricted by desire.

"Next, I ran my tongue from your clit to your tight little asshole and back to your clit again and just teased that sweet pussy of yours until it was sopping." This was no fantasy; my pussy was so wet that not even that thick tongue of his could soak it up. I began to smear myself against his hard thigh, letting him know how much I liked this dirty talk.

"Then what?"

"And then, after you begged for it good 'n plenty, I flipped you over and took you from behind. Not slow, but hard and fast. Rammed into you again and again so that my balls slapped up against you."

"Would you stick a finger in my ass?" I whimpered, running his shaft between my slippery labia so that the head repeatedly knocked my clit.

His eyes lighted on me. Suddenly, he grabbed me and tossed me over his shoulder. My bare ass to the moon, Neil carried me out of the truck as I shrieked and kicked in delight.

"You up for more?" Neil asked as he laid me on the hood.

"Only if you are, sailor." But I knew he was. The blind head of his hard-on was pushing into my belly button.

"Scoot your ass further up." His wish was my command. The smooth curve of metal cushioned my lower back. When he eased my legs over his shoulders, I couldn't think of a better position in which to get head.

Neil leaned down to take a long sip from my pussy, and his eyes peeked over the horizon of my curly mound. They looked at me so clearly. We watched each other as his tongue seductively circled my clit. As he began to suck on my little bud of flesh, tugging it rhythmically with the vacuum created between his sunken cheeks, I dropped my head back on the hood. Like grains of salt diluted in a vast, black sea, there were only a handful of stars in the sky. My vision began to blur as the tugging increased between my legs, and the stars above shimmered as if under water. Neil used his thumbs to further part my labia, and he massaged each fleshy lip as he opened me up most intimately. He examined me thoroughly with his inquisitive eyes and fingers and tongue. There was no part of my pussy he didn't carefully attend.

"Your clit is the most amazing color when you're excited. Did you know that? It's violet and pink, almost iridescent." He continued to squeeze my nether lips while peeling them apart to further expose my clit. I felt my whole pussy pulse like the organ of a heart. When his lips again met my beating center, only a few hard strokes of his tongue were needed to call in the tide. I opened my eyes wide to the night sky as I came, the orgasm long and rippling.

7

"You, *what?*" Verónica almost dropped the tray of salt and pepper shakers that she was carrying from table to table.

"Shhh, Verónica. The whole diner doesn't have to know!"

"Well, shit, Lola. If I had known you were going to run off and do that last night with *him*, I would've worried about you disappearing from the party like that."

Apparently, she hadn't been worried about where I went—until now, that is—busy having her own tryst with Icy Eyes on the foggy rooftop of the Victorian. I had actually expected my cousin to give me a high five when I told her about finally getting laid or even make some dumb joke about bringing a whole new meaning to the expression *lay on the horn.*

"Fuck, what is it, Verónica? Does he have an STD or something? We used a condom."

An old lady, her gray hair dyed a ghastly purple hue, looked up from her poached eggs in disgust.

"Here, have some salt." Verónica quickly offered in a lame effort to placate the elderly patron. She quickly pushed me on to the next table, out of scolding range.

"Verónica, what is it?" I whispered as she switched an empty pepper shaker with a full one.

"Remember, I'm *Betty* in front of the customers." Veronica pushed her finger into the pinstriped front of her polyester uniform where *Betty* was stitched in gold thread. All of us waitresses at the diner had fake names designated by our uniforms. I was Ruby.

"Okay, *Betty*, what is the problem?" She whisked the tray to the next table. I could tell she was annoyed with me, but I really didn't know why. I had five minutes before my shift started to find out.

"The *problem* is, he's my friend Teresa's boyfriend."

"What?!? He didn't tell me he had a girlfriend." I suddenly felt flimsy, like a cardboard cutout of myself. One greasy breath from a customer could have knocked me over.

"Well, I mean, they just broke up a couple weeks ago. But they're always doing that and getting back together." I remembered Teresa suddenly, like you remember a bad dream; in broad daylight, her hourglass waist and platinum hair haunted me. I had met her my first night at Tito's. Suddenly, I didn't feel so glamorous with my dyed black tresses.

I changed the subject as if this bit of information had no effect on me, though really I felt like crying. I could be such a girl sometimes.

"Nacho's a real psycho. What was he doing outside our apartment, anyway?"

"He probably just really likes you and wanted to see you. See why you haven't called him back," she responded coolly. Why was she being such a *puta*? I tried to tell myself it was because it was the end of her shift and she had hardly slept the night before having to get to work early. I was lucky to have the afternoon shift on Saturdays.

"Here." She practically shoved the tray in my hands. "Do you mind finishing this? I want to get out of here. I'm practically keeling over." Even when she was hungover and exhausted, my cousin's hair was perfectly tucked into her paper cap and her face smooth and flawless, like the powdered surface of a compact.

"Yeah, no problem." The tray wobbled in my unsteady hand, the heavy glass shakers clinking like crystal. I watched Verónica promenade to the back of the diner, blithely dropping her final checks on tables. One check fluttered to the floor, rotating in the air like paper windmill. I rushed over to pick it up.

Now I really didn't know what to think about what had happened between Neil and me. Not that I was naïve enough to believe everything he had said or even that he would come pick me up after work, which he had offered to do because he didn't want me to walk home alone in case Nacho was still lurking about. But when he dropped me off last night, dawn already freshening the air and gilding each blade of grass, I felt something awaken between our mouths as they yawned together in a lasting kiss.

I glanced down at his number, written on the inside of my wrist. *Won't wash off as easily,* he had said. I smiled and reexperienced the glow I had awakened with late this morning. The sun was actually shining in San Francisco today, almost too brightly, and I had felt positively radiant, inside and out, as I walked to work. Yet maybe Neil's heart did indeed belong to someone else. Maybe my fantasy of him had colored the world gold when in fact it belonged to a more complicated palate. One of the busboys, carrying a heavy dishpan, stopped in front of me.

"Table four is ready to order." He looked a bit like Nacho, with his shaved head and baggy pants. More like the boys from Tucson who picked me up in their lowriders and rapped along to their blaring car stereos. Not boys who looked like Elvis and listened to old country music and liked Nabokov.

"Thanks, Edmundo. Tell them I'll be right over."

What did Neil see in me, anyway? I was nothing like that girl Teresa, who was so hiply dressed and confidently coiffed. I didn't have time, however, to contemplate my insecurities. The hostess was seating a six-top in my section. San Francisco was waking up at two in the afternoon, hungover and blinking like a nest of baby birds. If I didn't feed them soon, those beakless mouths would begin their incessant clamor.

The hours passed by fast at first, served rapid-fire on plate after plate of omelets and hash browns. Later, as the sky began to darken, and the last of the brunch customers straggled out around dinnertime, the minutes trickled by slowly. Doubt began to drip like a leaky faucet until I had a pail full of uncertainty. *Neil wasn't going to come by. Who was I kidding?* Still, I fingered the tiny crucifix trapped sacrilegiously in my cleavage and prayed that he would show.

He didn't. I punched out at nine on the dot with my jacket in hand. I bummed a cigarette off Edmundo even though I didn't smoke and waited until I was around the corner from the diner to light up. A breeze extinguished my efforts. The fog had started to roll in and brought with it the chilly sea air.

"Those things'll kill you." My heart leapt like a puppy recognizing the voice of its master. Neil leaned against the front of his truck, his arms crossed in a manner that conveyed that he had been standing there a while, watching me struggle with the wind. He was dressed all in black—black jeans and a leather motorcycle jacket—looking hotter than hell.

"Um, yeah, I don't really smoke. It was just a long day, that's all." Relief washed me clean, and I sparkled.

"Cute dress." He stepped away from the parked pickup and traced the A-line down to its hem. The itchy polyester tickled my skin.

"I guess I'm a bit late. Sorry." He leaned down to kiss me full on the mouth. Taken by surprise, I barely kissed him back, and his moist lips pressed flatly against mine like a postage stamp to an envelope.

"Don't worry about it. I usually rush out of there the minute my shift ends." I was still holding the unlit cigarette, and he removed it from my hand and tossed it to the sidewalk.

"C'mon, let's get a drink." His fingers handcuffed my wrist, and I followed him to the truck, a willing prisoner.

"I thought you were driving me home."

He cocked a heavy eyebrow.

"Did you want to go home?"

"Well, if we're going out, I'd like to change out of this embarrassing uniform."

He started the engine. It grumbled like a crotchety, old man.

"No way, I want you in that little fifties getup. Until, that is, I take it off you ... *Ruby*." He touched my embroidered breast, and I puffed up to fill his hand. His palm rested there for a moment and then deftly slid across my chest to touch the vee of bare skin that dropped down my neck.

This time, I really kissed him back. I felt his thigh vibrate next to mine from the revved engine, and I held onto that hardy muscle as the slighter muscle of my tongue worked itself into his mouth. I was already getting slippery between my legs and swore I could smell the sex from last night seeped into the pickup's musty upholstery.

I pulled away first, remembering Verónica's words, and decided to play it coy. His lips still hung in the air for more, but I patted his thigh in consolation.

"Where are we getting drinks?" Realizing that our little make-out session was over for now, he shifted in reverse.

"It's a surprise," he stationed his free arm around my shoulders, "but I don't think you've ever seen anything like it."

8

Neil was right: nothing could have prepared me for La Estrella. The unassuming bar was not unlike Tito's in its anonymous façade and seedy interior. Everything about the bar was peeling, from the paint on the outside to the cracked linoleum squares of the dance floor on the inside. Middle-aged Latino men danced cheek to cheek with women whose makeup was applied thick and shiny like lacquer. I wondered if the couples would be able to peel their faces apart when the song ended.

It wasn't until Neil handed me a Tecate that I realized what was queer about the place. I was the only female—biological, that is—in the whole establishment. The ladies dancing and flirting in Spanish with men, many who resembled my father in their blue-collar wear and creased faces, were all in drag. These drag queens often towered above the men, wearing heels even higher than Verónica would dare and in sizes that must have been special ordered. Their voluminous hair—wigs, I suspected—added even more extraordinary heights. The one closest to me donned Tammy Faye eyes. I was impressed.

"C'mon, I want to introduce you to Ana." I followed Neil down a dimly lit corridor, which some couples found more private than the dance floor. They hung on each other like teenagers who, having no other place to go, resort to bus shelters and public stairways for their liaisons. I tried not to stare, but nobody noticed Neil and me anyway.

Neil knocked on a door with a star on it. It looked like it was cut out of aluminum foil. An effete voice inside granted us permission to enter. The room was like an incubator, all lit up with hot bulbs that framed mirror after mirror of two facing rows of vanities. The dressing room smelled distinctly of baby powder. Amidst open compacts of face paint and dresses adorned with ostentatious ruffles and sequins, sat a mermaid. Clad in a sea-green satin gown that tapered tightly at the calves before flaring out again like a fish tail sat the most stunning trick on nature. Her blond hair was long and hung in ringlets down to her breasts, which looked real to me—not the hair, that is.

"Neil, *mi hijo*!" She rose like Venus from a sea foaming with chiffon and taffeta. Neil kissed her politely on the cheek, which was accentuated by a liberal amount of bronzer. She peered over his shoulder curiously to where I was sinking into a drapery of feather boas.

"What's that you're hiding behind your back, darling boy?"

I stepped shyly into the glamorous glare.

"Ana, this is Lola." She gave me the once-over. Her fake lashes extended nearly to her powdered brow.

"Well, well, Neil. I guess us ladies here can't really compete." I smiled timidly, unsure if this was a compliment.

"Don't worry, doll. We never stood a chance with Neil. He prefers his chicks with*out* dicks." Her laugh was high and hyperbolic. Neil grinned and gave me a reassuring squeeze around the waist. I felt tiny in the presence of the two of them.

"Children, I must leave you. I've got a Selena song to perform. *Again.*" She swept a green boa over her shoulder. It undulated like a sea creature.

"Be good, *mi amor.*" She planted another one on Neil and then patted my cheek. I wasn't sure if it was a look of warning, or of approval, that Ana gave me under her violet-colored contacts. But it was a look exchanged between two women, the kind too subtle for men to detect.

After Ana's dramatic exit, I took to exploring her curious lair. My hands trailed over various palates of eye shadow and rouge, which dusted my fingertips with a rainbow of color. Deciding on a garish shade of turquoise, I used my pinkie to swipe my lids. Neil watched me in the mirror, transfixed.

"Never seen a girl put on makeup before?"

"Does Ana count?" I turned around and laughed. He was sitting on the cluttered surface of one of the vanities, looking even manlier surrounded by all those feminine accoutrements.

"How'd you find this place, Neil?" I felt strangely at ease in this little room, heated and humming with all the bright bulbs.

"An ex took me here once."

"Teresa?" I blurted out. Immediately, I regretted saying her name.

"Um, yes." His expression looked almost piqued.

"I met her with Verónica." I stumbled over the words, feeling as if I had to explain myself, although I really wanted him to do the explaining. "Verónica told me you two recently dated."

I waited for him to say something, but he just nodded. It was an awkward moment spotlit by the myriad lightbulbs, which the mirrors only served to reflect into infinity.

"I mean, you guys aren't still dating, are you?" I had to know for sure.

"Lola, come here." Reluctantly, I moved into the open triangle of space between his gaping legs. He snatched me by the waist and pulled me in close. His hand ran up and down my spine as if it were a trusty banister he was afraid to let go.

"I haven't been able to stop thinking about you since last night. I didn't even recognize myself in the mirror when I got home from dropping you off this morning."

"Really?" His hand cupped my cheek, and I fell into its caress with a pleasant sensation of vertigo. When I opened my eyes they rested on a blond wig sitting on a dummy head just behind Neil, and I realized he hadn't answered my question about Teresa.

"So are you and Teresa still dating?"

Neil looked sternly into my eyes and answered with a resounding *no*.

"I'm glad of it, too. That relationship was bad for me." Yet, he didn't go into much desired detail.

"But *you*, Lolita." He was making me feeling radiant again and my pelvis tilted toward him as if it were a giant ear, to better hear his flattering words. "You are so sweet and smart, not to mention sexy as hell. I can't stop myself from being drawn to you. I didn't think I could feel this way about someone again. . . ." His words faded into a kiss that started out soft and soulful but soon exploded open with passion, which tangled deep in our mouths and lodged in our throats, making it difficult to breathe.

My hands flew all over him, almost hitting him with their urgency to knead every surface of his hard body at once. He plunged down my dress and came up with two soft mounds of flesh. He began to lick my nipples, which peeked over the pink edges of my bra like rosy sunrises. I began pulling on him, on the fleshy lobes of his ears, on the slick ends of his hair. The desire simultaneously to devour him and be devoured by him tugged me down to my knees. I had every intention of returning the favor he had done for me on the hood of his truck.

As I unzipped his black jeans, he released an anticipatory

moan that filled me with a seductive feeling of power. I freed his cock, which wasn't too difficult, considering that, again, he wasn't wearing any underwear. I began my exquisite torture on his cock, very carefully nibbling on the flushed tip. Neil let out a sharply exhaled, *Easy*, but I knew he liked it rough, the way I did, in the hands of someone I trusted to bring me pleasure, albeit via a little pain. The head was so tender and pink that I soon gave way to licking it like frosting off the top of a cupcake.

"Take all of me in your mouth," he growled. I looked up at him, still only rolling my tongue slowly around the smooth, salty skin of the head to tease him. He moaned again and grabbed my hair threateningly. I picked up speed but still only focused my lubricating action on the tip. My eyes dared him to do something about it. He tried. As he attempted to thrust himself deeper inside, I anticipated his lunge and pulled back without losing my suction on the delicious tip.

"You little coquette," he cursed. This time, when he furiously thrust forward, I took him all the way in, sheathing him completely in my mouth. My hand flew to the base of his penis to stabilize my carnivorous assault on the shaft.

"God, I could come right now," he groaned. Proud of my prowess, I began to leak between my legs. I wanted him both to pierce me down there while simultaneously filling my mouth with his pointed flesh. I resolved this by pulling aside my cotton panties and sticking a few fingers easily inside my hot pocket.

"That's right, baby, touch yourself while you suck me." But I couldn't finger myself *and* give his cock the attention it deserved. I abandoned my dripping folds to use the pussy juices to rub his balls. This pushed Neil over the edge, and he almost toppled off the vanity on which he was so precariously perched.

"Oh, Lola, I'm going to come. Do you want me to come in your mouth?" Just as I was about to answer, my mouth thick with him, there was a loud knocking on the door. *Why did this always happen to me?*

"Are you two decent?" The telltale lilt of a female impersonator made Neil jump back and smash against the mirror. Fortunately, my reflex hadn't been to clamp down, and his throbbing hard-on slid out without incident. Quickly, he tucked it up into his pants where it refused to succumb to gravity.

I got to my feet just as Ana entered, and she caught me straightening my dress.

"What have you two been doing in my dressing room?" She eyed Neil's boner unabashedly and then winked at me. "Dipping into my makeup, I see?"

"Oh, I'm sorry." But she was smiling at the both of us, thoroughly entertained up to her severely arched eyebrows.

"Shoo, *moscas.* I've got a costume change, and I don't want you knowing my secrets." She waved her hand, putting on airs with her acrylic nails, for us to scatter.

"C'mon, Lola." Neil clasped my wrist, and we dashed out of the dressing room. I glanced back over my shoulder to say good-bye to Ana, but she had already turned from us to remove her wig. Underneath, her cropped hair was dark and straight like mine. I quickly looked away, knowing exactly how she felt as she studied her reflection in the mirror.

"I'm going to punish you for that." We were back in the truck, and Neil was burning rubber back to his apartment. The Chevy flashed through the night: a red, tremulous ball of fire setting off car alarms in its wake.

"For what?" I asked coyly, rubbing Neil's package through his jeans. His erection still hadn't declined. He swerved around a black sedan pulling out of a parking space. A near miss.

"For teasing my dick back there with that gorgeous mouth of yours." He quickly nipped at my neck as he gunned through a red light.

"Promise?"

"Promise, what?"

"To punish me."

His black eyes darted at me, and I caught them in a quiver. I could only imagine what would transpire when we reached his apartment.

I spotted the garage up ahead, and my excitement increased tenfold. The sight of its shuttered, metal gate made my nipples excruciatingly taut. Only a week ago, I had stood before this very garage, my nostrils widening with the manly whiff of automotive grease, and caught sight of this tall, handsome stranger so powerfully gripping a heavy-headed wrench.

Neil parked at the curb.

"No time to open the garage," he explained and hastily shut off the engine. Seizing my hand like a tool he would wield to his liking, Neil yanked me out of the truck. We dashed across the cold sidewalk to a drab-looking door next to the garage.

"C'mon, Lolita, hurry." He rushed me through the front door. A dark staircase led up to his apartment, the stairs covered in a velvety material that padded my feet as I dashed up them. I tried not to trip as Neil prodded me from behind.

"Good, my roommate's not home." As soon as he shut the door to his tiny apartment, Neil pushed me up against it. The room was almost pitch black, but he didn't bother switching on the lights. He crushed me against the closed door with the full weight of his body, and we kissed fervently in the dark. There was something so deliciously fresh about his mouth. The inside of his lower lip tasted slippery and cool, and I ran my tongue cleanly across his uneven teeth.

Without breaking our lip lock, Neil lifted me off the ground. I was light in his arms as he effortlessly carried me across the room. With my legs wrapped tightly around his waist, my dress rode up to my hips and the damp crotch of my panties pressed against his stomach. He was struggling now with the doorknob to his bedroom, and I tasted the salty bristles of his neck in long, thick strokes of my tongue.

The door sprung open to a small, messy room that pulsated with the neon sign of a neighboring bodega. In the bawdy glow, I noticed the walls were lined with mismatching bookshelves, most shoddily built and sulking under the burden of the written word. Neil banged me up against one of the shelves, his arms protectively cradling my back from the hard spines of the books.

"I have to have you right now. No time to strip," he announced and vehemently unzipped his pants while precariously balancing me on the ledge of the bookshelf. He pushed down his jeans just enough so that his stirring manhood safely cleared the jagged teeth of the zipper. His piece crested like the mast of a ship atop a giant swell, and I grabbed it instinctively. It was hot and swollen in my hands, the head scarlet with fever. Inexplicably, Neil wrenched my hand off his stiff shaft and twisted my arm over my head.

"C'mon, put it in me, *coño.*" I felt belligerent in the agony of my desire. My panties were wedged in my engorged crevice, and, with my free hand, I swiftly yanked the damp, twisted fabric to one side. My slit gaped open and hungry for his inflamed tip only inches away. But he ripped my hand away from my panties. They snapped back against my cleft with a sting of pleasure. Now both my hands were pinned above my head, my wrists bound easily in his sinewy, one-handed grip.

"First, I need to check your oil." He slipped a finger inside me, then another, with increased vigor. I struggled lustfully against his hand's steadfast restraint as he calmly pulled out his fingers to examine like a dipstick.

"Just as I thought, all lubed up to fuck." He sucked on his fingers, his dark eyes tunneling into me. This absolutely pushed me over the edge.

"I can't stand this anymore, Neil," I implored mournfully.

"Hold on." Without warning, he released his hold on my wrists. I lurched forward into his chest and heard a distinctive crinkle where my right palm landed. I fished into his shirt pocket and sure enough, I discovered a wrapped condom.

"How convenient," I cooed and ripped the packaging open with my teeth. His brandishing erection was temperamental and, with some difficulty, I sheathed it while keeping my perch on the bookcase. This time, it was Neil who tugged my panties aside, and I barely had a moment to grab onto the ledge before his cock plunged up into me. I felt absolutely cleaved by the thick girth of his member, and the tender walls of my passage burned as he penetrated me. I bit my lip, but a cry whistled through my clenched teeth.

"You can take it, girl. You've taken me before." He thrust back up. This time, I was more malleable, stretched out to encompass his solid rod as it prodded my pleasure center.

"*Más duro,*" I moaned, squeezing my thighs tighter around his waist to draw him further in. Realizing he didn't speak the language of my passion, I translated, "*Harder,* Neil."

A fury darkened his face, and he wildly grabbed the hair at the nape of my neck and rammed himself up my cunt. He pounded me hard against the bookcase, and paperbacks cascaded from the shelves. I splayed open my legs so his seismic thrusts could lodge even deeper into my fault line.

"I like that, baby, when you spread your legs like that." He assisted by pressing on my inner thighs to ease them even farther apart. This time he had the exact leverage to fuck right into my G-spot. He hit it hard.

"Oh, God, Neil. I can't take it. I really can't," I crooned with the lust of a girl who could definitely take it; and Neil continued to give it to me.

"What about if I put a finger in that tight, little asshole of yours. Do you think you could take that?"

I nodded naughtily, eager to be doubly penetrated by this man. He inserted his middle finger in my mouth, and I sucked it as I would his precious manhood. His pumping action between my legs slowed as he slipped the lubricated finger under the ass of my panties, which had somehow managed to stay on me, although askew. Neil's finger ran up my downy crack until he found the puckered entrance. With the broad tip of his finger, he pressed around the rim of my asshole in a massaging motion that relaxed me. Slowly, he pushed beyond the resistant flesh. Suddenly, I felt so filled up with his thickness, from both in front and behind, that I became light-headed.

"Oh, Neil." My murmurs were faint but euphoric, and Neil was now invigorated. He began pounding back into me, simultaneously groaning my name and cursing.

"I like how I can feel my cock in you, banging up against my finger in your ass." I felt that junction too, roiling my insides. My dizziness suddenly gave way to a marked sensation: somewhere between those two points of his flesh burrowed deep in me, an orgasm was squeezing out. Neil recognized the transformation on my face and sped up so he could arrive there with me.

He brought his face to mine. Our teeth gnashed with feral kisses, tearing madly into each other's lips. Then, from that riotous place between my legs, something shot out of me, wet and shiny like a bullet. It must have pierced him because he immediately collapsed onto me with a mortal moan. Not quite slain, Neil shuddered to life with a final, heroic spasm of his orgasm.

We slid down the bookshelf, sweat clinging to our clothes, our naked parts still joined. Carefully, Neil pulled out of me— the condom wilted as his passion subsided—and lolled back onto the floor. I draped over him listlessly and lay my head onto his heaving chest. With my eyes closed, I listened to his heart and lungs calm.

"Where did you come from?" he whispered into the softly pulsing chamber of his room. His languid fingers absently, but instinctively, combed my tangled hair.

"Funny, I was just wondering the same thing . . . about you, that is." Neil curled his biceps around me and gingerly kissed the top of my head. Strange, how after such ferocious sex, Neil held me in the most tranquil, almost chaste, embrace. The boy sure came in like a lion and left like a lamb.

I would have fallen asleep right then and there, lying on top of Neil in my sweaty, waitress uniform, if he hadn't picked me up and carried me to his bed, only a few feet away. With sensual affection, Neil removed every stitch of my clothing as I lay there, drowsy and limp. His clean, dry sheets wicked the sweat right off my skin as he slid my naked body under the covers. The mattress was so soft that my dreams were already sinking into it. As soon as I felt Neil's own disrobed body cradling mine, I fell fast asleep.

9

Waking up in Neil's arms, I suddenly panicked: how would I ever be able to leave San Francisco in just two months time when I couldn't even conceive of leaving my lover's bed this morning? I studied Neil in his sleep. I would never have thought him to be such a peaceful sleeper. Not one snore had escaped his heady lips all night. The sun, peeping through the broken blinds, stretched across his worn comforter, casting golden rectangles onto it. I ran my hand over the warmed, pilled surface that gently rose and fell over his body. Neil shifted in his sleep and pulled me closer to him underneath the covers. Our naked bodies were cool and smooth like sea glass worn edgeless by the ocean.

Neil's eyes opened without warning. Immediately, he studied my contemplative face.

"You look so pretty in the morning." His words were sleepy but earnest. He kissed me in the intimate cloud of morning breath.

"What are you thinking about, Lolita?" Neil could read me like a book.

"Oh, nothing." I shook my head with a forced smile. I was so happy in his arms, in his bed, in this tiny, messy bedroom of his, that I didn't want him to think anything was wrong.

"Something's wrong. What is it?" He was fully awake now. Gentle but alert.

I picked at a dried cum stain on his comforter and tried to choose my words carefully.

"It's that I've, well, just met you—and I *really* like you—but I'm only here a couple more months. . . ." I didn't know how else to say it without confessing how deep my feelings for him already ran.

"I know, I've been thinking about that, too." Neil rubbed my lower back rhythmically. It made me want to curl up in a chamber of his heart and go back to sleep and never have to think about this feeling ever ending.

"How far away is Tucson?" Neil smoothed the hair away from my forehead.

"Like eight hundred miles."

He sighed. "I guess I'll have to never let you leave this room. Hold you captive and bring you food three times a day. You'll have enough to read." He rolled on top of me and began kissing my neck emphatically. Being Neil's love and literary slave definitely held an appeal.

"What about my illustrious teaching career?"

He had moved down to kissing my breasts. My nipples perked like gumdrops between his nimble lips.

"Hmmm, I can be an apt pupil." I felt his flesh stiffening against my thigh as he sucked my pliable nipples into extended points.

I pulled him back up to me.

"Seriously, Neil." I loved the innocent look his long, black lashes gave him, even when he had a raging hard-on. "I think I'm falling for you."

"Ah, Lola," he sighed happily. "You are the most amazing creature. I don't ever want to let you go." His tattooed arms reiterated this by clinching my narrow body. I keenly rubbed his taut, colorful muscles. His plush lips sunk warmly into mine, giving me the courage to continue.

"I think I may be falling in love with you, Neil."

He looked at me as if I were a complete stranger. The shift in his expression was almost imperceptible and he continued to hold me just as he had before, but I perceived his distance all the same.

"I'm not sure if this is love," he struggled to pick his words cautiously, "but maybe just the feeling of not being lonely."

I felt as if I had been slapped in the face, and he immediately saw how his remarks had stung. He hurried to rationalize.

"I mean, sometimes, it's easy to confuse lust and love." His body felt heavy to me, and I felt trapped under the weight of his long limbs. To hide my hurt and embarrassment, I turned my face away from his searching eyes.

"Lola," he plied softly into my ear. He touched my chin and tried to turn my face back to his. A sense of pride deployed to my chin and resisted his advance.

"*Babe*." His warm breath on my neck threatened to melt my resistance. "I don't want you to think I don't feel strongly for you, because I do. And I am so crazy attracted to you." He squeezed me for emphasis. "But we've really just only met, and I don't want to jump the gun here."

I contemplated the expression *jump the gun* in the long silence that trailed his words. It did indeed feel like a race to me now; all of a sudden that was clear. I had two month's time to win this boy's heart, and I would sprint to the finish.

With this new resolve, I succumbed to Neil's soothing touch. He was massaging my exposed earlobe between his index finger and thumb in hopes of getting back into my good graces. His lips brushed my turned cheek. I let him try his submissive kisses all over the inert side of my face. Finally, I turned and gave him back my lips in full.

10

"Morning, *prima*."

Verónica pretended not to hear me as she noisily stacked plates into the kitchen cabinet. In an unprecedented crack at housework, Verónica had washed the buildup of dishes in the sink. They sat in dripping but clean piles on the counter. I went over to the fridge and pulled out a block of cheese and a carton of eggs.

"Verónica, have you seen my tortillas?" She had to answer me now. I was a foot away from her.

"Try the drawer," she suggested coldly. Sure enough, the tortillas were in the vegetable drawer underneath a wilted head of lettuce.

I cooked my breakfast burrito in silence. From time to time, Verónica glanced at me warily from the sink where she was vigorously scouring a pot. We hadn't seen or spoken to each other since our conversation at the diner on Saturday. Now it was Monday, and I had woken up to Verónica's clanging in the kitchen. As I groggily pulled myself out of bed, still exhausted from my weekend's tryst with Neil, I dreaded facing her. I had to remind myself that I hadn't done anything wrong: Teresa wasn't my friend, or Neil's girlfriend for that matter.

It wasn't until I voraciously tore into my burrito—sex with Neil had created a hunger in me that seemed bottomless—that Verónica broke her silence.

"So how was the rest of your weekend?" Salsa and melted cheese dripped down my fingers, which I greedily sucked clean before answering.

"Good. I hung out with Neil." I imagined she had that one figured out on her own when I didn't come home Saturday night.

Verónica had scrubbed everything in sight and begrudgingly joined me at the kitchen table. She stripped off the yellow dish-washing gloves and checked her manicure.

"Look, Verónica, I really like Neil. *Please* be excited for me." That was all I had to say. Verónica looked up from her nails. Her almond-shaped eyes widened with compassion, although they were rimmed with concern.

"I know, Lola. Neil's a great guy. I just don't want to see you get hurt, that's all. That one can be a real heartbreaker." She sighed with such emotion that, for a fleeting moment, I wondered if maybe she was speaking from personal experience.

"Don't worry. I can take care of myself, I promise." Then, I added gratuitously, "Everything is going so great. We are just so hot for each other. Neil seems really into me." I wondered if I was saying these things to convince my cousin or myself.

"Oh, that's wonderful, Lola!" It worked for Verónica. She clapped her hands and, in her excitement, got up from the table to hug me around the neck. "I'm sorry for being such a *puta*. Seriously, I want to hear everything. Don't you dare leave out a single, juicy detail!"

She pulled up her chair right next to me and began to pick off my plate, gobbling up all I had to say about my romantic, and *caliente*, weekend with Neil.

I told her everything. Everything, except for the part about gushing my true feelings to Neil, only to feel shot down in return. It was just a minor glitch, anyway, I told myself; we had made love just as passionately soon after and spent the rest of the day lounging around his apartment. He had even brought me breakfast in bed, running out to the café down the street to get me an egg sandwich and coffee. Nothing tasted so good as breakfast in a bed still steaming from our lovemaking.

"And he brought you *flowers*?" Verónica acted shocked. I had been, too, when Neil pulled the bouquet out from behind his back after special delivering breakfast. Even though the carnations were dyed blue and the daisies were missing half their petals, I had positively swooned at the gesture.

"So what did he say when he dropped you off?" I had gotten to the end of my fairy tale.

"Um, what do you mean?" We hadn't prolonged our kiss good-bye. Neil was late for his Sunday afternoon shift at Tito's.

"I mean, when are you two going to hang out again?"

"Oh, he said he'd call me soon." Verónica's eyebrow twitched but resisted raising warily. I ignored it as best I could and relished the last savory bite of my breakfast.

"I better go call my dad back." According to the post-its scattered around the apartment, my dad had been calling all weekend.

I dumped my plate in the sink, where it rattled around the empty basin, and grabbed the cordless from the counter. Verónica was busy watering the cactus from her drinking glass and didn't look up as I left the kitchen.

Phone in hand, I shut the door to my bedroom for privacy. I felt as if I were holding a loaded gun; my finger twitched, triggerhappy. Before giving myself time to think it through, I dialed— but not my father's number, although I really intended to do so. Neil's machine picked up. His voice sounded even lower on the recording. I tried to sound blasé as I left a message. *Hey, Neil.*

It's Lola. Just calling to say hi. Gimme a call sometime. I wondered if the tape could pick up the vibrations of an eagerly beating heart. After I hung up, I said a quick prayer that he would call me back soon.

I was back outside Tito's holding a staring contest with the bar's heavy door. The wooden number 9 still hadn't been fixed and continued to moonlight as a 6. It was a gloomy Sunday, and I cursed the seasonless summer of San Francisco. My knees were bare, remote from the hem of my short skirt, and knocked together like ice cubes in a highball glass.

Do I knock on the door? I shook my head at myself. *This isn't his apartment. It's a bar.* Yet, I felt like an unexpected visitor. If he wanted to see me, he would have called me back, right? That was Verónica's opinion on the matter. A week had gone by without a word from Neil. For the first few days I was hopeful, fueled by still-palpable memories of naked skin and damp kisses. At work, I fluttered about the diner, cheerfully waiting on customers and not even noticing my sore feet. Then, when the weekend came, I grew despondent and my feet, heavy. I was sure he would have called me by Friday to make plans for the weekend. Friday night came like a wrecking ball and knocked me flat on my back. All I could do was watch TV in bed, refusing Verónica's invitation to go out. The next day I did more of the same. Eventually, my thoughts became as blank as my stare at the television screen.

Sunday morning, though, I woke up brightly with a delusional hope. All week I had desperately wanted to see Neil, and now I could! All I had to do was stop by Tito's while he was bartending his Sunday afternoon shift. . . . My logic was transparent, and I knew it in the hole in my heart that was enlarging each minute I loitered outside the bar. I felt ashamed for lying to Verónica about where I was going. Who goes grocery shopping in a miniskirt and red pumps, anyway? I still had a chance to turn around; he would never know that I came.

I decided to leave a second too late. The bar door swung open and out walked Teresa. She didn't see me at first. She was looking back through the closing door to call, *Bye baby*, to someone inside. I wanted to push past her to see whom she was talking to: a friend, a drunk at the bar, her *abuela*—anyone, I hoped, but Neil. But I couldn't move. I was frozen to the sidewalk, whose cement glittered like ice crystals. She saw me, and the corners of her smile sharpened with recognition.

"You're in my way." I should've slapped her then. Slapped her for looking at me the way she did, with that haughty, knowing look. Slapped her hard for giving me the once-over, making me feel like a schoolgirl dressed up slutty for her first dance. I should have slapped her for talking to me like an ant she was about to step on.

Yet, surprising both of us, I moved out of her way. I stepped aside to let her pass because if I had said one word to her, either pleasantry or obscenity, I would have burst into tears. Strange, how I had not cried all week, but was now suddenly struck with a visceral pain in my gut, like an appendicitis, that made me want to cry out. I had come face-to-face with the realization of why Neil hadn't called, and I cowered before her cold, pristine beauty. What miraculously kept me from crying as Teresa smugly walked away, I could not say. The minute, however, she rounded the corner, tears cracked my stony resolve like a weeping statue of the Holy Virgin. I turned and walked slowly back to the apartment, barely able to see through my veil of tears.

11

I opened my eyes to a familiar pattern of tattoos. My sheets had fortuitously slipped from the shoulders of my sleeping lover, and I smiled at the sight of his smooth, inked skin. The moment of awakening was soft and downy like the underbelly of a bird, and I closed my eyes to linger in my dreams. I was dreaming of the desert. We were driving in Neil's truck right at that afternoon time when the desert is swathed with a pink, vulval glow. I caressed Neil's arm, strong like a boxer's. He was tan, almost as dark as . . . Nacho. My eyes opened again to the familiar pattern of tattoos. Gang and memorial tattoos. Nacho rolled over in his sleep. A garbage truck stopped outside my apartment and men yelled and the metal lids of trash cans clattered onto the pavement. Nacho's eyelids raised half-staff, struggled to flutter all the way up, but ultimately flagged. As he dozed, his tattooed women kept watch.

It was hard to tell time in our basement apartment. Although I had a window, it was at eye level with the feet of passersby. I could basically distinguish day from night, but not the gradations in between. August in San Francisco wasn't like

August in Tucson, where the heat woke you up soon after dawn. Music murmured through the wall, so I knew it couldn't be too early, since Verónica was already up. Slowly, I inched away from Nacho, and his hand limply fell from my breast. I tiptoed over him, trying not to rustle the sheets as I stepped.

Verónica's door was open, and my cousin danced in front of her mirror like a teenager. She wore an oversized Morrissey T-shirt that just covered her underpants.

"Knock, knock." Verónica whirled around, lip-synching as she beckoned me in. I flopped down on her leopard-print bedspread and flipped through a *telenovelas* magazine. Verónica was trying to learn how to speak better Spanish by watching the *novelas*. Sometimes I watched them with her and translated.

The song ended, and Verónica blew kisses to her audience of adoring fans. Her staginess reminded me of Ana, the drag queen at La Estrella. I was suddenly sorry I never got to see Ana perform.

"Hey, Verónica. Have you ever considered performing at La Estrella? You'd fit right in with the personalities there, especially with that big hair of yours." Verónica picked up a leopard-print pillow from her bed and hit me with it.

"*Puta!*" She threw another pillow at me, this one red satin and stitched with the words *Buenas Noches*. I tucked it under my cheek.

"When did you go there, anyway?"

"With Neil, remember?" I smiled to myself with the memory of that mischievous blow job.

"How could I forget?" Verónica rolled her eyes. She wouldn't let me pine long about Neil after I found out that he and Teresa were back together. Soon after, Teresa and Verónica got into a fight of their own—about what, I was never clear—and they were no longer friends. Verónica wanted me to erase Neil from my mind like she had her friendship with Teresa.

"So how's lover boy in there?" She cocked her head toward our shared wall.

"Getting his beauty sleep." Verónica laughed. Behind his back, we referred to Nacho as Sleeping Beauty. Whenever he spent the night, he always slept for hours after I got up.

"Sounds like he was a real Don Juan last night." Again, she gestured toward the thin wall.

"Sorry." I buried my face into her satin pillow. It smelled like stale candy.

Verónica was only teasing because she couldn't be happier that I was with Nacho. After things had ended so abruptly with Neil, she facilitated Nacho's return. Starting with his apology for acting like a psycho. For weeks, I spurned his advances: his roses, his offers to take me out to fancy dinners, his love letters written in Spanish, begging for another chance. Then, one night, when Verónica was out on a date, and I sat at the rickety kitchen table with a book and the cactus to keep me company, I realized that I was lonely. Neil just wasn't coming back. I called Nacho and told him I wanted to go for a ride.

"What are you *viejitas* gossiping about now?" Nacho stood in the doorway, rubbing his eyes. He hadn't bothered putting on a shirt, and I could tell Verónica was checking out his tattooed pecs.

"Look who's talking," Verónica bantered. "You're as ancient as a vampire, the way you sleep away the day."

"Well, at least I don't look like no Medusa." Nacho joined me on the bed and began nibbling my neck.

"Never heard that one before," Verónica shot back. Nacho ignored her to kiss every inch of my exposed shoulder until I started giggling. Who would have guessed that Nacho would be so affectionate? This was one of the many things that had pleasantly surprised me during the month that we had been dating. He also made damn good *enchiladas*.

"Eww, get a room." But Verónica left us in hers to take a

shower. She snapped her towel at Nacho's ass on the way out of her bedroom.

"How is *mi princesa* this morning?" Nacho tenderly rubbed my nose with his.

"A little hungover, but otherwise good." I touched his cheeks. They were always so smoothly shaven.

"You were quite the hot *mamacita* last night." I blushed. Admittedly, our sex last night had been hot. It had also been drunk; I had nearly blacked out when I was on top of him climaxing. Nacho liked me on top. He also liked going down on me, which he was attempting to do right there in Verónica's room with the door wide open!

"Nacho, not here!" He had my boy shorts pulled down to my knees.

"She takes long showers. She's got all that hair, you know." He was right, and his tongue was *so right*. It gently prodded my pea-sized flesh until it fully emerged from its shell. Nacho took a moment to steal Verónica's satin pillow from beneath my head and expertly placed it beneath the small of my back. With my pelvis tilted skyward, Nacho plunged his face back into my carnal mound. His nose nudged my clit, rubbing it and sniffing at the same time, as his tongue moved to penetrate me. I murmured something about *what if Verónica walks in,* but I succumbed as his tongue unfurled an inch or two inside me.

My eyes were closed, and I concentrated on coming. I was back on the hood of Neil's truck with my legs splayed open to the stars. As Nacho's tongue thrust into me, it was Neil's mouth I remembered. The way he sucked and sucked on my clit, his head buried deep between my thighs as if for eternity. His tongue had been relentless, and I had to surrender to its thick, punitive strokes. The lapping between my labia sped up and my desire neared the boiling point. Hot, wet bubbles coursed through my bloodstream and converged between my legs. I thought of Neil driving into me with the full force of his passion against the dash, his tattooed muscles bulging as he gripped the handholds of my body, and began to moan. A hand covered my mouth to stifle the telltale sound. At last, the quick flourishes of tongue between my legs released the pressure from behind my clit into rapid-fire spasms that riddled my body with pleasure.

As I lay panting, we heard the shower turn off.

"Better get you decent." Nacho pulled up my boy shorts but not before gently kissing my satiated sex.

"Thanks for breakfast." I swatted him with the satin pillow for his crudeness.

"Now *I'm* hungry." My stomach rumbled almost simultaneously with my words.

"Me, too," Verónica piped in. She was standing in the doorway with her hair dripping. It was deceptively straight when wet.

"Let's go to the diner." Both Verónica and I moaned at Nacho's suggestion. Why would we want to go there on our day off?

"C'mon, *chicas.* I'm craving some chili fries."

"*Chili fries for breakfast?*" Verónica and I spoke in unison, and then laughed our twin laugh. Nacho looked at us sideways and shook his head.

"Well, I'm going. If you two come, I'll buy you breakfast." Verónica and I looked at each other and shrugged. Why not? I'm not sure if Nacho realized that we got employee discounts.

"You driving?" Verónica loved Nacho's car: a black '64 Chevy Impala. Admittedly, it was a pretty hot car, and Nacho kept it in pristine condition. On our first, well real, date, he made me wipe off my shoes before I stepped inside.

"Course. C'mon and get dressed, Verónica. You look like a drowned rat." That being said, Nacho and I scampered out of the room.

* * *

Louis, our fastidious manager, hung around our table as we ate breakfast. I think he had a crush on Nacho.

"Lola, when are you leaving, again?"

"Two weeks, Louis. The twenty-third. You had me mark it down on the calendar yesterday, *remember?*" Verónica and I exchanged a look across the table; Louis definitely liked Nacho. His mustache was extra twitchy.

"Oh, Lola. Don't go!" Verónica whined pathetically, and then prodded, "Nacho, tell Lola not to go." Nacho glanced up from his food and scooted closer to me in the booth.

"Yeah, Lola, don't go," Nacho responded impassively, rather absorbed in the gory mess of his chili fries. I saw through his *machismo*, though. In bed the night before he had implored me to stay in San Francisco and be his girlfriend.

"C'mon, you guys. You know I can't. My teaching job starts in three weeks." To be perfectly honest, I was looking forward to getting back to Tucson. I never thought I'd miss the desert heat, but after this foggy, ambivalent summer in San Francisco, I was ready to go home.

"Who am I going to live with when you move out?" Verónica lamented and poked her eggs with a fork until the yolk broke.

"I'm sure you'll find someone, Verónica. You still have a couple weeks." I looked across the diner to where Edmundo, the busboy, had dropped a plate while clearing a table. It broke into large pieces when it hit the ground. The windows up front were large and faced the street. I was probably looking for him at that moment without knowing it; I had been, whether I liked to admit it or not, every day for weeks. At every loud rumble of an engine, my head would snap around hoping to see his truck. I never did. But now, when I least expected it, when I was thinking about how I couldn't wait to leave San Francisco, Neil appeared. My heart leapt and smashed against the pane as he passed by the window. To my astonishment, Neil placed his hand on the smudged glass of the door and pushed. Neil stood inside the diner, as Edmundo foraged around the floor for shards near his feet, looking around as if for someone.

When Neil saw me, I knew it was me he was looking for. I'm not sure what expression crossed my face, one of exhilaration or of horror, but Verónica saw it and curiously turned to the subject of my astonishment. She quickly whipped back around and looked apprehensively at Nacho who, fortunately, was lost in chili fries oblivion. At that same instant, Neil saw Nacho at my side. A grim line set his jaw, with just a flinch of movement in his cheek. He turned around and abruptly left the diner. My eyes desperately tracked the back of his head, black and polished like a bowling ball, as it diminished from sight.

Grossly unaware of what had transpired, Nacho looked up from his fries and, still chewing, smiled at me. His mouth looked bloody like a vampire's from the carnage of his chili fries. He tried to kiss me, but I pushed him away. He shrugged it off.

"Nacho, gimme some of those." Verónica swooped in with her manicured talons to swipe a fry. She glanced at me with a look that signaled, *Don't worry*. As she began to bicker with Nacho, distracting him for my benefit, I sat back, stunned by Neil's appearance at the diner. *Why had he come?*

he. He wiped his hands on a bandanna draped from his back pocket. It did no good; they were still black as sin when he grabbed my shoulders.

"Lola." He looked me dead in the eyes with emotion that can't be faked. It would have been so easy to kiss him, but my pride prevented it.

"What were you doing at my work?" I repeated again. He sighed and dropped his hands from my shoulders.

"Come sit down." He motioned me over to the open tailgate of the pickup. He helped me up, and I secretly relished his strong grasp on my arm.

We sat side by side with our legs dangling off the edge of the truck bed.

"I heard you were leaving soon," he explained, looking down at his grease-stained hands, "and I had to see you before you went."

"Why?" I needed to hear more than that. I had never seen Neil nervous before, and I nimbly lay my hand on his thigh to encourage him to continue.

"To say I'm sorry." Daring to look me in the face, he saw my eyes well up with emotion. Quickly, he took my hand, squeezing it, and spurted out what I needed to hear. "Lola, I am so sorry. I got scared. My feelings for you were so strong, so fast, that I freaked. I knew you were only going to be here for a couple months . . . I just didn't know what to do. So I bailed." He looked at me mournfully.

"What about Teresa?" I still hadn't completely given in, even though my heart was leaping from my chest, suicidal. He looked down at his hand, which had smudged mine with grease. He tried to rub my hand clean, but it only made it worse.

"I just can't explain that," he shook his head. "I guess it was just safer in some weird, messed-up way. But that's completely over now, I swear." I believed him.

"What about you and that guy?" He meant Nacho.

12

I had to find out. Curiosity ate me up for three days until there was nothing left but the naked carcass of my need to see Neil. This time, I went straight to the lion's mouth: the garage.

It was nighttime, but the hour was young and restless. I walked briskly down the damp streets with the confidence of a girl with nothing to lose. In a week and a half, I'd be leaving this grey city behind. As I approached his block, the fluorescent lights of the garage reached me like a beacon. There were no shadows in which I could slink, and the echoing heels of my tall, black boots announced my arrival.

Neil emerged from the gaping, crocodile jaws of the Chevy. His navy blue coveralls were covered in grease. I cocked my hip to one side and stood before him, dressed slimly in black. The look he gave me was so peculiar that I felt my poise momentarily falter.

"What are you doing here?" His smirk softened his words, and I knew that he was glad to see me.

"What were you doing at my work?" I haughtily echoed his question with one of my own. I took a step forward, and so did

"I guess it was safer," I smiled impishly. Without warning, Neil clutched the back of my neck. We kissed in such a moment of synchronicity that it was nothing less than magical. Our tongues wrapped around each other with reckless abandonment. Neil cradled my face with his blackened hands to steady our kisses, but they were too frantic. He fell back as I ripped open the snaps of his coveralls and shoved his broad chest with all my might. Straddling him, I pulled off my sweater and shook my long hair free.

"Wait a minute," he raised his head. "Let me close the gate." He lifted me off him, as if I weighed nothing more than a sack of potatoes, and gently tossed me to the side. He hopped off the back of the truck.

As Neil scrolled down the gate with a racket, I slid off the tailgate and walked around the truck. I could tell it had recently been waxed, and I ran my hand across its gleaming surface.

"What are you doing?" Neil was behind me, breathing down my neck.

"Just admiring your body work." I turned to him coyly. He was closing in on me, his broad chest bursting from his unbuttoned coveralls. He looked so wicked with his slick, black hair and dagger tattoo that it filled me with an erotic fright. I ducked around him.

Neil didn't chase me as I explored the brightly lit dungeon of the garage, examining the carts of tools and greasy auto parts. Instead, he stalked me with his rapacious eyes. I picked up a heavy wrench lying atop a red cart.

"You going to do something with that?" Neil leaned against his truck, arms folded patiently with the confidence that he would soon have me.

"Um, no. I just like holding it." I did like its weight. "Perhaps for protection."

Neil approached me fast.

"You may need it." He swiftly took the wrench from my

hands and dropped it to the concrete floor with a clatter. Grabbing me roughly by the wrists, he pulled me toward the truck.

"Get up there," he ordered. As I clambered up, he smacked my ass. I yelped.

"Shut up or I'll do it again."

"Promise?" I provoked. He jumped up after me and pushed me against the back window of the truck's cab. He yanked the hair away from my neck and sunk his teeth into the back of my neck. I gasped at each thrilling bite, and his hands reached around to fondle my breasts.

"Take off your pants," he whispered close in my ear, and then added, "and your panties." Still facing the back window of the truck, I shimmied out of my tight jeans and pulled down my panties. Neil, behind me with his erection pushing hard up against me, helped me strip off my shirt. Only my bra remained.

"Spread your legs." I felt cool air compress against my bare skin right before he smacked my ass. I cried out, but this only kept the spankings coming in short, stinging slaps. I started to crumble to my knees as if the moisture between my legs was sucking me down. Neil grabbed me by the roots of my hair to pull me back up.

"You like it when I slap your ass, don't you?" I could only nod hungrily for more.

"I'm going to tie you up, then," he threatened and turned me around so that I faced him. My lips were wet and limp in desire, but he cruelly ignored them. He unfastened my bra and sucked on each nipple before scooping me up, naked, in his arms.

Carefully, Neil laid me on the cold, metal bed of the truck. I gasped as my skin came in contact with the frigid surface. Neil wasn't altogether merciless and quickly grabbed a blanket, the kind that movers use to pad furniture, and placed it underneath me. His hands were rough but warmed my skin as he dug his fingers all over me. I knew that tomorrow his fingerprints would bloom into tiny, purple bruises. He raised my arms over my head and ran his tongue along the shaved part of my armpits.

"Let me get some rope. Don't move." He leapt off the truck and quickly returned with some bungee cords. He saw that my hand had snuck between my legs, three fingers shoved guiltily inside.

"I told you not to move," he growled and jerked my fingers out. You could *hear* how wet I was as my fingers exited with a succulent pop. Neil delivered a quick slap to my pussy. I gasped, shocked, but never so turned on.

Lusty and livid, I pushed my crotch up toward him for more discipline. He slapped it again, this time slightly cupping my mound in its entirety as his hand made contact. I moaned, and moaned again as he repeatedly struck my pleasure center.

Then, adoringly, he tied me up. The bungee cords hooked fortuitously into handles on the inner walls of the truck bed. Neil was careful to tie the silky cords tightly around my wrists. I spread my legs apart for him, but he didn't bind them. A cool draft licked my exposed quim. I opened myself up even more to him, hoping that the sight of my split slit would lure him in.

"Neil, I need you inside of me." I begged for it.

"Not yet, my Lolita. First I'm going to play with you some more until I know you really want it." My eyes widened as he pulled down the rest of his coveralls. His erection bolted straight out from his body. The boy seemed to have a distaste for underwear; he never wore any. Neil got on his knees to straddle me but still towered above like a Grecian statue, naked and hard as marble. He began to stroke his cock, smirking down at me as he did.

It was a magnificent view, Neil kneeling over me, powerful arms and chest and thighs all tensed around the pumping action of his hand. The bulbous head of his cock was turning violet under the fast jerks of his hands. Wildly, I tried to wrestle from my wrist restraints but they held fast. My singular desire was to stuff that pointed flesh in me.

"*Neil!*" His paw dove into my honey pot and emerged dripping. A moan whistled through his teeth and his self-inflicted strokes momentarily ceased.

"I don't ever think I've touched a pussy that wet before." Amazed, he plunged his fingers back inside. I tried to hold them there with all my might, squeezing my innermost muscles around him, but I was too slippery. Neil swore as his fingers slid out. He rubbed my excessive juices on my stomach, which was streaked with grease.

"I like how dirty you make me," I murmured. He smiled nefariously and continued to knead my stomach, my thighs, with his stained hands.

"That's cause you like it dirty, *puta.*" I burst out laughing. Apparently, Neil spoke a little Spanish. Neil grinned too, and then asked in all seriousness, "How do you want it?"

"Like *una perra*," I quipped. It took a second for Neil to understand, but when he did, he was quick to unhook the bungee cords. I slipped them off my wrists and rubbed my raw skin.

"I've got a condom in my purse." It was still sitting on the tailgate. I had borrowed the purse from Verónica, and she tucked a couple of condoms inside as I walked out the door. *For good luck,* she had said with a wink, giving me her blessing.

Neil struggled with the clasp, and I crawled over to him to open the purse myself. Digging through a mishmash of coins and matchboxes, I pulled out an intact condom wrapper.

"Let me." Half perched on his lap, I sheathed his cock, sad to see its ruddy head disappear but eager to put his safe sex inside me.

"Let's go to my master bedroom." Neil was built like a playground and he seesawed me into his arms and carried me the few feet back to the blanket. This time he laid me down on my stomach.

"I know you've always wanted to do it back here," he whispered into my ear. Already I felt his driving member part my tender flesh. I tilted my pelvis up and he eased into my tight center. He was so thick inside me that it nearly pushed tears out of my eyes. I felt so filled up with him.

"Oh, Lola. I want you. I want you so badly." He pumped inside me slowly at first, loosening me up.

"You have me, Neil." To assure him, I clamped my inner walls around his cock, guiding him in deeper with my undulating grip.

"Oh God, I could come right now." His balls were slapping against me with the rhythm of madmen. Then, all of a sudden, he slipped out.

"I have to have you on top of me, so I can watch you come." With his might, he rolled me on top. We both became unexpectedly quiet and watchful as I slowly lowered myself onto him. I rode him at a deliberate pace, dipping forward to kiss him. My hair fell all around us, and we kissed with our eyes wide open in wonderment. My clit discovered the subtle but hard ridge of his pubis, and I began to smear against it.

"That's right, baby. Use me to make yourself feel good." I hardly needed encouragement. I rubbed myself hard against his public bone until it hot-wired my clit.

"I'm almost there," I crooned.

The hairs trailing down from his belly button had become damp and matted from my efforts. Neil had stayed inside me the whole time and now began to accelerate his thrusts to catch up with me. I watched as his lower lip dropped and top lip curled, his mouth gashed open in pleasure. He was already lost in it, his eyes closed, but every pore open to me. I tossed my head back to join him in the abyss.

Our eyes were closed as we climaxed. There was no telling

of time or place, our bodies suspended in ecstasy. In this blackout, I felt something pop like fireworks against a night sky. Suddenly, I was awake—eyes open to the brightly lit garage— with a heat exploding inside of me like a stick of dynamite. I was deaf to my own wild noises. Neil below me was practically epileptic, his face contorted but godly. I was still pulsating from my own orgasm when he came, so hard that I felt the exact moment of his release in a spasm that shocked his body. A strange sound escaped his lips. It took me a moment to decipher: the sound of my name perverted by his rapture.

Neil curled around me and wouldn't let me go. We lay in the back of the pickup, secluded lovers basking in the faux sun of the fluorescent lights. Only the occasional sound of a car whizzing by reminded us of the world outside the garage.

"When are you leaving?" Neil nuzzled his face into the back of my neck, and his lips tickled my skin as he spoke.

"In a week and a half." He pulled my knees closer to my chest so that he could better spoon me.

"I didn't realize you were going so soon." He sounded genuinely regretful.

"Well, you snooze, you lose." I still felt a little jilted.

"Don't be like that, Lola." He squeezed me hard. I tried to wriggle free, but it was impossible.

"Can I come visit you?" I stopped my squirming.

"Are you serious?" I spun around in his arms like an eggbeater until I faced him.

"Totally serious. I can't just let you be gone forever now that I've got you back in my arms again." I looked at him incredulously, but I was too exhausted from our lovemaking to doubt him further. He pulled my hands flat against his heart.

"Really, Lola. I mean it." He kissed my nose until I smiled, fully convinced.

"Can I get a ride to the airport?"

"You bet, doll." Neil's kisses trickled down my sternum.

"On second thought, can I drive the pickup to the airport?" Neil looked up, skeptical. He rested his chin between my breasts.

"You think you can handle it?"

"I think I can handle it." I patted his bicep and reminded him, "I've handled *your* hot rod plenty." I reached down and made a grab for it.

"Well, I suppose I could let you take me for a ride."

With that said, I rolled on top of him, and clutched his stiffening stick, ready to shift into gear.

In a week and a half, I would be maneuvering the transmission of my other love, the red Chevy, driving to the airport with the windows rolled down—the wind wicking off the San Francisco Bay and through my hair and Neil's hand stealing under my skirt. It would be then that I would realize that Neil had been right about one thing: it hadn't been love between us, but rather pure lust. That shiny, hard diamond that can cut through anything, even the cubic zirconia we call love. But for now, Neil and I had days ahead of us to indulge fully in our lust, which was already rocking the truck bed beneath our bodies in the brightly lit garage.

China Doll

SUNNY

Dedication

To DeborahAnne MacGillivray.
A wonderful author, Web mistress, and friend.

1

Rand felt like a different man. A wild one, untamed, seething with feelings, with needs, with a gut-clenching want . . . for a woman's softness. Something to burrow into, bury himself in, press his face against. It had been so long, he'd almost forgotten what it felt like. The sultry hotness of Medan, Indonesia, was like an invisible hand of heat that wrapped around him, melting away the ice that had encased him for five long years so that he felt the tingling, burning pain of renewed sensation. Now the need, the want, the wild desire churned within, rising, rising, threatening to flood him like a powerful wave.

Men sensed it and stayed away. Women sensed it, too, and flocked to him, drawn by the tantalizing allure of danger. Nor did it hurt that he was a "wealthy Westerner." Perspective was a funny thing. Here, *any* Westerner was considered wealthy compared to the vast indigent population, even in an affluent port city like Medan on the western Indonesian island of Suma-tra. But, sweet though the local women were, he'd never paid for a woman before, and didn't wish to start now; nor for a man, several of which, who, after seeing the lack of feminine success, ventured Rand's way to try their luck. They weren't the only ones who wondered about him. There were Canadians, Australians, New Zealanders, and other Americans in the Hotel Danau Toba's dark disco lounge, some who'd come for leisure, others for business, and others like him, coming or going from Aceh's tsunami relief effort. The white women giggled, whispered, and wondered, but didn't approach him. Nor did he approach them, though for a brief moment he thought of doing so. It was like standing precariously on a cup's rim, watching the writhing bodies sway seductively to the pounding music on the dance floor, vibrant with life, energy, and passion as his control slowly unraveled and thinned, but still held by a tenacious wisp of thread. He was still in control—too bad—balanced on that narrow edge. And he didn't want any of these women or men. He tossed back the rest of his drink, about to rise, when she came in.

She looked like a fine porcelain doll, a China doll. She wore a vibrant red sarong and her long black hair fell in a midnight wash down to her hips. Her almond eyes, glowing black and uncertain, would have given her away had not the white purity of her skin proclaimed her a foreigner as loudly as if she had screamed it. Like moths drawn to a brilliant flame, the Indonesian men approached her. Rand watched them intently. Only two kinds of people came here. Those already with companions or lovers. And those looking for one.

She'd come alone.

2

The pulse, the beat, the *loudness* of the music was what hit Dr. Anna Huang first. Then the darkness, the dimness of light, the swaying bodies rocking to the deep, throbbing beat like supplicants worshipping before the altar of Baal.

Within seconds, she was swarmed like a queen bee spraying pheromone into the air. Two men, three men, four, suddenly surrounded her, their faces handsome, sharp, one androgynously pretty, another dark as burnished teak, the two others a lighter brown like bleached driftwood washed ashore. Hands touched her, reached for her. Anna had wanted a man, had come here looking for one, but, sweet Jesus, this was ridiculous.

They pushed her, pressed her back out the door she'd just entered. Or maybe she'd backed out. The deafening music muffled with the closing of the door, and her voice rang out in the silence. "No! Don't touch me."

Anna heard now what they were saying. Money. Amounts varying from 50,000 rupiah, five U.S. dollars, to 250,000 rupiah, twenty-five dollars, spewing forth like a bidding war from their eager mouths.

Maybe it was being in Indonesia, surrounded by Asian male faces, some frighteningly handsome. Maybe it was the bargaining she heard in their voices, the lust she saw in their eyes, their greedy, grasping, reaching hands, the overpowering mix of musk and cologne. Maybe it was the fact that for the first time in twenty years, she was willing to take a man once more into her body, on this night far away from home, from New York. All of it triggered memories, brought back that face—a chilling, handsome face that had died but refused to stay buried. The face of a striking Asian man whose exotic beauty cloaked a lying, poisonous tongue. *My rich American whore,* he had purred.

Heart pounding, sight nearly blinded, she shoved away the touching hands grasping at her. "No! I said no!" Panic sharpened her voice, but to no avail. Their eagerness did not subdue. Neither did their jostling for her, against her. She looked wildly around for help, but there was no one else in the empty hotel corridor.

A flash of disco lights. A blast of music bursting loud for a second and then fading away as the door opened and closed. Someone else exited the lounge, drawing no one's attention until he spoke—a rapid, smooth pattering in Bahasa, the national Indonesian language. He spat it out with gunshot sharpness, and the men surrounding Anna slithered away, back into the club, shooting resentful glares at the man who had sent them on their way. Escaping waves of loud music beat against her as the doors opened and closed with their leaving. And then it was silent. Just them. Anna and the man who had rescued her.

Tallness—and roughness—were what struck her first. Uncivilized. With sun-bleached sandy hair falling loose and wild down to his shoulders, scraggly-bearded and mustached, he looked like what the pretty Asian men should have chased away, instead of the other way around. An American, she thought, then corrected herself. A Westerner, at least. Here, in the jeweled archipelago of Indonesia, Australians and Aucklanders were more common because they were much closer. But whatever he was, he had come to her aid and Anna was grateful.

"Thank-you," she said.

He stared down at her. Only then did she notice his eyes. They were the only lovely thing about him, an odd, swirling hazel, with flashes of rain-forest green scattered among flecks of brown.

"What . . . what did you say to them?" Anna asked, because he remained silent and she was curious.

"That you were mine." The words and flatness of the deep baritone—he *was* an American—raised her hackles, turning gratitude swiftly into attack.

"I'm not yours!" Anna hissed. "Not yours, or theirs. I'm not a whore. I'm not for sale."

His hazel-green eyes crinkled slightly as he smiled, a hidden movement betrayed by the shifting of his unruly beard as his lips curved beneath the bushy growth. "You're mistaken," he said. "They weren't trying to buy you. They were selling."

Her anger faded away under the unexpected shock of his words. "You mean . . . those men were—"

"Selling themselves."

Anna flushed wildly. Somehow it was even more embarrassing than when she had thought it the other way around.

"But why would they approach me?" she asked, bewildered. "There were other Asian women in there, some of them Chinese like me. They weren't being propositioned."

"They knew you were a Westerner."

"How?" she asked with disbelief. "You, obviously, look like one. I don't." In fact, with her long black hair and sarong, she'd thought she'd blended in with the other natives. Just one of the other tens of thousands of Asian women here.

"Your skin gave you away. No native is that white. They knew you were a Westerner at first glance. And Western women are known to be rich, aggressive, and promiscuous," he said dryly, his beard shifting again as he smiled.

Anna's eyes narrowed then relaxed, when she realized he was deliberately baiting her. Not with the truth, but with what was perceived to be the truth here. "I've been in Indonesia for three weeks now and haven't been bothered like this before."

"You must have been in the company of Indonesian women."

Though it was more of a statement than a question, she nodded.

"They are the best deterrents to unwarranted male attention here."

It was that one word, *unwarranted*, that plucked a string of guilt in Anna. Actually, tonight's attention had not been unwarranted. She had, in fact, sought attention, deliberately dressed for it. She just hadn't expected this much, or this kind.

"A word of advice. If you wish to go back in there, go in the company of another woman. Not alone or you will find yourself stampeded once more." One last look and he was turning away, heading down the corridor, away from the closed doors and the faint pulsing music behind it.

"Wait . . ." Despite the roughness of his appearance, he had been kind. A gentleman. And he was the total opposite in all physical ways from the nightmare of her first and only lover so long ago. "You were . . . you were also in the lounge," Anna made herself say, heat reddening her cheeks.

Rand turned back to her reluctantly. It had been hard enough to make himself leave her the first time. She was a mix of both innocence and worldliness, of wanting and not wanting. He was conflicted enough himself, without having to deal with another's uncertainty. "Yes," he said, "I was also in the lounge."

"Were you also approached?" she asked, and the public hallway suddenly seemed less public, more intimate, with the asking of that question. With only the two of them, a man and a woman, locked in this pocket of carpeted silence.

"By women first," he said, "and then men." Again that slight crinkling about the eyes.

She smiled briefly in return. Then let it fade away. "Did you not want any of them?" she asked in a low, hoarse voice.

"No." Just that one clipped word.

Anna bit her lower lip, heart pounding. "What *do* you want?" she dared asked him.

For a couple of loud heartbeats, she didn't think he would answer her. But finally he did. "I want to touch, taste, and smell a woman," he said slowly. "To sink into her willing softness. And not have to pay her for her pleasure or mine."

Anna swallowed. "I'm a woman." Her voice dropped down to the barest of whispers. "I would not make you pay for your pleasure."

He walked to her. Rough calloused fingertips lifted her chin. But it was a soft touch, a gentle touch. "What about for your pleasure?"

Anna just shook her head, breathing in his clean, masculine scent. Natural, unadorned.

His hazel eyes stared down at her, pierced her. "What do *you* want, little one?"

She couldn't argue with the endearment, not when he stood a head taller than her. What did she want? To emerge from the cocoon where she'd nestled the last two decades of her life. To live again, to risk again. *To not be afraid.*

"I want a man's gentleness . . . and to know what gives him pleasure."

A sharp intake of breath. The withdrawal of his touch. "And if I said I would try to be gentle?"

There was kindness in those odd swirling eyes. *Dear God, please let this be all right. Please let this not be a mistake.* "I would say that it would be enough."

He held out his hand to her. "Then come."

Hesitantly, with a visible tremor, she reached out, took his hand, and felt his larger palm engulf her smaller one.

Willingly captured.

3

Silence beat the air as the hotel elevator swiftly lifted them up. Her hand was so small in his. The top of her head came only to his shoulder. Rand wondered what the hell he was doing.

Gentleness. She wanted gentleness. Rand wasn't completely sure he could give her that. It had been so long and he wanted so much. He closed his eyes. God grant him the strength. "Are you a virgin?"

She started, gave a short laugh. "No . . . but it's been a long time."

She looked so young, and he wondered for a moment if she was a graduate student. There were plenty of them out here. He wondered how long it had been for her, but didn't ask outright. Didn't tell her it had been a long time for him, too. That would only lead to uncomfortable questions for them both. Too intimate. An odd thought, really, when they were about to join their bodies as one.

"Were you raped?"

Ah, the questions this man asked. The impressions he had. "No. Just . . . betrayed."

The elevator dinged as they reached the twelfth floor. The corridor was both familiar and foreign to Anna. And the alienness of it was due entirely to the tall man, the stranger who walked beside her, her hand swallowed in his.

Who am I? What am I doing? What stranger is inhabiting my body? About to give that body away to a rough-looking man whom I just met with kind eyes and a gentle touch.

Too soon, they stopped before a door. Only their harsh breaths moved the air. His, deep. Hers, light and fast. Frightened. Determined.

"You can still change your mind," he said quietly.

She looked up at him, and the ghost of her past floated for a moment before her eyes, overlaying the bearded face, imposing the handsome, laughing face of a deceiver in his place—shining black hair, knowing black eyes. Foolishness, despair, humiliation threatened to swamp Anna again, as it always did. Her fingernails cut crescent grooves deep into her palms and the sharp, stinging pain helped push back that ghostly face. Steely determination firmed within her. She was a different woman now. And he was dead, though he haunted her still because she allowed it. But no more . . . no more. It was time, more than time, to lay the ghost to rest. Finally to face that which she most feared—intimacy with a man. Her greatest failure. Her greatest misjudgment.

She shook her head, chased away the vision with raw will, and saw once again, clearly, the rough face of the man before her, the American.

"No. I want this." And she did. She'd been a perfectionist all her life, used to excelling, to having things be perfect. It took the harsh reality of stunning failure to realize that things didn't always have to be perfect. Sometimes it was enough to just have things not be too bad. People learned, grew, changed. And, dear God, she wanted to change. It was as if time had suspended her, held her forever unchanged at the age of nineteen. Not only emotionally but physically. Twenty-one years had passed. Or rather passed her by. It was her birthday today. She was forty-one years old and her hair was still black, without a touch of white. The lines of time had barely touched her face so that she looked almost half her age. Her head knew it came from genetics—from her mother before her, passed on down to her daughter, Lily, all of them looking far younger than they were. But part of Anna could not help but feel as if time had been held in abeyance when she had bowed out of life, so that she was frozen forever as that foolish young girl of nineteen.

All she'd known since that one great mistake was safety. No more risks. And what was life, but risking?

The hotel key swiped down, a green light blinked, and the door yawned open—an uncertain future.

"Are you sure?" the man asked again, like a devil tempting her to be a coward once more. *Run. Hide. Hide away.*

And she wanted to, so badly that it was almost like a physical pull, and that instinctive desire to flee was what finally sparked Anna's temper, flared hot and firm her determination to see this through—to lay that devilish ghost to rest once and for all. *You're dead. Dead, you bastard. Nothing but ashes now. Leave me alone!*

Squaring her shoulders like a soldier about to enter battle, her gaze firm and unwavering, she said, "Yes. Yes, I'm sure. I want this." *Whatever it might bring.*

"Then come inside and take what you want."

4

Tenderness swept through Rand, pushed down the primal lust for a moment, as she stepped through the door and entered his room like a soldier girding for battle. Extraordinary elegance. Steely determination. A potent, powerful mix. But it was the uncertainty he sensed in her, the vulnerability that touched him most. Courage. There was courage in her, he realized. She was facing what she feared.

A grimace twisted Rand's mouth, shifted his beard as he followed that strand of thought to its logical conclusion—*he* was what she feared. And he didn't want that.

She'd stopped after taking a few bold steps into the room. Tensed as the door snicked shut. Trembled as he tread up behind her, beside her, then past her. This little one required a man's care, his patience and gentleness. He prayed he could give it to her.

Flicking on a soft lamp, he kicked off his shoes and lowered himself onto the side of the bed, feeling like a giant beside her smallness, trying to lessen his bigness, his threat. But the swollen hardness that tented his pants belied his harmless posturing. He opened a drawer, took out a foiled packet, and laid it on the nightstand. A statement. An invitation.

Harmless. Harmless. Gentleness . . . Rand chanted it like a silent mantra. He took a deep breath. "A man is easily pleased. Just being inside a woman, and his strokes will bring him to completion. I will be content just to be within you."

His blunt words brought an uncomfortable flush to her high, delicate cheekbones, stirring pity within him that he was careful to keep out of his face. *Ah, little one.* His blunt words were but the shimmering surface of what they would do before the night was over.

"But if you wish for gentleness," he continued softly, "I think it best, then, if *you* set the pace."

Anna moistened her dry lips. "What . . . what do you mean?"

"I mean what I said—for you to take what you want. Touch me, undress me. Tell me how and where you want me to touch you, if you even do. And when you are ready, put me inside you. Your pace. Your will." He smiled ruefully. "And I will try to bear it for as long as I can. No promises . . . but I will try."

His deep voice—earthy sincerity mixed with dry humor—eased some of the tension stringing her tight. And the novelty of the idea eased Anna even more, relaxed her. Stirred her. *Take what you want. Your pace. Your will.* Putting his strength, his desire—*his body*—under her control.

It was a gift. A generous, thoughtful, unexpected gift. Only a strong man, confident in himself and sensitive to another's need, could have made it. He was . . . surprising, this man.

Anna accepted the gift. Signaled her acceptance by setting her purse on the chair, by slipping off her shoes. By going to him, standing before him, unbuttoning that first button, then the second. By unveiling a lovely masculine chest, surprisingly muscled. A chest sprinkled with a dusting of golden fur a shade darker than his hair.

"Do you want the lights out?" he asked.

She lifted her eyes, looked into those amazing eyes. This close, she could see the flecks of honey-brown in the sea of blue-green aquamarine his eyes had darkened to. This close, she could smell the sweet musk and feel the heat rising from him. This close, she could see the thickness of his gold-tipped lashes. "No. I want to see you." *I want to see your face, memorize it. To know whom I'm touching, whom I'll bring into my body.*

Down her fingers traveled, unbuttoning, until there were no more. Until she had to tug the shirt from him, free it from his pants. Slide it from him to reveal shoulders broad and strong, skin darkened under the hot Asian sun, with no tan lines marring the lovely bronze hue. Just more of that light golden brown hair dusting down his arms, peeking out in a tantalizing bush from beneath his armpits, furrowing down like an arrow to where that most forbidden part of him lay swollen and bold while he sat there quiet in his yielding strength. *How much more a man you are.* And it called to her, challenged her to be woman enough to take him.

She took a deep breath, breathing his hot essence, his natural fragrance, into her, and finding it pleasing. Found with unexpected surprise that undressing him was not an awkward chore but a pleasant task, like unwrapping an exquisite present. She reached for his belt, freed it from its buckle, pushed free the button with shaking hands—eagerness, excitement, fear making her tremble. Heard the rasp of his zipper sliding down. Without comment, he lifted up and Anna pulled down his pants, undressing him like an infant. But he was no child. He was a full-grown man, long, ripe and full, the tip of him springing up, almost out from his boxers, but hidden still, by some kind act of fate.

She kneeled there like the supplicant she was before him, at his feet, her eyes level with that part of him that would enter her. Her mind knew the truth, that he would put that part of him inside her and that it would fit, but her brain refused to accept it. *How could that fit inside me?* Or did the gathered cloth of the boxers make him seem bigger than he was?

She closed her eyes and pulled down the boxers, felt the mattress give as he lifted his hips up once more. Then her eyes opened and she looked with horrified fascination at what bobbed before her, less than a foot away.

He was actually bigger. Not so much long, but wide and thick. Really thick. She was a doctor. She'd seen plenty of penises. But holy mother of Christ, this one was intimidating. It would be hard enough fitting it into her small mouth, much less down there where a size slender tampon felt uncomfortable.

She just froze, froze. Then her brain kicked in. If a seven-pound baby could pass through her channel, this male organ going in would be nothing in comparison. Anna knew that, she really did. She just didn't know if she believed it.

"You're big," she whispered finally, and swept her wide eyes up to meet his.

"Not unusually so," Rand muttered, cheeks flushed, eyes burning bright. The disbelief was plain on her face and he wanted to both laugh and groan. Having her kneeling there like that . . . her mouth so close to where he ached . . .

Sweat dampened his temples. Heat blasted from his body. He was naked while she remained fully clothed in vibrant, flaming red. Red, like her small, full lips, which he forced himself not to look at. Lips so close. So damn close to him that he couldn't help but tremble.

"You're trembling," she said softly, wonderingly, and all he could do was smile. Or rather, grimace.

The lines of strain and restraint were evident on his face. And the novelty of it—such strength held in check. Such want . . . for her, for her touch—moved something inside Anna, pushed away the fear. And beneath the fear was . . . curiosity. This strong man trembled . . . for her?

Her hands lifted to her sarong, but her eyes watched him as she began to unwind it from her body. She watched him watch her, her hands unwrapping, unveiling, slowly revealing in a graceful removing of cloth until skin beckoned, gleamed, was laid bare. The swath of cloth dropped to the floor, her armor gone. His eyes were riveted on her, and his trembling increased, so that he vibrated like a tuning fork, forcibly struck. He trembled . . . because of her body?

Anna looked down at herself for a moment, wondering what he saw to cause his cheeks to flush so, his jaw to tighten in that mixed agony of need and want. She saw only the usual paleness of her skin, the slender slightness of her breasts, the slim curve of her hips, the cotton plainness of her bra and underwear. Nothing alluring, no tantalizing confection of lace or satin to cause *that look* on his face as he gazed at her. He was staring at her breasts, heat almost like a palpable wave washing from his eyes. Those eyes lowered in an almost tactile caress, down her soft belly, her tender thighs, bringing a soft sigh from her, a clenching and unclenching from deep within her—an odd sensation.

She was lovely. Like a goddess from the moon with her thick fall of black hair, her crimson lips, her pale skin. Healthy, whole, her skin so white, alabaster pure, like new-fallen snow. Grace. She was the embodiment of it. Her gestures, her movement, the soft sway of her hips, her speech, her lips, her shybold eyes. He wanted to touch her, to have her touch him. Wanted it so badly that his fingertips tingled and burned with the wanting of it, and he had to dig them deep into the bedcovers to stop from reaching for her. *Dear Goddess, please touch me!*

As if in answer to his prayers, her hand lifted toward him. Then dropped away, so that he almost groaned aloud, closed his eyes for a moment. When he opened them again, it was to see her bra fluttering to the floor like a fallen bird, revealing the brown velvet of her nipples, beaded slightly, but not enough, not nearly enough. Her underwear pushed down slowly and her dark triangular thatch beckoned like a siren's call. *Come find me, discover me. Delve into my secret wet pleasure.*

He swallowed, sucked in a breath, caught the faint aroma of awakening female desire. She was . . . exquisite. Her breasts were small and high, made with tea-cup delicacy, with a tracing of blue veins like living lace beneath the marble whiteness of her skin.

Her hand lifted again to hover before him. "May I . . . touch you?"

Please. Yes. Touch me! But all he did was nod, a sharp brief gesture, not sure of what would spill out of his mouth if he opened it.

Like a blessing, her soft hand fell upon him, and he groaned, a low sound drawn from him against his will. *Dear God, it felt so good.* And then it was gone, lifted away.

"Did I hurt you?" she asked, startled.

"No, it felt good." *So fucking good!* "Don't stop." *Please, please don't stop.* He had to clench his jaw to keep from begging.

He felt her touch upon him again. Had to close his eyes, concentrate on taking a breath in, letting it out, then repeating the cycle as her slender hands touched him, explored him.

He was so hot. Like a living furnace made of flesh and muscle. Of masculine beauty. Hers to appreciate, hers to explore, hers to touch, savor, caress . . . because he allowed it. She reached out and took that gift. That pleasure. And it was pleasure, she found to her surprise, to touch him. To savor the heat and hardness of him. The softness. The rise and fall of his chest, the wispy tickle of his man-fur against her palms. The silky softness of his sun-kissed skin, so much darker, browner, against the whiteness of her hand. She loved the vitality of him, the wildness of his hair, the ruggedness of his beard, the burning of his eyes—like a flame lit from within, so that his eyes churned to sea blue, dark, mysterious, hinting of temper, of power. Of desire. All leashed beneath her will, so that she trembled. Her nipples tightened and tingled, causing her to gasp in surprise. *More,* her body cried, her hands demanded. And so she took more.

A small, delicate hand pushed, urged him where he wanted to go, and he toppled back onto the bed, a giant felled by a soft touch.

"Scoot up," she murmured, crawling onto the bed beside him. A breath, a promise. He did, until his head rested upon the pillow, and his body was laid bare atop the covers, hers to do with as she willed.

And what she willed was to lie beside him and stroke him, caress him, to continue to explore him as if he was the first man ever made. It was heaven. It was hell. And he could do nothing but lie there and tremble, and then cry out as her fingers grazed his nipples.

"Do you like that?" She was shy. She was bold. She was the essence of woman emerging into her power. And she was killing him.

"Yes." The dry rasp barely sounded like him. "Yes, I do."

She looked into his eyes and smiled as she ran her fingers over the small budding tips of his nipples once more, natural in her nakedness, reveling in his.

Then the shyness peeped back, and the black lashes swept down like a demure fan to cover those pleased, shining dark eyes. "Can you . . . touch me as I touch you?" A soft question. "Would you like to?"

"Oh, yes," he breathed and smiled, rolling to his side. She smiled back. But it slipped away when his callused fingertip touched her, feathered over her nipple peaks like coarse, abrading linen.

Her turn to gasp, to have those dark raspberry tips tremble beneath his hands, to peak even tighter, pebble even harder at that bare touch.

The touching, sharing of pleasure, gazes locked, so intense, so intent . . . dear God above, it was one of the most intimate things she had ever experienced . . . with this stranger who did not feel like a stranger, who had laid bare his body for her pleasure. And she had found it so—pleasure. Hers and his, both. This . . . if nothing else followed . . . this alone was worth it all. How much she had missed. Begging the question . . . was there even more?

It was no longer fear, but eagerness that drove her now, that tantalizing promise of more, even when another man had shown her long ago that, no, there was not more. But here, now, with this man, that hope, that allure, sparked, flared, like an ember dying, dying, but not gone, springing back to life. Bursting into a small flame of hope.

Her hands lifted away. So did his, reluctantly, with a last light brush that passed a tremor through her body. When it passed, when strength flowed once more in her limbs, she raised up over Rand like a shy, fearless angel. Her long sweep of hair fell like a wash of eager kisses over him, caressing him first in a silky wave, a brush, a fall across his body. Then her face lowered and her mouth, so soft, pressed against his shoulder. Her warm, trembling breath blew over him, prickling his skin with tickling pleasure. She chased the invisible trail of breath, followed them with those soft red-ripe lips across his collarbone. A touch, a flicker of tongue, a taste in the hollow of his neck that made him clench, tighten, then forcibly relax, as she continued down her path, learning him, his texture, his scent, his taste, sampling him like an appreciative gourmet delighting in her brilliant creation. Her creature. Breathing life into him, over him, making him pant and groan and shift beneath her— wonderful sounds of life.

"Do you like this?" Another kiss, another lick. Down, down his chest.

"Yes."

"This?" She took the small nipple bud she had stirred to life with her hands, and licked it with her mouth, grazed it with her teeth. Raised him from the bed.

"Oh, God, yes." A prayer. A groan. A deep masculine mutter.

She smiled and he felt the curving lift of those small lips against him. Then he felt nothing but her as she took his nipple fully into her mouth and sucked and sucked and pulled upon it like a playful kitten.

She lifted up, shifted her upper torso over him, and watched with eyes sparkling like dark, precious gems as he raised his head and prepared to repeat the caresses on her—their agreed-upon game.

Those eyes, so dark, so shiny as he rose up, closer, closer. His lips touched her shoulder, and he could no longer see her eyes. Could only feel her—skin so soft. Could only smell her—like sweet pleasure. Could only taste her—like newfound desire, awakening. Like fine sugar sprinkled with crystals of salt. Like the incomparable taste of willing, wanting woman.

"Sweet, so sweet," he murmured, kissing, licking, nibbling his way across her delicate collarbone, like his, but so different. So finely made. He feasted, like a man come across life-giving water after a long trek across a barren desert. Like a drunken man imbibing grape juice, fermented and aged, for the very first time . . . intoxicating. Making her breath shudder out past her lips. Making her shake and tremble gloriously above him, so frail, so strong. Woman. His, in this moment, as he was hers.

His lips—so hot, so soft, so wet, so firm—dear God, she'd never known, never known a man's lips could feel this way, could make *her* feel this way. Down they went. Down the soft rise of her chest. And beneath those hot tender lips, she didn't feel small. She didn't feel inadequate. She felt like a goddess treasured, like a bounty discovered. She felt cherished, like she had never felt before. And the warmth of that feeling brought tears to her eyes. Made water rise and well. Made her squeeze her eyes shut so all she could do now was feel, not see.

She felt the soft, ticklish brush of his beard like wiry silk across her chest. The brush of softer, silkier hair. Then hotness—such heat, such wetness, such gentle force—hotness engulfed her nipple, and tears were forgotten. *All* was forgotten as waves and waves of hot, sweet sensation swept over her, flushed across her chest, arrowed down like an invisible trembling wave, down, down to that secret place inside her. Making her clench, making her cry out, arch, tremble above him. Not in release, but in a taste of what was yet to come. "Oh!"

Tug and pull. Tug and pull. Like a relentless baby that had just found succor. But the feelings of these lips, this mouth, this tongue ... the feelings those wicked, wicked teeth inspired were not feelings she'd ever felt before. She wanted to twist, to groan, to pull him to her, to push him away. She shook, trembled, swayed above him as if a powerful wind had suddenly swept her, and it had. Desire. Hot, sweet, unfamiliar desire. The wetness trickling down her thighs shocked her, surprised her, lifted her up away from him, from those sweet sucking lips that did not wish to give up their prize just yet, so that she popped out of the forceful seal of his mouth with a jarring sharp sensation that was painfully pleasurable.

She swayed like that for a moment, half-sitting, half-kneeling, drunk with the punch of passion, with unexpected pleasure. Dazed. Eyes wide but unseeing.

Too far away. Like a magnet she drew him. Like the pulling north pole. Up, up he went until he knelt beside her, and saw the crystal drops that had leaked out of the corners of her eyes. Such bewildered eyes. Irresistible. He didn't even try to resist. He bent to her, drawn, like a lover, like a protector, to those tears. Her eyes closed as she sucked in breath after trembling breath, and he kissed her, feathered his lips over those lovely eyes and drank her tears. Salty, sweet. What were they? Tears of passion? Please, God, don't let them be tears of fear.

"Don't be afraid," he murmured. "I won't hurt you." Inadequate words, but he knew nothing else to say.

She laughed, a short, sharp sound. A sound more of surprise than of humor. Hurt. He *had* hurt her ... by showing how sweet making love could be with the right person. But how could he be the right person? This stranger. This rough, gentle, wild man.

She shook her head, bewildered, wondering. Dazed, confused. Lost but somehow feeling found. She kissed him, this sweet man. Tasted the salt of her tears upon his lips. Found the flavor of him to be lovely. Dark, honest, and clean. She moved her lips against his, learned their shape, their feel—soft but firm. Wanted more.

A touch, a sweep of her tongue, and he opened the seam of his mouth, inviting her to enter and explore. Soon, soon, but first ... She angled her lips lower, opened her mouth and sucked in the fullness of his lower lip. Ripe, tender, like delicious fruit. She savored him—with lips, with tongue, with teeth, with gentle firmness—fastening her teeth on the ripeness of him, nibbling, pulling, stretching him taut with some of the wildness that he made her feel. *Mine. You are mine.* And he groaned his want, his need, his desire. Only then, when he had given her his need—his pleasure—did she delve in to explore the bounty within. Wetness, silk. Hot breath that she took and gave back. A sweet tongue that she stroked and pulled and sucked into her own mouth.

And then it was his turn to explore. To learn her. To sweep across her small, even teeth—dainty like the rest of her—to find and dance and duel with that surprisingly wicked, agile tongue. She was like a cat, a mix of naughty and shy, minx and kitten. And God, he wanted to touch her, to put his hands upon her, but she hadn't touched him yet, hadn't given him permission.

But how he wanted, wanted, wanted to. And the wanting slipped out of him in a low harsh sound. God, she made him wild. She made him hot. She made him want to be gentle while he ravished her with sweet passion. *More. Give me more.*

She was drowning in him. In his desire, in his touch, in his taste. In the erotic feel of his tongue sliding against hers, rough, tender, promising more. Nothing but his mouth touched her. But that mouth, that tongue . . . He pulled his tongue out, then sank it back into her. Out. In. In a slow, steady motion that parodied the dance yet to come. He surged into her like a strong wave, moving in her mouth, across her lips. While down below, more secret lips swelled, ripened, grew pungent with wet, musky arousal that made her pull back, gasp, stare wild and bewildered and panting at him.

He trembled, swayed toward her like a rushing wave eager to fall upon her. But he held. Held. Oh, the restraint in him, this man so much bigger and stronger than her. His eyes burning and flashing with more passion than she had ever seen in a man. Yet, still, he controlled himself. Who was he? How could he make her feel so safe, so cherished?

"Please." The word was a harsh, grating sound pulled from him.

A man who begged for her touch.

Her eyes softened. She didn't want him to beg. She wanted to give him what he needed, to satisfy his want. She wanted to please him, pleasure him, as he had pleasured her already. More than she ever expected. More than she knew she could feel.

"Lie back," she murmured with promise in her eyes. He did, feeling vulnerable, exposed, open. Open to her gaze, which whispered down to that part that could not hide, could not lie. That had swelled up with heat and need, so taut that it lay flat against his belly, aching, just past the dimpling of his belly button, a heavy, burning weight against his own skin. Throbbing,

throbbing with its own heartbeat that echoed a whisper behind the beating of his heart.

Like grace, her hand descended upon him and touched him. Made him quiver, shake, clench his teeth. Made him weep from another eye. The single one.

"You're crying," she murmured and swirled that clear liquid precum over him, over his sensitive head, making him jerk, arch his back, almost break his teeth.

Those eyes, eyes that swirled with passion and wonder, looked up and held him in an unbreakable grip. "Am I hurting you?"

"No, it feels wonderful." His next words slipped out unbidden, unstoppable. "Just touch me more."

"Like this?" She slid those smooth fingers down him, and the feel of her touching him was like cool rain hitting parched earth, a wet, nourishing benediction, making him shiver, swell, jump beneath her hand. Making him want more.

"Ah . . . yes!" he cried.

She pet him like she was petting a living creature. Light fingering strokes, exploring, touching, learning him—his sensitive mushroom head that drew a low sound from him as she circled and circled him there. His thick stalk that she wrapped her small hand around and came up short, unable to reach thumb and fingers together unless she squeezed down on him. And not even then.

His back arched and he cried out, surprising her, pleasing her with his reaction. Oh, he liked that.

She tried it again. *Squeeeze.* Yes. A groan, a faster pulsing in her hand. More groans as she slid that tight hand down him. More groans, more clenching of teeth as she slid back up. Tighter, squeezing tighter, drawing out more moans, more groans. Making his tanned muscles sheen and glisten with sweat.

"Am I hurting you?"

"No, no. God, no. It's great." *Wonderful. Freaking fantastic.* And then it got even better as her other hand cupped him, squeezed his balls. "Oh, fuck!" The words came out of him blindly, squeezed from him with the wonderful sharp-dull sensation shooting from his balls.

Touching him like this was like touching his nipples, Anna thought. So sensitive. Would her mouth feel even better on him?

Wetness touched him. Heat, silk. Different yet so similar to what a woman felt like when he sank himself between her legs. Soft, luscious heat and wetness, tugging, sucking, wrenching a startled cry from him. A wicked tongue, laving, exploring. Oh God. Oh God oh God oh God . . . it felt so fucking good.

"No more," he gasped. "Please, no more, or I'm going to go and I don't want to go yet. Not until I'm inside you."

Reluctantly, Anna's mouth left him. He tasted different down there. And not unpleasantly so. Fascinatingly. Intriguing. Did he taste the same all over? Even lower? Questions that must seek an answer another time.

He sat up, his eyes hot, eager, avid. "Lie down," he said, voice gritty. And then it was her turn to shake, to shiver, to anticipate, while his eyes gleamed. "Your turn."

Her turn. *Oh, no.* But the rules of game had been set, somehow. He could touch her in the same manner that she touched him. *Oh, God.* She hadn't thought of that when she'd touched him there. She'd just wanted to please him.

Lying there like that felt incredibly vulnerable, with him over her, so male, so big, yet safe, restrained. Eyes holding hers, he smiled like a pirate about to plunder. To scoop up treasure that lay naked before him, waiting for him to discover, to take. And take he did. He lowered his head down to where that most secret part of her lay hidden, and she closed her eyes, unable to watch. Only able to feel. That first touch. His hand, a fingertip, made rough from physical labor stroking her springy curls, smoothing through them. Making her jump at that first touch, so sensitive. Jump again as he dipped that finger lower. *Oh, God.* Even more sensitive down there, at those hidden lips, swollen, wet. *Sweet Jesus!* Pleasure speared through her like it never had before, parted her legs, panted her breath, clenched her fists into the bedding. Rippling, rolling, shivering pleasure as he played with her deftly, delicately. *Oh, oh, oh!*

Her hips lifted, rolled into his touch, begged him for a deeper delving. He gave it to her and it was her turn to cry out "Oh, my God!" as one finger slipped into her—male, thick, wider, much bigger than her own. He slid, wet and slippery and hard into her, and she sucked and clenched about him, trying to stop him, trying to hold him, but he pushed in deeper. *Oh!*

She held still, suspended, her hips lifted up like an offering to him, legs splayed wide, incredible sensations flooding her, almost overwhelming her, as he pushed in even more, then pulled back out, leaving her hollow, bereft, empty, aching, until he filled her once again. Slow glide in, pushing his way gently in, making room. Pulling out in that unending dance, in the most primal rhythm of life, of desire. She trembled, taut, suspended on the brink of something huge, something monstrous, a great force like a tidal wave swelling up within her. Another slow push in of that finger—deep, deeper than he had been before, all the way in, touching a certain spot—and she toppled, crashed. Broke apart. Crying, spasming, clenching that thick finger tight within her, her whole body shaking, vibrating, inundated with sharp, piercing, overwhelming pleasure that burst over her in a flooding wave of crashing sensation, tingling her fingertips, her toes. Clenching, clenching, clenching. And then it was over. The rolling waves of ecstasy receded, leaving small rippling aftershocks echoing in the wake of that great smashing wave. She was boneless, utterly spent, gasping. Only able to breathe. Only then able to see—a face with eyes like the churning ocean gazing down at her, hot above her, his face so flushed that he looked sunburned, as if her passion had burned him.

"What . . . what was that?"

"That," he murmured, his face lowering, "was your first orgasm."

5

He moved between her legs, in the space Anna had unconsciously created for him. She felt the heat of him first, that hot, hot skin hovering over her, between her open legs that were splayed wide and wanton. Only then did she become aware of her position, but not enough to care. It took energy to care and she didn't have any just yet. All she could do was breathe and recover. Learn to feel again. Feel first, then move.

Feeling returned with his touch. The touch of his hair whisking like gossamer silk over her thighs. The touch of his hot, puffing breath falling upon her like a prayer, a soft tingling benediction, blowing over her wetness, bringing her into awareness of that wetness and the first touch of embarrassment. It was as if his breath infused energy back into her. And then he touched her, really touched her. With the wiry silk of his mustache, the tingling brush of his beard, the press of his soft lips firm against her. *Oh!* Just firm enough, soft enough, not to tickle, not to hurt. Just there against her swollen lips, her wetness, the liquid expression of her desire peaked and satisfied, but once again rising like a phoenix from ashes. Rebirth. Renewal.

Feeling returned with a pulse, with a press of lips, with a wafting of hot breath across her, blowing over her, stirring her sticky hair, her sticky renewing desire. She was too sated to tremble. To boneless to move. But she could feel—his lips, his tongue, hot like the rest of him, sweeping out, tasting her, licking her in sure, steady sweeps. Not too much, not too little. Just right. He swept up her sticky length, then back down, lapping her like a cat lapped cream. A deep sound rumbled from him, passed up her legs, thrilling through her, making something deep inside her clench once more. Stirring her back to life from her sated bliss, building hunger back up with each lick, each lap. Her hands drifted down to feel the softness of his hair. Beautiful, smooth, a pleasure to touch and hold and stroke as he stroked her with that steady, gentle, but not too gentle tongue. Up again. This time, he burrowed a little deeper, as if her touching him had been a signal. He burrowed deeper and found a hidden pearl. Hard, taut, over-ripened like a sweet fruit ready to burst again.

"Ohhhh." The word-moan-sound was pulled from deep within her with the rasping of his tongue over her ripeness. And then it was gone. She relaxed once more as he licked and lapped his way back down, over her thickened lips that tingled once more with life and sensation beneath his rough-gentle ministrations, enervating her with odd languor even as she began that pleasure-seeking climb once more. She knew what it was now, that feeling, that pressure, that building, building force. And she no longer feared it but welcomed it. Yes! More . . .

"Aaaahh!" He touched her once more, there, burrowing deep and finding that secret, sensitive plumpness. Touch, taste, swirl, away . . . like washing waves advancing and retreating from a sandy shore. Then something new, as if the sound of her cry had prompted him on to his next step.

His tongue pushed into her opening, like a thick, gentle marauder, seeking treasure and finding it. She gasped.

He pulled back out, retreating with a last gentle swirl of his tongue at tender, shivering tissues, hidden, discovered.

Out, down, around that hidden button that shot sensation after blinding sensation through her, in her. Then a lower, deeper delving. A stabbing of the tongue. In, around, out, dancing in her sheath. Making her groan.

Her hips lifted in the delicate dance of desire, building, building, making her feel empty, needing something inside her—his finger, his tongue. Anything. Just more.

As if another signal had been given with the rise of her hips, his hands came up to grip her waist, to control her, open her more, so that he could dip his stabbing tongue deeper into her, push into her more, retreat back out, making her cry out with want, with need, as he left her, her hands fisting desperately in the softness of his hair. "No! Don't go," she cried, lifting herself up to that incredible mouth.

Like a sweet reward, he parted her once more. With a jolt, she felt his teeth clamp around her at the base of her ripened pearl. He bit down lightly and then sucked her into the hot, wet cavern of his mouth.

What she had felt before was pleasure. What she felt now as he bit down and pulled and sucked and laved at her ripe swelling was ecstasy so fierce, so hot, so overpowering, it bordered on the sweetest kind of agony. It burst from her, a sharp explosive climax, rocking through her with almost punishing pleasure, filling her up, then spilling out, bursting from her, over her. Rocking her up, rocking her over, then crashing her down in gentle bucking waves, leaving her awash with amazement that he could do this to her. She, who was no virgin, who had borne a baby that was a woman full-grown now.

Anna had never known this was possible. And she felt like weeping now that she knew.

6

It was the quietness that finally stirred Anna. That opened her eyes and turned them to him. He lay beside her, his body tense and tight, while hers felt boneless. Her body sated, his unfulfilled.

One tanned arm was flung up, covering his eyes, as if that somehow helped his body contain his weeping need. Clear, liquid desire oozed from the swollen head of him. He'd been so kind, so patient, so gentle. She wanted to please him now, in turn, as he had pleased her. And so, though her body was sated, fed so well that it no longer needed or wanted, she reached up over him and plucked up the foiled wrap that had lain there so patiently waiting.

The shifting of the bed, the ripping sound of paper made Rand lower his arm. He throbbed, he needed, he burned. And yet he was happy. She had been so beautiful, so surprised in her release. She had surrendered so sweetly to him, to his pleasure, had lain so trustingly beneath him as he had probed her first with his finger and then with his tongue. The taste and feel of a woman, this woman, the feel of her hands gripping his hair as she shuddered beneath him—even now the memory of it filled his heart, made bearable the aching unfulfilled need of his body.

His eyes flew open to see her poised above him, her skin flushed, her lips passion-reddened, passion-sated, passion stirring once more anew.

"Your turn." She smiled and his cock lifted hard and heavy against him at her words. At her action.

She pulled the ring of rubber firmly over his thick crown, rolled it down to his base.

She shifted up, settled over him, straddling him, her long hair falling in an inky wash over his waist, his stomach, his thighs, wisping over him like a thousand kisses. Another smile, and something darker in those mysterious eyes of hers: knowledge. Waiting pleasure.

"Touch me," she said.

He didn't wait for another invitation. His hands filled with the sweet delicacy of her breasts. His thumbs rose to brush and explore her rosy tips, finding hardness there among all the softness. Her eyelashes fluttered down like butterfly wings at his touch. She sighed, a slow release of breath, then opened her eyes to peer down into the very essence of him, of who he was. Who was he that he could make her feel this way? Gently she pulled him back, angled him up, lowered down onto him, watching him as she touched him to her, as he probed her, as she rolled him in her wetness, over her moist pouty lips, and then through them.

She held him with her eyes as she slowly took him into her body with effort, with grace, with steely determination. She had to fight to push him in, to get the thick head of him to enter into her willing but tight body, so long unused. He wanted to throw his head back at the sweet, swallowing tightness of her, but her gaze refused to release him. And so he watched her. Watched her watch him as she took him into herself like a sweet dream, like finding heaven when he had been so long in hell.

Heaven became hell when she finally pushed the fat crown of him in, surrounding that part of him in weeping wonder. In hot bliss. In tormenting stillness. And then in excruciating slowness.

Dear God, he felt so big. He *was* big, despite his denial. Big and hard, so hard. Like steel. She panted, relaxed, pushed down. If only she could get him all the way in! She swiveled his hips, moved in testing increments up and down. Such small, careful movements, not wanting to dislodge him after working so hard to get him in this far. She leaned forward, over Rand, and pushed down, gasping when his head lifted up and he latched upon a taut nipple, his mouth replacing the roughness of his hands, pulling, tugging, sucking on her, sucking a groan out of her, tightening her around him, squeezing a vibrating groan from him, transmuting that painful sound of pleasure through her breasts, shafting it down to where he joined in her, that tiny bit. It was lovely, it was breathtaking, his mouth upon her, the edge of his teeth around her hardness like a sweet promise. She felt a hot gush of her liquid honey spill over him, its purpose to make it easier to slide in. But the clenching tightness of her sheath snug around him resisted his entry.

Reluctantly, she pulled back away from him. His eyes rose back to hers, watching her as she danced over him—swivel, lift, gentle rise, firm push down. Lift, push, around and around, with barely any progress.

He'd said all it took to please a man was to be inside a woman. But he hadn't said how hard it would be to get him in there.

Her hand came down to measure him, to feather up, then down to his base. She almost wanted to cry with frustration. Not even halfway in.

He looked like he was in agony, jaw muscles bunched, eyes blazing like jewels set afire, body clenched all over. Tight with restraint, with being gentle.

"Help me," she pleaded.

His hands lifted from her hair where he had buried them, like black silken ropes sweetly binding him. A harsh breath. "Can I be on top?"

"Yes."

With a lunge, a twist, he rolled and she was suddenly beneath him. His hands on her hips kept them locked together so that he was still in her. He began to move and she was the one who had to close her eyes now. *Oh, my God.* Maybe it was not having to do the work. Maybe it was being on the bottom. Whatever it was, sensation washed anew within her like burned ashes stirred to life, combusting once more into flames that licked over her entire body as he moved within her with gentle force, with gentle power, pushing into her with steady strength, making her yield to his slow invasion, yielding her softness to his hardness. Making her realize that this . . . this was truly being a woman. Taking him into her, surrounding him, swallowing him up. But it was her cup that spilleth over. With incredible sweetness, with incredible sensation, with hot, bursting pleasure. The movement, the joining, the physical presence of him in her, around her. So right. Suddenly she wanted it all. Lifting her hips, she surged up, impaling herself on him so that he was fully sheathed within her. Her body to his. His hips against hers. Her curls mingling with his. And the sight of him buried deep, disappearing inside her, sent a quiver, a clenching within her. Pulled a sweating curse, a moaning groan from him.

Eyes locked with hers, he began to move in her. And it was a joining more intimate than anything she could have imagined. The fierce agony on his face, the press of his sweat-dampened body against hers as he braced himself up over her on his arms. The movement of him pulling slowly out of her—heavy, hard, slippery hot—was even better. Rippling pleasure, incredible friction. Her hands came up to grasp his hips. When he started surging back into her, her hands slid down to palm his tight, flexing buttocks as he pushed. He was so hard, both inside and outside where her hands caressed him, kneaded him. Her knees came up, bridging his hips, and that angle made it easier, opened her up more, so that he came even deeper into her, glazing both their eyes, blurring their vision until nothing else mattered but the motion, the union. In, out, rocking inside her, around her, over her. His breath striking her face. His body plunging into her open, more receiving channel. Less tight, more space. A faster pace. That climbing once more. Clenching, tightening, relaxing . . . to begin that dance again. Apart, together, in her, then out. Until she was lifting her hips in rhythm to his, meeting his thrusts with her own, plastering herself to him, grinding against him. But it wasn't enough, not enough. He was being so careful. And it was killing her.

"More!" she gasped—begged—as he left her, surged back into her. "Don't hold back, don't hold back."

Eyes gleaming, sweat plastering his hair to his temples, face so tight—he obeyed her. His rhythm sped up, loosened as if free, the force of his thrusts doubling, tripling, taking her breath. She exploded, burst like fireworks set free, a hot wash of ecstasy lifting her up, lifting both of them up as she clenched so tight around him that it felt as if a hot inner fist were squeezing him. And then he burst, too, in a wonderful, wracking, shuddering release, crying out, creaming out, spurting within her. A moment of rapture, then blind heaven, sinking into the softness of her. Having her wrap her arms tight around him, holding him, drifting in the sweet aftermath for a countless moment. One breath, two, and he found enough strength to roll off to the side so that he wasn't crushing her.

Her eyes opened, dark and languid.

"What's your name?" he asked, and she didn't think to lie.

"Anna Huang."

"Anna," he murmured. "My name is Rand. Rand Weatherby. A pleasure to meet you."

"Yes," she said, and kissed him.

7

The joining of their bodies, their release . . . it was as if it freed them of the awkwardness, the unknowingness. Now they knew each other, and the knowing seemed to give them permission to touch, to kiss. To talk.

"Were you coming or leaving?" he asked, stroking her thick pelt of hair as she lay curled up against him, her head resting on his chest, her hand stroking over his shoulder, down his arm.

Her hand, that soft hand, stopped moving, stopped touching him. "Would you like me to go now?" she asked in a careful voice.

He scowled, pulled back so he could look into her eyes. "Hell, no. I want you to stay. Can you stay?" he asked softly, persuasively, his voice so at odds with the fierceness on his face.

She went with his voice. "I'd like to."

"Then stay." The displeasure smoothed away from his face. "I was asking about Aceh Province. You're here as part of the tsunami relief, right?"

Anna nodded.

"Are you coming or leaving from Aceh?"

She relaxed then, letting the tension flow from her, allowed him to put her hand back on his chest, allowed him to rest his hand once more on her hips, stroking, brushing, in a languid, liquid movement up and down the small rise and curve, connecting them in touch though he stayed that small distance away to watch her face.

"Leaving," she said.

"Me, too. I spent eight weeks in Aceh Besar, in the village of Terbe, building new houses."

"I was in Abidin Hospital in Banda Aceh for three weeks, treating the injured."

"Are you a doctor?"

Anna rewarded him with a smile. "Yes," she answered. Most people would have assumed that she was a nurse simply because she was female.

He smiled back, comfortable, relaxed, totally at ease, his rough, callused hand moving up and down her side in gentle, soothing strokes. "What type?"

"Family practice."

His eyes crinkled in that familiar way. "The whole shebang, huh. From babies to the old folks."

"Yes, I like it that way. The continuity of it."

"My kid brother's going to be a doctor, too. He's in his last year of medical school at Johns Hopkins. Me, I like building things. I'm an architect." His eyes suddenly gleamed with humor. "You look surprised."

And she was. "You don't look like an architect," she said, putting it mildly. With that hair, that body, he looked more like a construction laborer. But his eyes were filled with kindness and perception, with keen intelligence.

The beard shifted as his mouth curved up in a smile both hidden and revealed by what lay over it. "What, all the hair?"

She nodded, laughed a little. "Yes." Lifted a hand to stroke "all the hair." The crinkly touch of his beard tickled her palm, making her giggle. And the sound of her giggling was so unlike Anna, she stilled in sudden surprise.

He was smiling at her, pleased that he'd made her laugh. "I let everything grow out the last couple of months here."

"And you labored with your hands, didn't just push a pencil around."

"No, I also hammered and lifted. It's been so long since I did that. It felt good." He stretched, long and languid. "Helping people felt good."

"Yes, it does."

His hand lifted to scratch his chest and she followed the movement idly with her eyes, then froze as she caught sight of the line of paleness on the fourth finger. His left hand.

Stupid, stupid, stupid, she muttered to herself as her eyes slowly lifted up to his narrowed ones, to his lying, cheating stillness.

He was married.

"It's not what you think," he said, his voice low as he saw where her eyes had fixed.

"No, I didn't ask." And she should have. Not his fault. Hers. "But I can't be with you anymore if you're married." Anna swallowed and sat up, suddenly, terribly conscious of her nakedness, of the sticky wetness still between her thighs. *Oh, God.*

"We would not be here together like this if I were married." His voice was deep, gritty, touched with pain. "She died. A year ago."

A long, slow breath eased from Anna. "I'm sorry."

"Yeah, so am I. Though in some ways she'd already died five years earlier."

He looked so desolate. The grief in him was real and sharp and drew her back into his arms to hold him, stroke him, comfort him. "I'm sorry." *For doubting you. For her dying and leaving you.* "I'm sorry."

A sigh shuddered out of Rand and he held her tight and found himself finally able to talk about it. "We were married for one year before her car accident. Her name was Dianne. She was an artist—gifted, vibrant, so full of life. The accident almost killed her. Maybe it would have been best if it had." He took a deep breath, said flatly, "It left her brain-damaged, with the mental capacity of a one-year-old child. I hired attendants to look after her in our home. I kept her alive when I don't think she would have wanted to be, not like that. Unable to walk or talk, or feed herself. With horrible contractures. She would have hated knowing that she was like that. I pray to God that she didn't. And I kept her like that for five long years before she finally died. I kept her with me because I didn't want to be alone. Because she was first my wife, and then my child. And when she died, I lost everything. My wife, my child, my family."

He pressed his face against her hair so that she wouldn't see him cry. So she could only hear the thickness of tears in his voice, but didn't see them. He blinked, concentrating on not letting the wetness spill from his eyes.

Her voice drifted to him like soft velvet, her words a soothing, healing balm. "You did nothing wrong in caring for her. She would have done the same for you had you been likewise injured, and you would not have hated her for doing so. You promised to love her and care for her, in sickness and in health. And you did. You kept your vows. Survivor's guilt." She laughed, and it was a harsh sound. "It's a real bitch."

Curiosity stirred Rand from his own hurt, made him tilt her face up to his. "You sound as if you know."

Darkness stirred in her eyes. "Oh, yes. I know. Only my guilt is for being happy. Happy that the bastard died."

"The man who betrayed you?"

"Yes."

"Who was he?"

She lifted up so that his hands fell away from her face, so that she rose above him, looked down at him. A hand lifted, touched his face in gentle apology. "I don't want to talk about him."

"What do you want?"

"I just want to be with you tonight."

"Okay," he said softly, making her smile, making her bend down to kiss him, to press her red lips, swollen from their kisses, against his lips, brushing softness against softness, firmness against firmness. Tender, seeking, promising. Leaving him dazed.

"Stay here," she whispered, and he watched her leave the bed and walk gently to the bathroom, her hips swaying gracefully in natural fluid movement. Water ran and splashed, the toilet flushed, and she returned with a damp washcloth in hand.

"Let me care for you, now," she said and moved the cloth down his shoulders, over his chest, down to the part of him sticky from his own ejaculate after he had disposed of the condom.

Beneath her silky touch, under the rasping brush of the washcloth against his skin, he began to stir, to thicken and harden.

"I want to touch you more, explore you more," she said.

He grew even fuller beneath the caress of her words.

"I want to lick you, taste you. I want to roll your balls in my hand, feel you spurting in my mouth, and taste you sliding down my throat when I swallow you down into me. That... that is what I really want."

"Jesus," Rand breathed, prayed, not entirely sure which. He bit back a groan but couldn't stop himself from flexing beneath her hand, an eager bob.

"Is that a yes?" she asked.

"Yes. Hell, yes."

She smiled. Like a cat who had licked the cream and was about to swallow it.

8

Anna lay between his spread legs on her stomach, propped up on her elbows. He was semihard, which meant that he lay flat for the most part, only just beginning to lift, to angle up instead of down, like a series of eager nods . . . up, down, lift, fall. Not too thick yet. Just plump, without being too hard. The tip of him was cushiony, like the extra padding on your ass to protect your bones. But here, a man had no bones, just hardness and softness. Especially there at the crown, like donning a helmet before the big man dived in. The image shone laughter from her eyes.

Seeing the laughter made Rand both eager and wary. Pleasure awaited. But how long he had to wait for it decided how painful the climb would be before reaching the blissful summit. By Anna's languid movements, she wasn't in a headlong rush to reach that cresting peak yet. Nope, that smile said she wanted to play. Bad, good . . . he wasn't sure which. Maybe both.

She ran a finger over the tip of his crown, inspecting it up close and personal. Without volition, he jumped beneath her touch like a diver springing up and down on a board about to lift up into an arching dive, startling a husky laugh from those lips so close to him that he felt a groaning pull deep within him.

"Whoa, partner," she said, and grasped him firmly with her left hand to keep him still while she continued to explore. To run that finger once more across the top of his crown, smooth over the small bumps lining his upper rim, and dip down over that flaring edge, running a light finger behind the helmeted head of him, making him squirm in uncontrollable movement.

"Hmmm ... sensitive here," she murmured. "How does that feel?"

Easy answer. "Good. But your mouth would feel even better."

Another husky laugh. Another hot gust of breath hitting him. Another uncontrollable flexing lift of his rigid length, straining in that small hand that controlled him, that kept him there at that angle, pointed downward, toward her mouth.

He watched with rapt fascination as her red mouth parted, as her pink tongue came out and ran over where her fingers had touched him, licking in a sweet glide over the sensitive rim of him, shuddering a breath out of him, making him close his eyes for a moment as if to savor the brief pleasure before letting it go to await the next.

"You're right," she said, dark eyes capturing his, "my mouth does seem better." Gone was all the uncertainty. In its place was a siren licking, teasing, exploring. Pleasing both herself and him.

Another languid lick over the top of him, down the side of him. She swept her devilish tongue beneath the crown of him, hitting a sweet spot, uncovering a hidden plexus of nerves that speared a hot flash of heat through him, making his eyes widen, making him surge up into her hand without thought, just reaction.

"Good?" she asked, eyes wide and curious, a small smile curving those lips.

"Yes," he gasped.

She took him at his word and did it again. Lick, lave, just there, burrowing deep behind that flaring rim. Seeking out that secret treasure . . . his pleasure. Making him tremble, cry out. Making him want more.

Softness touched the tip of him, and pressed. He looked down, met those dark, siren eyes watching him, while inches below, he was pressed up against her mouth, a long rod that looked poised on the brink of entering her, knocking there at her gate. The sight of him big and fat against those beautiful small lips sent a hot wave of sensation rushing through him like a tingling pulse. But her lips were closed. The soft cushion of her lips pressed against the cushiony head of him, testing, teasing. Then that mouth parted slightly and her tongue blinding sought him, explored him, while she watched him. Delicate strokes. Searching out, finding that single hole. Exploring its little dimensions with the firm tip of her tongue, making him writhe, speeding his breath, his heartbeat, racing the pulse beneath her hand where she held him still for her enjoyment, learning his pleasure.

It was so hard not to move, not to push himself between those waiting lips, so red, so moist and tender and hot. Because taking, moving, was what men naturally did, without thought. Instinct. A primal impulse to conquer. Not to yield. Yet yielding was sweet and right, here and now with her. There was sweet satisfaction to be found in watching the petals of her confidence slowly unfurl, watching the woman in her bloom. Heat, passion, hungry taking—that would come another time. For now he yielded and suffered and enjoyed. This night was hers.

Like a reward, like a temptation she could not resist, those red lips parted even more and moved over him, taking him in, surrounding him in wet heat, in moist silk, bathing the crown of him, enfolding him in a tight seal. Pushing down, pulling back. Sucking, pulling, tugging, over and over, just past the head of him and then back down, while she swirled her tongue over, around, and under him, arching his back, making him cry with aching relief, with hot gasping pleasure.

"Oh, yes . . . Oh, God . . . so good . . . Anna!"

Hearing him cry out her name made Anna suck harder, more fiercely. Made her thrum her pleasure deep in her throat, vibrate it against him, into him.

Against his will, Rand's hips began to rock the tiniest bit, as if he'd been so good, so good, for so long and he couldn't help moving just a little, a tiny bit, moving in her rhythm, sliding in and out of the hot silk of her mouth. In and out, but not deeper. Just moving, sweet friction, in the rhythm of life, of love.

She was the one who took him deeper, as if her small mouth had had to relax and soften, then she could take more of him. Suck, lave, stab, swirl, her mouth sliding down to meet her hand at the halfway mark where she held him tight. Her other hand rising to grip him below that first hand, squeezing him even tighter, sliding down to the base while he slid in and out of her hungry, sucking mouth.

She watched him through half-slitted eyes, gleaming, as if the movement—hers, his—sparked her own desire. As if his panting, straining pleasure stoked hers, quickening her breath, quickening her pace, deepening her force, her pulling. Hardening her surge down his shaft, swallowing him up. Tightening her pull in her wet, mouthy retreat back. Bringing him to the very brink.

It was so good, so good, so fucking good that he didn't want to give it up.

"No, no, no . . . not yet. Don't make me go. Please, not yet," Rand muttered, groaned, writhed as another clever sweep of her tongue slid over that hidden sweet spot underneath his rim. He didn't want to let go because when he did, it would be over, and he didn't want it to be over. He wanted to ride that biting, cresting pleasure, surfing it like a giant wave, building, building, a delicate dance, a precarious balance, not going over yet. *Not yet, not yet. Please, God, not yet.* He fought his pleasure, fought to hold on just a little bit longer.

Her gentle, sweet, wild man. He looked glorious, rough and wild, his jaw tight, his body straining, shaking, aching. Wanting, wanting, and yet holding back. Silly man.

Like a threat, like a promise, her lower hand gave one last squeezing caress, so hard that it almost rolled his eyes back in his head, and still he didn't go over. He hung on like a man sliding down a precipice, desperately clawing the slippery slope of desire with fingernails dug in deep to slow his inevitable descent, while below him, satisfaction yawned like a hungry lover beneath him, waiting to shatter him. Waiting for him to fall, sweet, stubborn man. Making her want even more to push him over, to make him come, to feel him spurting inside. To see if that small seep of his pleasure tasted even better, richer, when it was full and abundant and liquid in her mouth, rolling down her throat.

Her hand left him, trailed lower, and he tensed even more, his muscles bunching so tight that every tendon, every sinew, every hard, ridged curve stood out in prominent relief, in loving delineation as that slender hand moved lower to softer climes. Tender fingers slid over his aching sac, cupped his balls firmly.

Sweating, trembling, cursing, he waited for her to squeeze him. But she didn't. Instead she pulled him, gently. And the steady, thready, pulling sensation on his tightly drawn balls, in addition to the licking, sucking, pulling, and squeezing of his arousal, made his mouth open and round. Made a low harsh sound pull out of his gritty throat. And then . . . then . . . when he was drawn tight as a wire . . . *Then* she squeezed and rolled his balls together in her small white palm while she swallowed him down, swallowed him up. Squeeze and pull, and he was gone . . . coming, shooting, shaking, shattering in her mouth.

Quivering, pulsing in her hand. Leaping, pulling, lifting up, drawing tight like a living, throbbing thing in her hand, in her mouth.

Then she finally tasted him, felt the force of his ejaculate empty into her waiting, tasting, sucking self. She felt him jet into her, splash against the back of her throat, slide down. And yes, he did taste better. His groans were richer, his surrender sweeter, than anything she had ever tasted, ever known. Hers.

He was gasping, unable to get enough air, breathing by reflex only, not thought. All thought had left him. His soul had left him for a moment, for a brief time, torn from him, flung up high into the heavens, reaching for the sky. Touching it for one blind, shattering moment. Then he was plummeting back down and she was waiting for him, catching him, holding him safe in her arms. He gripped her solid realness tight against him, shaking and shaken, buried his face in the midnight blackness of her hair, breathed her in. Softness, woman. His.

"Stay with me," he said.

Her soft hand stroked his back. "Yes."

Arms wrapped around each other, skin against skin, heart beating against heart, legs entwined, they slept.

9

The stirring of the air more than any sound awakened Anna. She opened her eyes, saw a stranger standing by the bed, and screamed.

"Anna, what's wrong? Baby, it's me."

She knew that voice, knew it intimately. But she didn't know that face.

"Rand?"

"Yeah, it's me. I shaved." Lips curved up. Teeth flashed white.

She saw his naked, unbearded smile for the very first time, and it stole her breath for a moment. *He* stole her breath. Dear Lord above, he was beautiful. Like an angel fallen from the sky. Like an old master's sculpture brought to living, breathing life, so beautiful he was unreal. Striking, stunning. A man who would draw all eyes, both men and women, to him when he stepped into the room. A man who was even more handsome than her lying, deceptive first lover.

He was looking at her shyly, expectantly, a total stranger but for his eyes. His beautiful green eyes . . . those, only those she knew. Not the chiseled face, the lean cheeks, the strong jaw, the full mouth. It was like looking at an old familiar map and finding yourself completely lost.

Handsome face. Lying tongue.

Dark Asian eyes looked out of that face for a moment. Another's features shimmered like a translucent mask over the face staring down at Anna, making her heart pound, her mouth dry.

Go away, go away. You're dead!

Rand's smile faded. He had wanted to please her, to be handsome for her. But she didn't look pleased. She looked scared.

Carefully, he reached out, took her hand. She was trembling. "Say something," he said, concerned.

"You're *young*." Dear God, so much had been hidden, only now revealed like a joke, like a great cosmic prank. *Young, young. Younger than me.* Five years or more were shaved off with that beard. She had to ask, had to know. "How old are you?"

He frowned at the question. "Old enough." Then more gently, "I'm thirty-one."

She closed her eyes. *Oh, dear God. Ten years younger than me!*

"What is it? I know I looked older with the beard. Did you have a thing for older men?" He said it half in jesting, half in real question.

Do you have a thing for older women? was the real question.

Wanting to cry and laugh at the same time, she shook her head.

He stroked her hair tenderly back away from her face. "Hey, I'm sorry I took you by surprise like this. I wanted to please you. Not freak you out." He smiled crookedly.

She didn't smile back. Just looked at him. Looked at him but didn't see him.

"Are you sore?" he asked.

Was she sore? "Yes."

"Let me run a bath for you. You'll feel better after a bath." A tentative smile and then he left her.

She watched him pad away. Only when he disappeared into the bathroom did she find herself suddenly free again, able to move, able to breathe. Able to panic. *Oh God, oh God, oh God.* She wanted to run screaming from the room. Instead, she forced a calming breath inside her tight, aching chest. Inhale, exhale. Silently she slipped out of bed. Picking up the sarong from the floor, she wrapped it quickly about her. Not the neatest job, but she was covered. Grab the underwear, bra, and purse, ease the door open. Then she was running, fleeing, a ghost's laughter chasing behind her.

Rand came out of the bathroom, felt the emptiness of the room and somehow knew Anna was gone and would not be back. He ran to the open door. The hallway was empty, deserted. Ran to the stairwell, found that empty and silent as well, and returned to his room, hurt, worried, panicked.

Why had she run? Everything had been fine, more than fine. It had been wonderful between them. Until he'd shaved off his beard and mustache in a stupid, vain gesture of wanting to please her. A hand lifted to run over the smoothness of his chin.

What had made her run? Only she could answer that.

The real question now was: Was he going to run after her? A woman he'd met and bedded for one night.

The answer was the same as the one he'd given before.

Yes. Hell, yes.

10

The hustle and bustle of New York City felt odd after the lush tranquility of the rain forest. Of Indonesia. She'd been home for over a week now. She busied herself in her medical practice by day, stared up at her ceiling by night. She was her normal self during the daytime, but when darkness fell, it was as if someone else possessed her, kissed her, made her body ache, her heart throb.

And when she awakened from fitful dream after fitful dream, it was his name she whispered, "Rand."

The nights were unwillingly his, but she banished him during the day. Or tried to. Oddly, it was during the empty stretches of time when she wasn't busy, when she walked out into the crowded streets for lunch, that she would catch a glimpse of tawny, sun-streaked hair in a crowd, or a sweep of broad shoulders. Her heart would speed and she would race quickly after him, looking, searching, but not finding him. Never him. Always someone else. And the discovery, the desperate chase, the questioning look from a stranger's face would make her feel foolish and sad.

She'd left him. Fled like the coward she was. Because of vanity, insecurity, fear of herself and of him.

Had she been right? Had she been terribly wrong?

If it had just been one thing, and not two . . .

His beauty, perhaps, she could have gotten used to. Funny that now, looking back, his beauty was the lesser evil. But his youth . . . Not three years, five years, or even seven years. But ten years younger than her! Dear God, it made her feel like a lascivious Mrs. Robinson. She didn't want to be the older woman corrupting the younger man. She felt foolish and old. And then plain foolish because of her silly pride—vanity. She'd never known before how truly vain she was, and how empty it would leave her feeling.

Sometimes, lying in her bed alone at night, restless and empty and yearning, Anna thought of hiring a detective to look for him. She knew his name, his age . . . a smile twisted her lips . . . that had to count for something, make it easier to find him. But then she'd wonder if he even still remembered her. Had he moved on to other women? And there would be other women, abundantly so. They would flock to him with that face, that body, those eyes. She missed his eyes most. She missed his arms around her, the weight of his leg over hers, the beat of his strong heart against her ear, his clean scent. One night and it was as if he'd burned himself into her, chased away her ghost. One night and all she could think of . . . remember . . . was him. No other. The old wound had healed. But a new one had taken its place.

Her age was all that kept Anna from searching for him. It was different to be young and desperate, but old and desperate was not the same thing. It was more desperate, more pitiful. That silly pride again. Or was it just being plain stupid and cowardly? She ran. That was what she did, what she had always done. Only she was doing something new on top of that—ruining it first before he could ruin it. She was defeating herself . . . it was a sobering realization. She was forty-one years old. Her chances of finding happiness were slim already, but she, herself, was making them none. No chance at all.

He had made her happy. Had let her tease him, explore him, when the one before him had not. He'd given her pleasure, while the other had taken his and left her only emptiness, frustration, sadness, shame, and finally fear.

Was the way men made love reflective of themselves?

Find him.

Anna thought of it constantly, and the slow-passing days and long, empty nights didn't lessen the urge. Only grew it stronger. Seven more days passed, and then she caved. She would hire a detective. She would try to find him. To apologize, if nothing else, for leaving him so abruptly. To thank him for pleasing her so. And to see if there could be more pleasure, more time together. Even a brief taste more would be better than the emptiness she had now, and the reaching out for him, the battling down of her fear, was triumph in itself.

As if her resolve were penance enough, the restlessness left Anna, and she slept soundly for the first time since leaving his arms.

During lunch the next day, Anna called a private investigation agency not far from her office and made an appointment for the following Monday. It was Friday. The weekend yawned long and forever before her with only a social event that night and another one on Saturday to fill her time.

Her parents were surprised at the time she was spending with them now, attending several parties with them the weekend prior, when before she had avoided these high-society gatherings like the plague. Social chitchat. Empty talk to fill empty time wearing diamonds and pearls. But it was better than being alone and thinking and remembering. And aching.

Anna felt a little guilty when, at the party that night, her mother squeezed her hand and said, "Anna, I'm so glad you're getting out more. It seems I was wrong, not wanting you to go. That trip to Indonesia seems to have been good for you."

Oh, mother. If only you knew.

"Darling," she said, a smile on her lovely face. "There's someone who wants to meet you."

Anna cringed upon hearing those words every mother loves to utter. "Mama, I don't think . . ."

"Hello, Anna."

That low, honey-rough voice transported her for a moment back to sultry Medan, to a more primitive time and setting, so that the gentle murmurings around them dimmed and their sophisticated surroundings faded. Slowly Anna turned and looked up into rich, forest-green eyes.

He was growing back his beard, she noted inanely in that suspended surreal moment. A light shading of hair that served to accentuate rather than hide his face, his beauty. He looked like a rakish pirate now with that slight growth. Or a dark, dark angel. Was he truly there beside her? Like a dreamer, she reached out and touched him, felt his warm hand close around her smaller one. Real. He was real.

"Rand . . ."

"You two know each other," Anna heard her mother say, but she couldn't look away from the mesmerizing pull of those green eyes. Couldn't concentrate on anything but the feel of his rough calluses rubbing against her palm. He was real. In front of her. Here.

"Please excuse us, Mrs. Huang," Rand murmured and drew Anna away.

"How interesting," Mrs. Huang said softly, turning to the elegant matron beside her, who was also gazing curiously at the departing couple. "You must tell me all about your fascinating son, Mrs. Weatherby. An architect, did you say he was?"

"Hmmm . . . oh, yes," Mrs. Weatherby replied, turning to her, her eyes gleaming with interest. "And your daughter is a doctor, I believe . . ."

11

She looked stunned, surprised, shell-shocked, as she had once before. Rand's stomach twisted. His grip on Anna's hand firmed. This time, though, she wasn't running away. He wouldn't let her.

He guided her to a waiting car outside. The driver sprang out and held the door open for them.

"Your car?" Anna asked.

"Yes, get in."

Docilely, she took a seat, slid over to make room for him. The door shut, encasing them in silence.

"Your apartment or my place?" Rand asked, not trusting himself to say more.

Anna swallowed, looked blindly ahead of her. "My apartment."

Without surprise, she heard Rand give the driver her address. They drove in silence, sitting beside each other, not touching, but excruciatingly aware of each other, of each breath taken and exhaled.

The car pulled to a stop and the trip that had taken so long suddenly seemed too short. His hand wrapped once more around hers as the door opened and they stepped out. "Thank you, John. I won't be needing you the rest of the night."

"Good night then, sir." A tip of the hat and he drove away.

A murmured greeting to the doorman, and then the elevator was taking them up. That little surging lift, another interminable stretch of time, and they reached her floor. He walked beside her, and the hand wrapped around hers was both security and shackle. The grip was loose and easy, but strong. Anna doubted she could break free from that hand unless he allowed her, but didn't put it to the test.

The thick door shut behind them and then they were alone, inside where she lived. He released her then, watched her walk around the spacious living room turning on the lights. It was a lovely building, prewar, an architectural wonder lovingly preserved. And the inside was even lovelier, new blended with old. Tall windows, high molded ceiling with artful plasterwork, gleaming hardwood floors, Persian carpets, touches of cream and gold. Tasteful, elegant, rich. Like the woman.

Rand looked at her from across the room. "Are you happy to see me?" he asked, wistfulness seeping into his voice despite himself.

Anna stilled for a moment. "Yes," she answered, but still she didn't look at him. Toward him, but not *at* him.

"You don't seem happy," he said, walking toward her, and still she didn't look at him.

She froze, standing there like a deer caught in blinding headlights. But he only sat on the sofa, and again, he was like a stranger. An elegant one now in his beautifully tailored blue jacket and brown slacks. A white silk shirt opened at the neck, bringing out his rich tan. Black onyx and gold winked from his cuffs. He was comfortable, casual, sophisticated.

"How did you find me?" Anna asked.

"Your address was in your passport."

That made her finally look at him. "You looked in my purse?"

He nodded. No guilt, no apology.

"Then why did you wait so long before coming to me?"

He must have sensed or heard some of the plaintiveness, the longing within her. His eyes softened. "I had a report run on you. I made myself wait for that, first."

"A report?" Anna said, a tremor in her voice.

"Yes."

"So you know—"

"That you come from banking wealth, that you have a daughter, Lily, a former NYPD detective, recently married. That her father is listed as unknown. I know that you are forty-one years old. Happy birthday, Anna," he said softly. "You should have told me it was your birthday that night."

She just shook her head, lips trembling.

"Why did you run?" A gentle question. But his eyes . . . his eyes weren't gentle. They were roiling, a blue-green turmoil. "Why did you leave me when you said you would stay with me?"

"I . . . I did stay with you for the night."

"I never said it was just for the night."

What was he saying?

"Anna, come here, please." He held out his hand to her and she went to him, sank down onto the soft cushions beside him.

"Does it bother you so much, my age?" he asked.

"Isn't the question really: Does *my* age bother you?" She looked into his eyes, then glanced away. "I know I look much younger. I should have told you, said something."

"Why? It wouldn't have mattered then. It doesn't matter now. Is that why you ran?"

"Partly," she confessed. "And partly because of how beautiful you looked."

A sharp indrawn breath. "Tell me why that scared you away."

She looked down. "I've only had one other lover beside you."

"Lily's father?"

"Yes. I met him in China the summer after I turned nineteen. I left China engaged, thinking I'd found true love, discovered I was pregnant when I returned to New York, and was eager to share the news with my parents and to start the process of bringing him over to America after our marriage. My parents were shocked, horrified, totally against my union to a poor, nameless man from a small village in China. But I was so stupidly, foolishly in love. He'd been so handsome, so kind and attentive, pledging his love and devotion to me. It wasn't until I saw pictures of him with other women that I realized that handsome face hid a lying tongue. My parents had hired a detective in China, and the pictures he took were too explicit for me to mistake what my fiancé was doing with them. Not just one or two women, but four in the short month since I'd left."

Rand's arm came around her, warm, comforting, strong. "I'm sorry, baby."

Anna breathed in his scent, burrowed into the warm comfort of his neck. "But that was nothing. Nothing, really. I had a beautiful little girl, and I wanted her to know her father. So I took her to see him in China for the first time when she was six. And he was wonderful with Lily, buying her presents, fussing over her. Kind, attentive. He was good at that. I brought Lily to see him two more summers and each time we came, I gave him two thousand dollars because he was Lily's father. Two thousand dollars was a lot of money back then—three years salary for a successful businessman, which he was not. But that last summer, he found out how truly wealthy I was, and two thousand dollars, a fortune before, suddenly wasn't enough."

"How did he find out?"

"Lily told him." Anna lifted her head up and smiled sadly. "She wanted her daddy to marry her mommy and come live with us, and she thought he'd want that, too, if he knew how much money we had. So she told him. And the bastard kidnapped her. Told me if I wanted 'the brat' back, I'd have a hundred thousand dollars waiting for him the next day. He put Lily on the phone, pinched her and made her cry out so that I'd know she was still alive."

"Oh, baby. I'm so sorry."

The kindness in his eyes made tears well up in her eyes. She blinked them back furiously. If she cried now, she wouldn't finish the rest of the ugly story, and she wanted it out of her, now, while she was still able to tell it. "I didn't trust him. And he sounded so ugly on the phone, had hurt Lily purposely. I called the police. They were in place the next day. After I'd given him the money, he put a gun to Lily's head, said he changed his mind, that he wanted more. And when he did that, they shot him and killed him."

"He deserved to die," Rand said roughly.

And then she did cry. The tears spilled over, the telling of it bringing back the ugliness of that day.

He rocked her, soothed her, rubbed her back, stroked her hair, murmured, "Shhh, baby, shhh. It's all right."

"I'm sorry, I'm sorry," Anna choked. "When I saw your face, after you'd shaved, you were even more handsome than him. And not just handsome, but beautiful."

Rand stiffened, drew away. "I'm not like Lily's father."

She scrubbed away her tears with her hands, looking so vulnerable and young. Twisting his heart.

"I know . . . I know that now. It was just a knee-jerk reaction. Handsome face, lying tongue. The two things always went together in my mind. But you're so different, so different from him. Only when I found out how much younger you were than I . . . I panicked and ran. Why did you come after me?"

"I want to spend more time with you, Anna."

Her heart paused, gave one painful beat. "Oh, Rand. I want to spend more time with you, too. I was going to hire an investigator to try to find you."

He stroked the side of her face tenderly, and a tight knot inside him unraveled when she pressed her face into his hand, rubbed against it.

Smiling tenderly at him, she said, "For however long or short a time you want me for, I'm yours."

His eyes gleamed and his voice thickened with emotion. "I'm going to hold you to that." A promise. A warning. "I have something to confess, also."

Anna stilled. "You slept with someone else."

An odd look. "No." A low careful rumble. "Have you?"

"No."

He blew out a relieved gust of breath, pressed a hard kiss to her forehead, then drew back to look into her eyes. "Anna, what I'm trying to tell you is that, like you, I've only had two lovers. One of them, my wife. The other was you."

"What?" Somehow this surprise was the most unexpected of them all. Men, especially beautiful men, just weren't like that. "Why?"

"I didn't want any other woman . . . until I saw you."

It was unbelievable, yet she believed him. It was just so unexpected. Mind-boggling, in fact. But when you received a gift from the gods, you didn't question it to death. You just accepted it. And were very, very grateful.

"Oh, Rand," she breathed and kissed him.

He kissed her back. "I'll grow my beard back."

"No," Anna cried. "I love your face."

"Do you?"

"Yes, don't hide it."

"All right. What about my age, baby? I can't change my age."

"Unfortunately, I can't change mine, either," she said wryly.

"I wouldn't want you to, even if you could." He suddenly grinned. "Besides, you make a terrific Mrs. Robinson. Real wicked."

Anna slapped his arm, blushing hotly, though a smile teased the corners of her mouth. "Oooh. That was so mean. You're going to have to pay for that." She pounced on him and he allowed himself to fall back beneath her slight weight, laughing.

"Are you going to have your corrupting way with me now?"

Her eyes narrowed. "If I'm Mrs. Robinson, that makes you my boy toy."

"Boy toy?" His eyes positively sparkled.

He was asking for it. She decided to give it to him. Deliberately, with a wicked leering smile that would have done Mrs. Robinson proud, she smoothed both hands down over his butt. "Nice ass," she said, and squeezed hard.

He coughed-choked for a moment, his face flushing with desire and embarrassment, delighting her.

"Hmm. Maybe there are perks to being the older woman here that I should explore." She left those wonderful buns of steel and moved in front, on to more interesting exploration. "Ah, yes," Anna murmured, finding him long and thick, ready and aroused. She smiled at him and his eyes burned like green fire suddenly ablaze. "A wonderful boy toy. Come here, lover. Come give me some joy."

He growled, surged up suddenly, twisted, and pinned her beneath him. "It sounds like a challenging job. One requiring a lot of stamina and endurance. A strong back and an unending well of creativity and drive."

"Umm, yes, drive. You up for it?"

"I certainly am." And proved it by rubbing himself against her notch, making her lashes flutter down at the lovely grinding sensation of him pressing there. "I'll take the job," he muttered and swooped down to capture her lips.

They tasted and touched, licked and nipped, while their

hands flew over each other. Her zipper rasped down. He lifted away, pulled down her long dress. Glued his mouth to her hungry one while he blindly found the clasp of her pearls, unhooked them, set them safely on the coffee table while she sucked and sucked on his tongue, making him groan. He came up for breath, gasped wildly, gazed hotly at her sprawled beneath him, her lips red and swollen, curved in a teasing, tantalizing smile that only a woman could give a man, driving him mad with desire. Panting, breathless, he shrugged out of his jacket with more haste than finesse, driven by a terrible need to feel her skin naked against his. Driven by the same need, she yanked his shirt free from his pants, then used his shirttails to pull him back down on top of her. His hands dove into her hair, sent pins scattering on the floor. Her hair fell loose and long while she ripped off his belt, pushed down his pants and underwear so that he spilled free and hot and hard in her hands. She pulled on him, then when he moved forward at her beckoning, she pushed him back down, their joint actions moving him in her soft strong hands, holding him so achingly, wonderfully tight.

"Anna," he growled, groaned, reared up to push his pants completely down, then cried as she lifted up and took his thick shaft into her tiny mouth, making him curse, pant, throw back his head and make an arching sound of pained pleasure that was so sweet to her ears. Almost as sweet as the taste and feel of him in her mouth. Spicy. Addicting. A wonderful full load going in and out. Both hands played with his hard arousal while she licked and laved that cushiony, sensitive head, seeking out his pleasure.

"Oh, God, baby. Please, no more. No more," he groaned, even as his hips moved in uncontrollable tiny surges, his hands in her hair. Their rhythm. That familiar yearning, straining, gentle, dancing rhythm.

She hummed in disappointment, in acquiescence. One last lick and suck. Later. She'd taste him again later.

He shuddered, swayed. What was he doing? Oh, yes. The

bloody pants. He kicked them off, stripped off her pantyhose, bra, and underwear, baring her finally, blessedly naked, and fell upon her with hands, lips, teeth, and tongue like a starved man greedily gorging, filling his hands with her delicate flesh, drinking down her cries. Teasing, tasting, laving her tongue, then moving down to nip her responsive nipple. Wetness, hardness, taste, smell. His arousal and hers. Silky hair down below, a parting of her soft folds. Sliding into her with one finger and then two, stretching her, preparing her, while he sucked and pulled on that lovely nipple, throwing her over the edge.

Her turn to throw back her head and arch her back, lifting them up, so strong, so unexpectedly strong, clamping ferociously down on his fingers, milking them in a sweet release as she shook and shuddered so beautifully beneath him and around him. They sank back down and she shivered as he drew his fingers gently out of her, watching him with slumberous eyes, so dark, becoming even darker as he licked his fingers, tasted her, and found it good. Her eyes drifted closed.

Condom. He needed a condom. Where the hell was it? His eyes fell on his pants and remembrance kicked back in. His wallet. He retrieved his pants, found the little foiled packet, and sheathed himself in one stroke. Walked back to her, slid over her, between her opened legs.

"Open your eyes, sweetheart," he urged and watched as those thick lashes fluttered open once more.

Gently, firmly, he pushed into her. Easier than the first time, but he still had to work to get inside her, just barely.

"Hold on to me, baby," and with that gentle warning, he lifted them up to his feet, and started walking.

Anne stirred from her lethargy. Walking? Where was he going?

"Oh!" she uttered, as she felt him slide inside her a little more with his movements. Another "Oh!" then her back was pressed against the wall behind, and he was pressed into her in front, his hands on her hips, holding her up, holding her immobile so she couldn't move, just hung suspended like that, impaled by him, feeling so stretched.

"Are you all right?" he breathed, his voice strained.

"Yes, no. I don't know." She whimpered, wriggled against him, barely able to move. How far was he in? Her hand moved down, found him, moved up a frightening amount of length before she felt him end inside her, her lips stretched wide, tight and taut around him. Her hands blindly caressed him there where they joined. She squeezed him, wringing a groan from him. Looking into his eyes, so close to her, she said, "You feel so hard, inside and out."

He rested his forehead against hers, his breath falling in hot pants across her lips. "You feel so incredibly soft and tight."

"Do I?"

"Yes." His hands shifted on her hips. "Hold still, darling. I'm going to let you take a little more of your weight."

Anna didn't know what he meant, until she felt his hands loosen on her hips so that he was no longer holding her up, supporting her weight. Gravity was. But gravity doesn't support, it pulls you down. Slowly, slowly she sank down over him, and the sensation of it closed her eyes, her own weight sinking her down, pushing him slowly, inexorably in, stretching, stretching, stretching her. Torturously slow, torturously full, impaling herself on his thick pole, tight softness yielding to unyielding hardness. She slid down over him in flowing increments like hot molasses and she felt him push his way into her, thick, hard, and unrelenting. Doing nothing more than letting her own weight sink her down on him. *God!* The slowness of it was torture of the most exquisite kind, feeling every measurement of him entering her, leaving her panting, wanting to writhe, wanting to buck against him wildly.

"Does it hurt?" he gritted, teeth clenched.

"No!" It felt good. The sweetest agony.

"Just a little bit more." His hands grasping her hips, holding her still, he bent his knees, tightened his buttocks, and surged into her, sheathing himself all the way to the hilt.

She twitched, shivered, cried out. "Oh, God, you're killing me. Move, please move." She wrapped her legs around his tight behind, and squeezed him even more into her, against her.

He groaned, laughed, rocked against her. "Loosen your legs a little, baby, and I'll move."

She loosened her cinching hold and he finally began to move. He pulled out, out, out. And then pushed in, in, in. Killingly slow. And all she could do was take it, her hips pinned against the wall by his hands. Her head fell back. Her back arched at the exquisite rippling sensation of feeling him surging into her. The slow drag and heft of him pulling out. The thickness of him forging unhurriedly back in, like a heavy ship parting reluctant waves.

Hot wetness covered her nipple, sucked her into the wet silk of his mouth, tugging, sucking, gently biting, one hand coming up to cup and caress, squeeze and play with her other breast. Lovely, but he'd stopped moving. She chewed her lower lip in frustration. *Oh, God.* Why didn't he move! She swayed against him, danced upon him, shimmered her hips in shallow, rocking surges against him, just enough to feel beckoning pleasure shimmer like a promise. Just enough to tease herself crazy as he feasted upon her breasts with leisurely sucks and pulls. But not with the force, power, speed she so desperately needed. Urgently craved.

She gasped, she moaned, she whimpered, she begged. "Rand, please. Please, help me."

"Like this?" he said, and did that slow pull out, that slow push back in again. Then stillness, him buried deep and thick inside her, her helpless feet dangling inches above the ground.

She squirmed, writhed upon him, clenched her inner muscles tight, felt him flex inside her. "Please, Rand. Help me!"

"Yes," he murmured tenderly, kissed her gently. "Soon."

The word lifted her eyes disbelievingly to his. Soon? She would die soon.

He looked strained himself, muscles bulging tight with his restraint. But his eyes . . . his eyes held a rock-hard resolve. "I'll help you, baby, after you promise to make an honest man out of me."

He did another one of those slow pull-and-push things again, keeping her strung out on the torturous rack of slow pleasure. Her eyes widened at his words sank in. "You . . . you want to *marry* me?" Anna said in bewilderment.

He circled his hips inside her. A twisting, grinding, lifting motion at the end that almost made her eyes roll back.

"Yes, darling," he crooned. "More than anything else. My ring on your finger. Your ring on mine."

She couldn't grasp it, could not comprehend it. It was so hard to think. He wanted to *marry* her? She was older, he was ten years younger. She didn't even know where he lived. "It . . . it's too soon. We just met." She gasped as he did another of those circling lifting motions inside her. She whimpered, wailed. "I can't think like this."

"Then don't think, baby. Just say yes." He swiveled-lifted his hips again. "I can stay in you like this all day until you say yes," he murmured against her lips, a sweet, menacing promise, and flexed inside her.

She trembled against him, quivering helplessly, held up by him, on him. Pinned by his will. By his cock.

Gentle lips whispered over hers. "Say yes."

It was too much. Too little. Sensations bombarding her, then leaving her cold, shivering, wanting. Unable to think, only feel and crave and desire.

"Say yes," he breathed against her. She felt him thick inside her, his body tight against her, more than capable of keeping her strung out like this all day, driving her slowly crazy until she said yes.

In that moment of weakness, in that moment of want, she gave in to what her heart most desired. "Yes," Anna whispered. "Yes, I'll marry you."

His eyes blazed. Blue-green fire. He gripped her face and kissed her passionately, tremblingly, his heart thudding violently. He kissed her wildly. "Baby"—kiss—"Darling"—kiss—"Anna"—kiss—"You won't regret it."—kiss—"Promise you." Another hard kiss. And then he began to move, and she didn't regret it. How could she when he looked at her like that? Like she was his entire world, his entire desire. He was suddenly the one shaking, the one wild, the one out of control. He pulled out and thrust into her hard, fast, like he couldn't get deep enough, close enough, lifting her up the wall with his driving force, pushing the very breath out of her. But who needed to breathe when you could feel? . . . His hands behind her, protecting her, cushioning her. His thickness surging again and again into her, slick and hard, strong and deep, filling her with fierce, shooting pleasure. Stringing her tight and tighter around him, clenching his heaving, surging length, trying to hold him, grip him tight when he entered, as he left, when he returned home again and again.

Then Anna was the one fighting it, not wanting it to end, not wanting to go over. But it was like trying to stop a flood from sweeping you away. It crashed over her, rolled her under, threw her up, light, weightless, suspended in a still, infinite moment of time. And then she was convulsing and shattering in an endless orgasm that smashed pleasure through her, over her, out of her. Splintering her apart while he moved strongly within her, holding her. Then it was her turn to hold him as he heaved and bucked and shuddered and groaned in his own climax. To feel the strong pulses of his ejaculation throb from his base up through his shaft and out. To feel the tiny electric pulses of his satisfaction push against her own sensitive tissues. And it was wonderful.

He treated Anna like a cherished lover or a beloved wife, washing her, drying her, tucking her into the soft covers of her bed and snuggling beside her, her head resting on his chest, the lovely *ba-boom, ba-boom* of his heart a lulling dear rhythm beneath her ear.

He stroked her hair. "The first time I saw you, I thought you looked like a perfect little China doll with your porcelain-white skin, jet-black hair, and red lips."

"A China doll," Anna murmured. "Surprisingly accurate. Something put carefully on a shelf, hidden behind protective glass, sheltered by my parent's love, contained by my own fear." She ran her hand idly down his chest. "But that glass shattered when my daughter almost died two months ago."

Rand stiffened beneath her, lifted her chin so he could see her. "How?" he asked roughly.

"Lily helped break up a human smuggling ring. But the head of the Chinatown gang she brought down got away and came after her. I was in her apartment when he broke in, looking for her. He waited for her holding a knife at my throat until Lily arrived."

"What happened?"

"He cut me then, made me bleed, using me to get her to come to him."

Rand pulled the sheet down, baring her. "Where?" he demanded, dark rage in his eyes.

Her hand lifted to two thin lines on the left side of her neck, so faint Rand hadn't noticed them until now. Now, pointed out, they were so ugly, so glaringly obvious. His fingers trembled as he touched those marks, ugly not in appearance, but in what had put them there. A little deeper and the bastard would have severed her carotid artery. Killed her.

It left him shaken and enraged.

"He was going to hurt my baby," Anna said. "I couldn't let him. I hit him between the legs, dropped down and rolled away from him. My Lily took it from there."

"Is he in prison?"

"Yes."

"Good," Rand said, jaw clenched tight. "May he rot there."

A soft hand came up to stroke the shadowy line of his jaw. "It wasn't so bad. No, that's not true. It was bad. But it was a good thing. It was the first time in my life I'd fought for anything. I fought for my daughter's safety, and then fought for her happiness. She was like me, after what her father did to her, never trusting men. She loved Wes, the FBI agent who helped her break up the smuggling ring, but she was going to walk away from him. I told to her reach out, to risk her heart, and she listened to me. Me! The hypocrite who'd only risked her heart once and lost and never dared risk it again. She shamed me, and I couldn't go back to being that China doll. I couldn't step back onto that protective shelf again."

"Is that what you were doing that night in Indonesia?"

"Yes. Afterwards, I went a little crazy. I left the practice in my partner's hands, traveled to Indonesia to help with the tsunami relief. And it helped me, healed me, made me ready to tackle my biggest fear—intimacy once more with a man. I wanted to break free of those chains that I'd let my own fear bind me in. I was a China doll that night you first saw me. But I no longer am. I no longer want to be."

Rand kissed her, held her tight against him. "You're so brave. But I'm glad, so glad you waited for me." She felt so light and precious in his arms. And she'd almost died. The realization frightened him. "I don't want to wait," he said roughly. "I want us to be married right away. Tomorrow—no, tomorrow's Sunday. The next day. Monday."

"Monday?" Anna pulled away from him, dazed. "I don't have a dress."

He smiled. "We'll get one tomorrow."

"We don't have a license."

"We'll get that first thing Monday."

"Rand, I can't marry you in two days. I need more time than that."

He rolled her over suddenly, pinning her. Spreading her legs, he pushed gently into her. She was still soft, still wet.

"Say yes," he said, his jungle-green eyes glinting with determination.

"Oh, God. Rand, no. Please don't do this," she begged, squirming beneath him, arching up, taking him in, feeling him slide in deliciously, wickedly slow. He felt different, somehow. Better.

He pushed all the way in, then held still. "Say *yes.*"

"Please, Rand. I can't think like this."

Buried deep inside her, his hips swiveled and lifted. "Say *yes.*"

She whimpered, groaned. Then gave in. "Okay. Yes. Rand, please!"

He did. He proceeded to please her. And himself. With slow deep thrusts. With penetrating forays.

"Do you want children?" Rand asked, his face taut, his eyes tender.

"What?" God, it was so hard to think.

"Do you want children?" he repeated, strain evident in his voice as he continued to move in her, a steady gentle rhythm, allowing her to moisten, heat, soften more.

Children. His child. Her heart turned over. "Yes, I'd love to have your baby."

Rand's eyes flared with heat, with tenderness, with love. "Good, because I'm not wearing a condom."

"Oh." Anna blinked her eyes in surprise as she wriggled around him, clenched tightly about him as if to hold him still with her inner muscles and examine him. "Is that why I feel you more?"

"Ah, baby," he groaned. "Do that again."

She did, making him groan again, move faster inside her, long surging strokes.

"Yes," she panted, lifting up to meet his thrusts. "Harder!" Gasp. "More!"

The bed was creaking beneath them, in rhythm with their thrusts, the headboard bumping the wall in accent to his deep and deeper drives inside her, damp skin slapping against damp skin, her moaning, him groaning.

"More, Rand, more. Faster!"

He took her at her word and began pistoning into her. Hard, hot, thick, and complete. A wild impassioned taking, his lips swallowing up her cries, and then swallowing up a drawn nipple, achingly tight and sensitive. His teeth clamped down strong around her pebble hardness, bit down gently as he rammed sharp and deep into her with the full driving force of his hips and buttocks. She crested. Burst apart. Rippling, rippling, rippling endlessly around him, milking him dry. He arched back and spurted hotly within her, shooting his seed inside her. Tense man became boneless mass, sinking down, covering her with his relaxed weight. All too soon, he stirred, tried to lift away.

"No!" Anna cried, legs tightening around him. "Don't go. Stay inside me."

His weight crushed her back down into the bed. "I'm too heavy for you," he muttered, his face half-buried in the fragrant spill of her hair.

"No you're not."

"How's this?" He shifted a little onto his side, so that she bore less of his weight.

She stroked his hair. "Good." Anything was good as long as he was still inside her.

They dozed. When she shifted her legs into a more comfortable position, he stirred, lifted his face, looked at her, his face sweetly relaxed with satisfaction and contentment.

Tears suddenly burned the back of her eyes.

"Anna, are you crying? Oh, God, did I hurt you?" he asked, eyes wide, a bit wild.

"No, no. I'm happy," she sniffed and laughed. "You make me so happy. A baby," Anna whispered, and wondered if they had made one just now, created new life.

His big hand splayed over her belly, a protective gesture, encompassing it. "If it's a boy, we're going to have to name him Randolph. I hope you don't mind. It's a family tradition for the first son to be named that."

Anna smiled. "Randolph Weatherby, the—what—third?"

Rand's smile was a trifle embarrassed. "The twelfth. I'm number eleven."

"Randolph Weatherby," Anna murmured, frowning. "That sounds familiar."

"Paper," he said.

"What?"

"Weatherby labels, paper products. That's, uh, the family business."

Her eyes widened in surprise. Weatherby. No wonder it sounded so familiar. It was usually blazoned in big, white print beneath their triangular logo. In fact, she had a box of their white address labels next to her printer. And she'd seen a picture of Randolph Weatherby, Rand's father, on the cover of *Fortune* magazine six months ago.

"You're wealthy," she realized, stunned. His family, in fact, was possibly wealthier than hers. And they'd had their money far longer. Old money, not new like hers.

Rand frowned. "Yes, I'm wealthy. So are you."

"Then why do you want to marry me?"

He stilled for a moment. Dangerously still. When she finally awakened to the threat in him, it was too late. He had her pinned, her wrists manacled above her head, his body hard, fully on top of her, in her, a throbbing, stirring presence between her legs. His hot, angry breath hit her face like blows.

"I want you to marry me because I want you to be my wife, my family," he said, his voice hard. "Because I love you, you little fool. Not because I need your money."

"You love me?" Anna said, bewildered.

His eyes softened. "Yes, is that so hard to believe?"

"Oh, Rand." A catch of breath. "I love you, too."

And then Anna was flat out crying, sobbing. Her wrists were freed and she found herself clinging to him.

"Oh, God, baby. Please don't cry," Rand said tenderly, desperately. "I'm sorry, I didn't mean to frighten you. Don't be afraid. Please don't be afraid of me."

A slim hand smacked his shoulder. "You didn't scare me." Not too much, anyway. "I'm just"—sniff—"*happy*."

He rubbed her back. "Oh, darling. Do you always cry when you're happy?"

"I don't know," she hiccupped.

Rand kissed her tears gently away. "That's okay. We have a whole lifetime together to find out."

Together. Such a beautiful word. "Love me, Rand."

"I do," he said and began that beautiful dance once more. The dance of their love, of their pleasure. Of their togetherness.

Turn the page for a sneak peek at
BLOOD ROSE, by Sharon Page

Coming soon from Aphrodisia!

aside as he stalked toward her, his ridged abdomen rippling. He wore no small clothes. His magnificent legs were formed of powerful muscle, lean and hard.

And his cock. Serena couldn't look away. It curved toward his navel, thick and erect and surrounded by white-blond curls. She knew it would fill her completely, stretch her impossibly, and she knew it would be perfect inside.

Mr. Swift reached the bed first. He smiled, his teeth a white gleam in the darkened room. His hand reached—she followed the arc of his fingers with breath held—and he touched her bare leg. *Oh!*

"Miss Lark." He dropped to one knee. "Let us dispense with the pleasantries and begin with the delights." And with that he parted her thighs and dove to her wet cunny.

Candlelight played over his broad, tanned shoulders and the large muscles of his arms. His tongue snaked out, slicked over her, and Serena arched her head back to scream to the ceiling.

So good!

Boot soles sharply rapped on the floor. Leather-clad knuckles gently brushed her cheek. Lord Sommersby. She flicked her eyelids open as Mr. Swift splayed his hands over her bottom, lifted her to his face, and slid his tongue as he tasted her intimate honey.

Lord Sommersby looked so serious, but he never smiled. He required encouragement so she held out her hand to him, but her smile vanished in a cry of shock and delight as Mr. Swift nudged her thighs wider, until her muscles tugged, and feasted on her. His lips touched her clit, the lightest brush, and pleasure arced through her. She tore the sheets with her fisted hands, heard silken seams rip.

Then squealed in frustration as Lord Sommersby lay his strong hand on his partner's shoulder and wrenched Drake Swift from his work.

"She is a woman beyond your ken, Swift. A woman to be both pleasured and treasured."

Pleasured and treasured. Serena could not believe she'd heard those words from the cool, autocratic Earl of Sommersby's lips. He thoroughly disapproved of everything about her, didn't he?

And then the earl was gloriously nude. The hair on his chest was lush and dark and the curls arrowed down his stomach into a thick black nest between his thighs. His cock was straight and hard and remarkably fat, and it pointed downward, as though too heavy to stand upright.

A sweep of his lordship's arm and his rich purple mask flew aside, revealing dark brown eyes, narrowed with lust, and a predatory determination in his expression that made his fine features harsh. "Out of my way, Swift."

"I think the lady wants *me* to finish, Sommersby." With an insolent grin, Swift rolled back onto his lean stomach and lowered to her sex once more. She lost all her breath in a whoosh.

To have two such beautiful, naked men argue over which would lick her to ecstasy . . .

It was almost too much to bear.

Lord Sommersby bent and licked her nipples. Of course this was a dream, for she lifted her breasts saucily to the earl and spread her legs wider for Mr. Swift. His lordship sucked her nipple at the exact instant devilish Mr. Swift slid fingers in her cunny and—dear heaven—her rump.

Her heart pounded; her nerves were as taut as a harp's strings. "I will let you bed me," she gasped, "If you let me hunt with you."

Drake Swift laughed, and thrust *two* fingers in her quim and ass. "You were made for this, lass. For naughty fucking. Not for hunting vampires."

How illicit and wonderful it was to be filled, to feel invaded with each thrust of his fingers. Serena looked to Lord Sommersby.

"I would never risk your life," he said.

"But you know it is what I want most of all," she whispered.

"Is it?" Drake gave a roguish wink that set her heart spiraling in her chest.

In the blink of her dreaming imagination, both men were kneeling on the bed at her sides, looking down on her, their smiles hot and wild.

Mr. Swift's cock approached her mouth from the right, his lordship's from the left. The two huge, engorged heads met in the middle, touching right over her mouth.

Serena had never seen anything so erotic. So wildly arousing that she forgot about decorum, about bargaining, about hunting vampires.

What would it feel like to run her tongue around and between the two heads?

Their fluid was leaking together, making them deliciously wet and shiny—

What on earth was she doing? This was scandalous!

Her mouth opened to protest.

They moved to push their cocks in, parrying for position. Serena lost herself to the moment, shut her eyes, and stuck out her tongue—

Something sharp pricked her tongue. She pulled back, shocked by the pain, as thick liquid spilled into her mouth. Hot, with a strange yet impossibly familiar metallic taste.

Blood.

Icy horror snaked through her veins and she forced her eyes open.

The men were gone. They'd vanished and a young girl sat on the bed in front of her. A child dressed in a fragile white nightdress with loose, tangled golden hair.

Anne Bridgewater. Little Anne, who had died young—she remembered holding Anne's cold hand, laying her face to the girl's quiet chest . . .

As though floating over the scene, she saw herself twine the blond hair around her wrist to expose Anne's slim neck. Anne cocked her head, and her sweet scent of youthful skin flooded Serena's senses. Pain lanced her jaw and fangs shot out.

She was a vampire! Serena tried to resist, tried to fight, but she saw herself press her pointed canines to the girl's fresh, clean skin. The pulse thrummed beneath, fervent and strong, and the rushing blood sang in her ears.

Against her will, she bent to the young girl's neck . . . but everything tilted and a sudden light poured into her room. Havershire Manor. She was in her old bedchamber and Mrs. Thorton was tossing her half-packed case out the window while Mr. Thornton paced in front of the fire. Neither seemed to care that she wasn't wearing a stitch of clothing and she desperately tried to cover her body with her long black hair.

"You are in love with her," Mrs. Thornton screamed at her husband.

Serena fought to protest but she could not force the words out. She had done nothing wrong . . . nothing but read poetry with Mr. Thornton, and walk with him, and fall in love with him . . . and let him kiss her once—but nothing more.

Mr. Thornton raked his hands through his hair. "The wretched girl bewitched me."

His wife wheeled around and pointed at Serena. Her triumphant laugh rang out around her. "You'll starve in a week, you little fool."

She woke on a scream. Serena found herself bolt upright, sheets tangled around her legs, sweat pouring between her breasts. She pressed the flannel to her skin, to soak up the rivulets as she gulped down air.

Not again! So much for dosing herself with laudanum—it hadn't helped at all. Foolishly, she ran her tongue over her teeth. No sharp points, of course. No fangs. And she had never, ever hurt Anne Bridgewater.

Serena kicked back the covers and jumped down from her bed. She rubbed at her eyes, scratchy with sleep. She hadn't slept properly for four weeks. Not since coming to London, meeting Althea—Lady Brookshire—and joining the Royal Society.

She flung open the velvet drapes. Her bedroom in Brookshire House overlooked Hyde Park. Beyond the line of trees, pink touched the sky, promising dawn. How could she look upon the rising sun if she were a vampire? How could she stand in the sunlight?

But the erotic dreams of the magnificent Lord Sommersby and that enticing rogue Drake Swift—didn't they prove she was not a normal, proper Englishwoman?

She leaned against the window, staring out at the shadowy green park. She had promised she would not give in to her baser nature this time. Twice she had fallen in love and she'd ended up in disaster. She thought she'd loved William Bridewater, Anne's older brother. He'd come to her bedroom, kissed her senseless, and she wanted him. Wanted him with the same urgent fiery need she felt in these dreams. And that need had got her banished from the house. Then there had been Mr. Thornton, and his poetry, his brooding pain as they walked together, his stories of his wife's madness and rejection. She, the simple governess, had fallen deeply, impossibly in love—

She was never going to do that again. She could never do that again.

With the daylight spilling over her, Serena folded her arms beneath her breasts and paced to her bedside table. She slid open the drawer and drew out the small stack of folded pages. The edges were torn and curled and smudged by tearstains.

My dearest A,

I am writing to express my fears in regard to the behavior of S.L. She shows an unhealthy interest in men; she is brazen and wanton and disobedient. Often she slips out of her room at night, and returns only at dawn. One afternoon, a fortnight prior to my writing here, S.L. pricked her finger on a rose's thorn. She put the wound to her mouth and suckled—not of great concern perhaps—but I saw her return to the same place in the garden the next afternoon, deliberately wound her finger, and delight in suckling the blood from her flesh—

I greatly fear that your concerns are quite accurate estimations of the truth. You do see, do you not, why I beseech you to bring her to London, to keep her under your watchful eye? Dear Anne is devoted to her and the child is fragile and impressionable. I am not at all certain how to proceed—I have raised S.L. as a daughter, but she is not normal. Subhuman, in my opinion, and I fear, a danger to us all—

I must fervently await your reply,

> *Yours in devotion and admiration unsurpassed,*
> *Mrs. Ariadne Bridgewater.*

Every instinct inside her yearned to rip the words to shreds. But she couldn't do that—she needed these copies she'd made. There'd been so many of these letters, written to *dearest A.* She'd found them last week, neatly filed away in chronological order, in one of the bookcases in the Society's vast library. Letters written by Mrs. Bridgewater, the woman who gave her food, shelter, the woman who had raised her—the only 'mother' she had ever known. A 'mother' who thought her subhuman.

Who thought her a vampire.

Serena tipped her face to the weak strands of daylight, closed her eyes. Still hazy from the opiate, she struggled with the questions that plagued her day after day. 'Dearest A' was the elderly Earl of Ashcroft—the most powerful man of the Royal Society for the Investigation of Mysterious Phenomena.

To think she'd believed every word of Lord Ashcroft's story when he'd brought her to London a month ago. To think she'd believed he would teach her to slay vampires. *A tragic secret has been hidden from you, Miss Lark . . . the truth is that vampires killed your parents . . . but I will help you learn the truth, if you serve the Society.*

Lies. All lies. She'd been so thrilled to come to London, to stay with Lord and Lady Brookshire, to join the Royal Society. Ashcroft must have known she had been tossed out of the Thortons' home without a reference and had no place to go.

Worse, her parents hadn't been killed by vampires. The letters had made it clear. Serena's throat closed. She shuffled through the copies she had made but didn't look down at the words. She didn't need to, she'd cried over them so often the words were burned in her head. *I suppose this is exactly the kind of behavior we should expect,* Mrs. Bridgewater had written, *from the daughter born of a vampire and a mortal.*

Serena shoved the letters back into the drawer and shut it tight.

What did Lord Ashcroft want with her? Why had he kept her alive?

Was he waiting—waiting to see if she changed?

Would she? For all the books in the library she'd poured over, she didn't know. She didn't know if she could start out as a mortal and become a vampire without being bitten.

Serena stalked back to the window and pulled the curtains shut, filled with a sense of purpose. She was not going to wait; she would not be meek and docile and simmer in fear. If she wanted the truth she would have to bargain for it. And the journal of Vlad Dracul would be a temptation Lord Ashcroft wouldn't be able to resist. Once she had it, she would trade it for the truth about her parents, the truth about herself. And her life, God willing.

All she had to do was break into the brothel to find the journal. It was a deadly risk, but worth it. She had to find out the truth.

Was she the child of a vampire or not?